One Foot In Front of the Other

Sue Woolley

ACCENT

First published in 2020
by HEADLINE ACCENT,
An imprint of HEADLINE PUBLISHING GROUP

1

Cataloguing in Publication Data is available from the British Library

ISBN 978 1 7861 5986 1

Typeset in 10.5/13pt Bembo Std by Jouve (UK), Milton Keynes

Printed and bound in Great Britain by Clays Ltd, Elcograf S.p.A.

HEADLINE PUBLISHING GROUP
An Hachette UK Company
Carmelite House
50 Victoria Embankment
London
EC4Y 0DZ

www.headline.co.uk
www.hachette.co.uk

One Foot
In Front
of the
Other

To my Soberista friends . . . you know who you are

Chapter One

The last day of the creative writing conference had come all too soon and it had gone well, or so Claire had thought. She hummed to herself as she packed her case, ready to vacate her room after breakfast. Good job she was a light packer. She would return home with many inspiring ideas, not to mention useful hints and tips about how to write well-rounded, consistent characters and different approaches to storytelling. It had been wonderful to catch up with her old friend, Philip, whom she'd known since university.

A few minutes later, she was sitting in the wood-panelled dining hall of St Thomas's College, narrowing her eyes against the dazzling sunlight streaming through the windows, drinking her first cup of strong black coffee – reflecting that it was such a luxury to drink good coffee without having to grind the beans and load the Gaggia – when Philip sat down opposite and smiled at her.

'You were so funny last night!' he said in his soft Welsh voice. 'You abandoned English and started speaking gibberish!' He chuckled again.

Claire froze. Her cheeks felt hot, her eyes darkened, and there was a roaring in her ears. She struggled to breathe, to respond normally. As though from a great distance, she heard her neighbour, Tricia, chime in: 'Yes, it was hilarious! Helen and I had to take you up to bed, get you undressed, and tuck you in.'

Despair filled Claire's heart. Why did she not remember this? Summoning up every ounce of gumption she possessed, she raised

1

her head, and met Philip's kind, concerned grey eyes. Philip was always kind.

'I'm fine,' she laughed. 'I must have had one glass too many. How silly!'

Her laughter sounded fake even in her own ears. She turned her attention to her cereal bowl. The next few minutes were a triumph of acting skills, as she pantomimed enjoying her meal, even though the tasty cereal had turned to dust and ashes in her mouth.

'I've really enjoyed these few days – I've learned so much!' she said.

'Yes, me too. I can't wait to get back to my whodunit,' Philip replied.

'I've only just started my novel – but I think I'm going to have to re-write it from scratch, after all I've heard.'

She stood up.

'Got to go. I haven't finished packing, and we've got to vacate our rooms before the first session.'

Leaving her crockery on the table, she flashed a smile at her friends, then walked down the hall, back straight, head held high, her heels clacking on the parquet floor. As soon as she was out of sight, she broke into a run, fleeing to the privacy of her room.

Claire sank down on the narrow bed, her head in her hands. Hot tears, fiercely held back downstairs, were trickling down her face. She brushed them away.

How had it come to this? She was having such a good time. Her reading had gone well, and she had just been relaxing with a few friends and a couple of glasses of wine. Perhaps she *had* drunk a little more than usual, but surely not that much? *Why* couldn't she remember what happened?

She concentrated hard. The last thing she remembered was talking and laughing with Philip, Tricia, Helen, and the others.

Then . . . nothing.

She had woken up this morning feeling fine, apart from the customary dry mouth and the pain in the small of her back, which she

2

had ignored. As always. She had been vaguely surprised at how neatly her clothes had been folded on the chair and had congratulated herself on being less tipsy than usual.

But now this.

She, Claire Abbott, who was always so careful to present her best self to the world, had behaved like a complete idiot in public, in front of people whose good opinion she valued. To make things worse, they had found the whole incident amusing. Amusing! For which she should be grateful. At least they weren't ostracising her, mocking her. But God alone knew what they were saying behind her back.

Most frightening of all, she couldn't remember a thing about it. She had read about alcohol-induced blackouts but had never thought that she would have one.

What to do now? How could she face them again? She had failed, failed herself, failed everything.

She had been thrilled when Philip had contacted her, inviting her to the conference, had enjoyed meeting other budding authors, learning new skills. She had been looking forward to returning home and working on her long-neglected novel. She had even dared to dream it might be a fresh start for her after the turmoil and grief of the past few months.

And now she had screwed it all up by getting drunk – drunk! – in front of people she hardly knew. Could she ever hold her head up again? How was she going to bounce back from this one? She remembered other occasions when drinking too much had made a fool of her, wrecking her own self-image of the cool, confident woman she liked to present to the world. Memories she had carefully filed away in a closed and locked box in the deepest recesses of her mind. Her forty-fifth birthday, when she and Jack had thrown a cocktail party at home, and all her friends had come, dressed in their best. It had started so well – everyone chatting and enjoying themselves, but as more and more cocktails had been consumed, she had felt herself increasingly isolated from the gathering. Some time after midnight, she had gone to the downstairs cloakroom and been

3

violently sick, after which she had staggered upstairs and put herself to bed. The party had carried on without her, and she had suffered a hangover from hell. The photos posted on Facebook the next day had been excruciating to look at – her face slack, her eyes empty. And her friends' teasing comments had been worse. She had never been able to forget it, although she had sure as hell tried.

Then there had been another party, this time at Lucy's, and another pie-eyed Facebook photo opportunity – this time with her bra straps clearly visible and the same vacant expression on her face. Her face burned at the unwanted images these memories conjured up. Each time it had happened, she had sworn, never again. But then the next invitation would arrive, and the same sad pattern would occur.

But she had never blacked out; never been unaware of her behaviour. This was something new, something shocking. She buried her face in her hands and sobbed, both hands over her mouth, so that nobody would hear.

She glanced at her watch – 9:48 – the first session would be starting in just over ten minutes.

In an attempt to pull herself together, she went over to the tiny handbasin and splashed her face with cold water. Then she re-applied her make-up, nodded to herself in the mirror, picked up her case and bag, and headed back downstairs.

Somehow, she got through the final morning, taking part in the plenary, ignoring the heavy weight in her stomach. If she was quieter than usual, the only one who noticed was Philip, and he was safe as houses. After lunch, for which she had no appetite whatsoever, she prepared to leave.

'Bye, everyone! It's been such fun!' she said, with a bright smile. She exchanged hugs with the people she knew, promising to keep in touch.

'Are you OK, Claire?' Philip asked.

'Yes, I'm fine, really! Only a bit tired. I just need to get home and relax.'

After a moment too long; he nodded.

'You know your own self best. Be well.'

He hugged her and let her go.

Gratefully, she walked out of the hall and through the beautiful college grounds to her car. Hopefully the alcohol would have left her bloodstream by now. And she'd had two good meals to soak it up. She had to risk it; she couldn't wait to leave, to be alone, to put the whole rotten fiasco behind her. She thought it brave of herself not to break into a run. She opened the boot, dumped her case, and slammed it shut. She got into the car, put the key in the ignition, and stuck *Led Zeppelin IV* in the CD player. In an instant, 'Black Dog' was booming in her ears, forcing her to fight back the tears that threatened to blind her.

She scrubbed at her eyes, turned on the engine, blew her nose, engaged first gear. She'd be home in three hours or so. Then she'd have time to process this nightmare. But, for now, one thing at a time. Slipping the clutch, she drove off, loose gravel crunching under her wheels.

The drive home was familiar and tedious – country roads to the M40, north past Oxford to Warwick, then hang a left to the small Worcestershire village in which she and Jack had spent their entire married life.

Except that Jack was no longer there. She now shared the space with only Baggins, a neutered tabby cat with an assortment of bad habits. She hoped he would be there to greet her, stropping against her ankles, butting her legs with his big head. These days, he was the only family she had.

She could not get accustomed to the pain of Jack's absence. Every time she entered the house they had shared for so long, she still half-expected to see him sitting in his usual place in the lounge, his long, rangy body hunched over his laptop. Or standing in the kitchen, making a lavish mess, creating some exotic dish for them both. They had always divided the cooking between them – she did the baking, he did the savoury stuff. Learning to cook palatable meals for one had been another unwanted task, these past months.

5

It had been nearly a year since his death, but the pain was still acute, like a wound that wouldn't heal. Sometimes it subsided to a dull ache, but at others, it hurt so much she could not endure it, and would head out in the car, because the emptiness of her own home was too hard to bear.

But this day, it was a place of refuge for which she was longing. Once on the motorway, she put her foot down, and had to consciously ease back, when the needle swung past 90. She didn't need a speeding fine on top of everything else. She decided to switch to classical music to slow herself down.

It was hopeless to try the radio on this road – it would buzz and crackle, spoiling the relaxing music of Classic FM. She rummaged through the CD case with one hand, oblivious of the dangers, and found Einaudi's *Eden Roc*, which she reckoned would be sufficiently soothing.

She tried to concentrate on her driving and the countryside. It was dreary at this time of year – not much new growth on the trees yet, everything was grey and morose. And, to add to it all, it had started to rain.

She knew that, in a few weeks, this sad vegetation would be reclothed in new green to celebrate the return of the spring sun. But for herself – well, she couldn't see it happening, especially after this morning.

She turned on the car's headlights and wipers, hoping it wouldn't get too bad before she reached home.

Then she was through Evesham, driving down the well-known lanes towards the village. Jack and Claire had chosen this place carefully – it had to be within easy reach of a main line railway station, so Jack could get to the City – but they had both wanted to live in real countryside.

The village of Brandleton was ideal. She used Evesham for her weekly shop and Worcester was not too far away, if she needed a wider choice. It was a typical West Midlands village; there were two pubs – the Red Lion and the King's Head - and a little Co-op with a post office inside.

There was also a small infants' school, which they had never needed to use. Their only child, a daughter, had lived for six days. Laura, as they had named her, had been born brain-damaged, and had scarcely come into the world before she slipped quietly out of it again, leaving her parents bereft and heartbroken. The labour had been a difficult one, damaging Claire internally, and she had never conceived again, to her abiding regret. But this was an old grief, settled deep in her bones. She didn't want to think about it; not when the loss of Jack was still new, urgent and compelling.

She drove past St Mary's, in whose graveyard Jack now rested, before turning into Bredon Close and, with a deep sigh of relief, parked her car on the drive.

She looked up at the house – a typical 1990s three-bedroomed detached, with a small garden in front, and larger one behind. She was home.

At least no one could take this away from her – it was one time that Jack's job in the City had been a godsend. A combination of some informed speculation and razor-sharp timing during the dot-com boom meant that the house had been free of a mortgage since 2000, even if they'd had to pay the taxman a small fortune in capital gains tax.

Claire was so grateful. Whatever happened, the house was hers, lock, stock, and neglected garden. A place she could hide away from everyone.

Like now.

Sighing again, she opened the car door and straightened up She took her case out of the boot and walked to the front door.

As soon as she opened it, Baggins was weaving in and out of her legs, obviously delighted to see her. She had been away for four days and, although he was always free to come and go as he liked, through the cat flap – and the neighbours fed him twice a day - Claire felt he had missed her.

Dumping her case on the hall floor, she scooped him up in her arms. 'Have you missed me?' she said, stroking the top of his head with her chin, marvelling as always at the softness of his fur. 'Of course you have.'

7

Then he wriggled, so she let him go and headed into the kitchen to give him his supper.

She washed his dishes, put out a fresh pouch of Sheba – he was a fussy cat – and refilled his water bowl.

Then she sat down at the kitchen table and poured herself a glass of wine. It was wine o'clock, after all.

One hour and a bottle of Shiraz later she was feeling better. As usual, the wine had worked its magic, taking the edge off the pain. At least it was Saturday tomorrow.

She had better eat something. Heaving herself to her feet, she wove her way over to the fridge. She rootled through the freezer for a long-life ready meal, which she could heat in the microwave. Anything more ambitious would be unwise.

She powered up her iPad, opened another bottle, poured out another glass, and logged on to Facebook. Spooning in the gloopy pasta carbonara, she tried to concentrate, but Philip's kind, concerned grey eyes kept coming between her and the screen He had posted about the writing conference. As he had tagged her, she liked the post but didn't add any comments.

She wandered through to the lounge, iPad and wine glass in one hand, bottle of wine in the other. She spent the next couple of hours fooling around on Facebook or doing a jigsaw on the iPad.

By half past nine, Baggins was curled up fast asleep on her lap and her second bottle of wine had dried up.

'Come on, mate,' she said. 'Time for bed.'

Chapter Two

A persistent scratching on the bedroom door woke Claire up. Baggins was reminding her it was well past his breakfast time. She sat up and swung her legs down to the floor, wincing at the pain in her head and the brightness of the morning sun filtering in through the bedroom curtains.

For a moment she couldn't remember why she had drunk so much. Then it all came flooding back. She had blacked out at the writing conference. She had read of such things, but it had never happened to her. Why would it? She was not a serious drinker, after all. She just liked a glass or two of red wine in the evenings. Many people she knew drank as much or more than she did.

Shrugging on her fleecy dressing gown, she shambled down the stairs, nearly tripping over Baggins in the process, and into the kitchen, to be confronted with the table, still littered with last night's detritus.

She fed Baggins, then put the bottles by the sink to be washed out before recycling and the plate and wine glass in the dishwasher. Feeling nauseous, light-headed, and headachy, she drank a glass of Recovery.

Then it was time to shower, get dressed, and unpack her case, which still sat on the hall floor. She lugged it up the stairs and dumped it on the landing.

After a steaming hot shower, with lashings of her favourite Lush Twilight shower gel, she wandered back into her bedroom naked and stood in front of the mirror. She had always tried to take care of herself, eating carefully most of the time, exercising regularly. The result was a slim, toned figure, even if grey was creeping into her dark blond hair and wrinkles were softening her face. Not bad for 53, though. Really, not bad at all.

Her headache now subsiding, she got dressed in jeans and her favourite turquoise jumper - its bright colour always cheered her up - made the bed, then heaved the suitcase up into the bedroom and unpacked. She sorted the contents systematically, putting her dirty clothes into the washing basket and hanging the rest up in the wardrobe. Cosmetics went back into the en suite.

Then she walked back downstairs and spent half an hour restoring the kitchen to its usual pristine state. Breakfast was a bowl of granola with some Greek yoghurt, berries, and a large mug of coffee.

She had the whole weekend ahead of her. She worked part-time – Mondays, Wednesday mornings, and Thursdays. With her generous stockbroker's widow's pension, she did not lack for money, and only worked at the library because it got her out of the house and into contact with other human beings.

Putting yesterday out of her mind, she decided to walk down to the Co-op for some meat and fresh veg, so she could cook a couple of decent meals over the weekend.

The walk through the village was always a quiet pleasure. Every time there was some beauty to notice. Today it was the new green of leaves starting to bud.

She spotted a shy bunch of snowdrops poking their heads up through the soil and enjoyed the endlessly changeful pattern of the clouds in the pale blue sky. She was sure to meet somebody she knew; and even those she didn't, would exchange a greeting and a smile. Today it was one of her neighbours, taking her dog for a walk, well bundled up against the cold.

'Hello, Pam! Cold, isn't it?'

'Yes, but it's lovely weather for dog-walking. How are you, Claire?'

'I'm really good thanks – just back from a fantastic writing conference at St Thomas's College. I'm determined that this is the year I'm going to write that novel. How are you?'

10

'Oh, you know. Mustn't grumble. Ron's not been so well lately.'

'Oh, I'm sorry to hear that. What's wrong?'

'It's his heart. His heart rate will suddenly go crazy, for no apparent reason. He's getting some tests at the General next week.'

'Oh dear. I hope they manage to sort him out. Modern medicine can work miracles these days. Oh well, I'd better go – I'm on my way to the Co-op to do some shopping. Nice to see you. Please give Ron my best wishes.'

'Thanks, Claire, I will. Bye now.'

It took another ten minutes to get to the shop, and another ten to choose what she wanted, queue up, and pay.

Home again, she put the shopping away, then brewed herself another strong cup of coffee. Taking it through to the lounge, she fished out her notes from the conference. and read through them.

It had been a random decision to attend the conference. For as long as she could remember, she had yearned to be a writer. She was surrounded by books all day at work, and read voraciously. But her own words never seemed to be as good as other people's, somehow.

She was a member of the Evesham Writers' Group, which met in a local church hall. Once a month, members had to produce short stories of up to 1,500 words on a topic given by Duncan, the group's leader. They then read them aloud to the group and received constructive criticism. Writing the assignments had always been a joy and her stories were usually well-received – but she had never taken them any further.

She had started a novel when Jack had become ill. She had it stored on her laptop – who knew where – and when Jack died, she had shoved the hard copy into her writing bureau, never wanting to see it again.

Then Philip had told her about the conference. He had kept in touch with Claire and Jack sporadically, mainly through Christmas cards and Facebook.

Philip lived in the South West and was a member of a writing group there. When Jack had died, he had travelled up for the funeral and kept in gentle contact with Claire ever since.

A few months ago, in October, Philip had emailed her:

Hi Claire,

Long time, no see! I've just heard that there's a Creative Writing Conference happening at St Thomas's College in February, and I've decided to go along. Why don't you come too? I remember you always used to enjoy writing back in the day, and it would be lovely to see you for a few days and catch up. Here's the link, in case you're interested.

http://www.stthomascollege/writingconference/booking

Hope to see you there!

Philip

The email had come at exactly the right time. Claire was past the first desperate grief of Jack's passing and needed to find some meaning in her new, solitary life. Without thinking about it too much, so that she wouldn't have the chance to duck out, she had clicked on the link, filled in the application form, and sent it off. As a result of which she had spent the last four days feeling alive for the first time in months. Writing could be what she was looking for.

Then the blackout had happened. Could she ever hold her head up again? As shame washed over her in a burning tide, she hung her head, tears stinging her eyes. She had to face up to what had happened but didn't know where to start. Who could she talk to about this? Who wouldn't judge her and write her off as a poor, sad alcoholic?

She ran through her list of friends. Lucy, her best friend, with whom she shared most of her life, would not understand – she drank more than Claire herself and had no problem doing so.

There really wasn't anyone else she could trust with this sort of thing.

Then inspiration struck, and she reached for the phone.

Fingers shaking, she keyed in the number of Beryl, her spiritual director. She had been seeing her for the past three years after she had confided, in all the chaos surrounding Jack's illness, in Ruth, a friend from church, just how far from God she was feeling.

Ruth had suggested she try spiritual direction. 'It's not like counselling, not about trying to solve a problem, or fix anything. Your director's job is to walk alongside you on your spiritual journey, helping you to discern where God is in all this. They don't judge, they don't fix, they simply listen. I've found being in direction invaluable.'

Claire thought about it for a couple of weeks, then went on to the diocesan website to find a spiritual director. She picked Beryl's name more or less at random but, over the years, the bond between them had grown and deepened. Beryl had been a quiet refuge, and Claire valued their relationship enormously. She could trust Beryl with anything. She would help her to work it all out.

Eight rings.

Nine rings.

Ten rings.

Finally, someone answered the phone.

A man's voice.

'Hello?'

Claire cleared her throat. 'I'm sorry to bother you on a Saturday, but I was wondering whether Beryl is around? It's Claire, one of her directees.'

'Hold on a minute, love. I'll get her.'

She heard him calling, then the sound of footsteps on parquet.

Then, blessed relief, Beryl's light voice: 'Hello, Claire. Are you all right?'

'Oh, Beryl, thank God you're there! I so need to talk to someone, and you were the only person I could think of. Such an awful thing has happened.'

'Don't worry, it's all right. I'm glad you called. Do you want to come over or will the phone do? I'm going out later this afternoon, but if you want to pop round now, I can give you an hour.'

'Are you sure you don't mind? I wouldn't bother you like this, but I'm so stuck. I need to make some sense of all this. I can be with you in thirty minutes. Are you sure?'

13

'That will be fine. I'll have the kettle on. Drive carefully.'

'Thank you so much, Beryl. I'm really grateful.'

A little more than half-an-hour later, she was ringing Beryl's door-bell. Five minutes later, they were in Beryl's study, with its over-flowing bookshelves, and the sweet smell of the pot-pourri that Beryl made herself, ensconced in two armchairs. Beryl took a sip of her tea, then laid the cup carefully back on its saucer.

'All right, Claire, what's wrong? Tell me the story.'

Claire took a deep breath, then it all came pouring out – how much she had enjoyed the conference, how good it had been to meet Philip again, and then, how everything had turned to disaster. She held nothing back – the blackout, Philip's teasing comment the next morning, and how devastated she had felt.

'I just feel so ashamed,' she said. 'Nothing like this has ever happened to me – I don't drink that much. Just a couple of glasses of red most nights to keep the loneliness at bay.'

'Tell me about your drinking.'

Claire looked up with a start, her mouth dropping open. 'What?'

'Your drinking, Claire. Tell me about it.'

'My drinking?'

Beryl nodded. 'Your drinking. And the truth, please.'

'I suppose it's been getting worse since Jack died. When he was alive, we used to split a bottle of wine most evenings, you know, to unwind at the end of the day. But never more than that.' At least, not that I'm going to admit. 'Some days, we'd stick to tea and cocoa.

'After Jack . . . afterwards . . . I've felt so alone in the house. I've taken to drinking some wine most nights. To take the edge off.'

She paused, took a few deep breaths, made her decision, then said in a rush, 'Well, if I'm honest, I've been drinking every night. And recently, it's started to escalate. I'm really worried that I'm turning into an alcoholic or something. But I can't be! I mean, it's not as if I pour vodka on the cornflakes, is it?'

She took a sip of the now-tepid tea. 'And anyway, I don't drink any more than Lucy, or any of my other friends. And they're not alcoholics. So I can't be. Can I?'

She sat back in her chair, breathing deeply, waiting for Beryl's response. Would she judge her too? The whole thing had been a mistake, she should never have come.

'I hear how worried you are,' Beryl said. 'And I think you are right to be. From what you've told me, you're drinking much more than the recommended guidelines. What do you think you should do? Where is the Spirit in all this?'

This was Beryl's way. She always forced Claire to think things through for herself.

For a moment, she was silent. 'I don't know! I feel so lost, so ashamed. How can I ever hold my head up again?'

'If you truly want my advice,' Beryl said, 'I think that the best thing for you to do would be to sit with the shame, write it all down, and see where that takes you.'

Claire stared at her. She had been expecting to come away from this meeting feeling better, and now Beryl was asking her to face her demons head-on and admit to herself what a failure she was.

'You're joking!' she cried. 'How can I do that? That would mean admitting what a failure I am.'

'You're not a failure, Claire,' Beryl smiled. 'You know that. But you *are* in a bad place and the only way out is through. Ask God for help. You can do this.'

Claire's shoulders slumped. 'All right,' she said. 'I'll try.'

'No one could ask more of you. I believe that with God's help you have the courage to do this. He will help you to choose life. I will be holding you in my prayers until we meet again. Remember, you're not alone. Bless you, Claire.'

Claire stood up, gave Beryl a swift hug, then thanked her and headed back to her car feeling better for having shared her story, but daunted by what Beryl expected of her.

She drove off, itching to get home to Baggins and her journal.

Chapter Three

After a hasty and belated lunch, which she barely tasted, Claire went into the third bedroom. It had been Jack's office when he had worked from home, and had been simply furnished. A large desk, on which Claire's laptop now sat, a comfortable office chair, a writing bureau, and a couple of tall Ikea bookcases in a pale, blond wood.

In the last few months, she had taken it over as her creative space. The bookshelves were now filled with her special books gathered together from all over the house: classic novels, books about writing and art, reference works, biographies of favourite artists and writers. She had brought a Queen Anne armchair up from the lounge, so that she could read in comfort.

Her art materials were stashed in the small, walnut writing bureau wedged in the corner under the window. It had been Jack's gift to her to mark their silver wedding anniversary four years earlier. On the top was an antique-style desk light, together with her favourite photo of herself and Jack, both looking healthy and relaxed after a long walk on the Malvern Hills.

She had re-painted the austere magnolia walls a delicate and peaceful pale green and had brought in a couple of low-maintenance pot plants and a variety of Yankee Candles, which she loved to light when she came up here to write or draw or paint. As she lit one now – Midnight Jasmine – its sweet scent perfumed the air.

Beryl's words were echoing in her ears. 'I think that the best thing for you to do would be to sit with the shame, write it all down, and see where that takes you.' Sitting down at the bureau, she

16

opened her journal and started to write. She preferred the slower process of writing longhand, when she was journaling – it helped her to think.

Gee, Beryl gives me the nicest jobs to do. But I have been told to sit with it, so that's what I'm doing, two days after it happened.

I know exactly why I felt shame. Firstly, for someone like me, who is always so careful to present their best face to the world, to have been out of control of the public image I am presenting is scary and frightening. But worse, I don't remember slurring my words and can't understand why the amount of drink I had affected me. It can't have been that much, because I was up bright and early the next morning for breakfast. However . . .

The real reason is I have been drinking more and more since Jack died. Sure, I have tried to have some alcohol-free days, but I glugged two bottles of wine last night, and if I'm honest, I can't truly remember the last alcohol-free day I've had. In other words, I've been drinking at home again, alone.

But there's no way I'm an alcoholic or anything near it! Lots of my friends drink wine every evening. Surely there's no harm in it? I have a good job and am completely reliable as an employee. Last night wasn't typical – I rarely drink more than a bottle . . . I guess that's a bit much . . . but hey! It's not like I'm picking fights or throwing up or carrying a secret flask around with me, or anything like that. What's the harm?

Then why am I feeling so bad about it? Time for a bit of self-honesty, Claire! You know you're drinking too much, too often, and alone; all the things that magazine article the other week said were danger signs. But you haven't wanted to know that.

Shit. I wish I could do what Geoff did when he became a Bahá'í, and knock it on the head altogether. Bahá'ís aren't allowed to drink so he just took the pledge and that was it. I wish Christians couldn't. I'd love to make a vow to somebody and feel bound to keep it. Maybe I should go and see him and talk it over. And maybe, just maybe, it's God I should be making the vow to. But I feel a strong need to be heard and witnessed by another human being. And I wish somebody would take it out of my hands and forbid me to drink ever again. It's so very hard to find the discipline to do it myself when, in my secret heart of hearts, I don't want to. I love the taste and smell of red wine.

Please God, help me with this. I can't do it on my own.

She stopped and read what she'd written. So far, so good. But a long, long way from the whole story. If she was going to get to the bottom of this, she would have to go back to when she first felt uneasy about her relationship with red wine, her usual tipple of choice. It must have been three or four years ago when signs of Jack's illness first appeared.

Like her, he had come to terms with the fact that they were going to remain childless. Which had drawn them even closer, if that were possible. They had only each other – neither had brothers or sisters. Jack's parents were dead, and Claire's had emigrated to New Zealand when her father retired, because her mother was a New Zealander, and her elderly grandparents had needed somebody to look after them.

It had all started so innocently. They were blood donors and gave blood every six months. One August day, Jack had done the usual finger-prick test to check that his iron levels were high enough and had been disconcerted when the nurse shook her head.

'I'm sorry,' she said. 'You can't give blood today. Hadn't you realised you're quite anaemic?' Then she had given him a leaflet about anaemia and suggested he made an appointment with his GP.

'Who would have thought it?' he said to Claire later that evening. 'I suppose it must be down to the blood I've been losing the last couple of weeks when I've been on the loo.'

'You've been losing blood? How much? How often? Why the hell didn't you tell me?'

'I thought it was just piles,' he said, shrugging. 'Still, I suppose I'd better give the GP a ring in the morning. Good job I'm working from home. Don't worry so, Claire! I'm sure there'll be a simple explanation.'

That had been the start of it. When his GP heard his symptoms and examined him, she referred him to Worcester Royal Infirmary for a colonoscopy. Which had been moderately unpleasant but not too painful.

Then the results had come back. Jack had rectal cancer.

That night they had wept together, cuddling close, whispering reassurances. It was still in the early stages. There was every chance he would survive it.

At first, it had seemed to respond to treatment, and Claire's hopes had been high. Jack would get through this.

But then it had come back in a more aggressive form and, although the doctors had thrown every sort of treatment they could at it, it had been to no avail. Over the two and a half years of his illness, Jack's health had deteriorated.

He changed from an active, vibrant 49-year-old to a full-time invalid. He had hated it as much as she had, bitterly resenting the loss of his health and vitality. It had been up to Claire to be the strong one. She had managed, but the price she had paid had been high. She had numbed her anger and frustration with red wine.

Now, after everything, something had to change. She had to make a choice.

And she wasn't looking forward to it.

She was startled out of her thoughts by Baggins, who had nudged open the door, jumped on to the bureau and was rubbing his head against her. She glanced at her watch.

'Good grief! It's five o'clock.'

She had never known a cat like him. He seemed to know, within a five-minute margin, when it was time for meals. He was more reliable than any clock. She had been sitting, lost in thought, for more than two hours.

She stretched and went downstairs, gave Baggins his tea and prepared her own meal. She ate early these days. She'd knock up a chilli con carne, enough for four meals, eat one portion and freeze the rest.

Methodically, she assembled the ingredients so that she would not have to keep dashing to the fridge and cupboard once she had started. 'Setting your stall out properly', her mother called it.

She chopped the onions and red pepper, scrubbed the garlic, took the lids off the canned tomatoes and red kidney beans, and lined up the spices and measuring spoons. She had discovered she didn't mind cooking savoury food, so long as it was one pot plus accompaniments. Soon the chilli was bubbling away in the large frying pan. She put the timer on, so the rice would be cooked in time.

Then she opened a bottle of wine. She wouldn't drink it all but, after the mixed emotions of the day, she deserved a drink. As the first mouthful hit the back of her throat, she began to relax. She was determined to carry on with the task Beryl had set her – but, first, she'd unwind a little.

Two large glasses of wine and one rather tasty chilli later, Claire trailed back up to her study. She had a feeling she had journaled about her alcohol intake before, so she looked back through her old journals to find the entry, which would save both time and original thinking.

After a few minutes' search, she found it:

7th March
It is time to face up to the fact that I drink too much red wine. I drink between half a bottle and a bottle every day, which works out at between 33 and 66 units a week, or between two and a half and nearly five times as much as the recommended 14 units per week. One bottle of my favourite Californian Red is 9.4 units. I am becoming only too accustomed to waking up with a dry mouth and a pain in the small of my back. So it's time to say 'STOP' and mean it. No wonder I can't lose any weight. Even at the lower estimate of half a bottle or three glasses a night = 21 glasses a week = 2,100 empty calories. And the truth is it's probably closer to 4,000.

The idea of giving up wine completely horrifies me, which is a danger sign all by itself, but I think I'm going to try moderation first. Because I do love the smell and taste of red wine.

So: from today, I resolve not to drink from Monday to Friday, and to have one bottle of wine at the weekend, spread over the two nights. Let's see how it goes.

Claire read the date in disbelief. Nearly five years ago! So she couldn't blame it on Jack's illness. And here she was, in as bad if not worse a pickle. She reached for her current journal, and started to write, scribbling down whatever came into her mind:

Moderation – that's a joke! I have to face the truth of one thing: I Cannot Moderate. I have spent most of my life (and certainly all my adult life) almost completely at the mercy of my desires (or appetites). 'I want', 'I need', or (worst of all) 'I deserve' have been fairly constant companions, especially in relation to things I put into my body. 'Because it's there' has always been a good enough reason to indulge myself, to allow myself a treat, because I deserve it. I'm beginning to understand I have been using food and alcohol as a reward, without ever really specifying why.

And then, when the drink has been drunk and the chocolate/popcorn/whatever eaten, I feel guilty for choosing to give in to temptation.

Was she being too harsh on herself? God knows, the last few years had been incredibly stressful – the rounds of radio- and chemotherapy, the recurring, desperate hope that this time the treatment would work. Then the final months, when she had known that Jack was dying, and she'd had to be the strong one, the one in control, the one in charge, the safeguard between her beloved and the rest of the world.

Was it any wonder she had turned to drink and sweet things for comfort? Didn't she deserve a little happiness, no matter where it came from – even a bottle?

Shuddering, she picked up her pen.

I wonder whether God has been nudging me in the right direction for months, by rubbing my nose in the Quaker advice 'A simple lifestyle,

*freely chosen, is a source of strength.' If I think about all the ramifica-
tions of that one, I'll be moving in the right direction.*

*The three most important words are 'simple' and 'freely chosen'. The
last two remind me I'm a rational, intelligent human being, perfectly free
to make rational, intelligent choices about what I put into my body,
instead of listening to my appetites or trying to numb the pain away.*

*I'm 53. No matter how much I drink to avoid it, I need to face up
to the fact that Jack is dead. I'm on my own now. There's only me to
look after me. It's about time I woke up and treated my body with some
respect, as a temple rather than a waste-bin. I know in my head and
heart this is true. I have to find a way to get my will moving in harness
with them. But I can't do it alone. Who can I ask? Who will help,
without judging?*

*I know Beryl believes God can help, but these days, I'm not sure
He's there. I haven't been to church for ages. Hardly at all since Jack
died. If it wasn't for Beryl, I'd have given up on God long ago. But
she helps me to hold on to some remnant of belief. Maybe I ought to go
to church tomorrow, to reconnect. I wish I had her certainty that God
is there for me. After all, Jesus dined with wine drinkers — I'm sure
that's in the Gospels somewhere. And he did turn water into wine at
the wedding feast. So maybe He wouldn't judge me, after all. Yes, I'll
go, and give it a try. What is there to lose?*

That decision made, Claire closed her journal, turned off the
desk light, and headed downstairs, where Baggins, and the bottle of
wine, were waiting for her.

Chapter Four

After a leisurely breakfast, Claire wrapped up and walked briskly down to St Mary's, the architectural pride of the village. It was small but beautiful, with many original features, as the church leaflet had it, her favourite of which by a long chalk were the exquisite stained-glass windows.

The last time she had been in the church had been for the traditional Christmas Eve carol service, which had moved her to tears. Before that, only twice in the last twelve months: first for Jack's funeral the previous March, after which she hadn't been able to bear to go there for months. Second, for the All Souls' service at the beginning of November, but that was it. Maybe it was time to get back into the church habit.

She was warmed and reassured by the refrain of the chosen psalm 'For his steadfast love endures forever'. The Gospel reading was from the Sermon on the Mount where Jesus talks about the birds of the air, and how God looks after them.

The message she heard, was 'Don't worry; you're not alone. I'm here. I'll help you through this.'

The peace of the old church seeped into her bones, and she relaxed.

What a difference an up-to-date translation of the Bible made. Reverend Martin, their new vicar, had gently introduced *The New Revised Standard Version* instead of the traditional *King James Bible* into his services. The mainly elderly congregation had been shocked and unsettled at first and the poet in Claire missed the glorious, sonorous language of the seventeenth century. But she had to admit

23

the new translation made the readings much easier to understand, which she presumed was the point.

He was, after all, supposed to be sharing the Word of God.

Her attention snapped back to the service. It was time for the final hymn and the blessing. During the notices at the end, Reverend Martin announced they would be holding a special service on Ash Wednesday, at 10.30. She had not realised the beginning of Lent was so near. She had been out of the loop for so long.

She could try to give up drinking for Lent! Why didn't she think of it before? With Ash Wednesday coming, it was such a gift! She'd be much more likely to stick to a resolution if she started on the first day of Lent. Of course, she'd have to see whether Miriam would swap her half day with her.

It was a sign. If she could manage to give up for six whole weeks, that would prove she didn't have a problem with alcohol. Wouldn't it? When she got home, she'd search the internet for some books about stopping drinking.

Coffee hour was the congregation's usual social time. People she hardly knew came up and welcomed her back and soon she was involved in a lively conversation about the spring play, which the village drama group were planning for the first weekend in May. This year they had fixed on an Agatha Christie.

'I'm really looking forward to it,' she said. 'They always produce plays to a very high standard.'

After a while, she excused herself, and went over to Reverend Martin.

'Reverend Martin, I was wondering whether it would be all right for me to attend the Ash Wednesday service? I know I haven't been to church for a while, but I'd very much like to, if that's OK with you?'

He smiled down at her. 'Of course, Claire, you would be most welcome! Is there anything you'd like to talk about beforehand?'

Claire shook her head. Damn him. How could he know? She smiled back. 'No, no. I just thought I'd like to come along this year.'

'That would be fine,' he said. 'If you change your mind, my phone number is in the church newsletter.'

So she picked one up on the way out.

She read the newsletter over lunch. A notice on the inside back cover caught her eye:

SPIRITUALITY BOOK CLUB

Would you like some fresh inspiration for your sacred
journey? Why not join our new Spirituality Book Club?
We will be meeting monthly, starting on 9th March.
Bring yourself, the book of the month, an open mind
and heart, and a notebook and pen.

Book Club Facilitator: Ruth Evans
Book of the Month: *Sensible Shoes* by Sharon Garlough Brown
When: 2nd Thursday of the month
Where: St Mary's Church Hall
Time: 7.00 p.m. – 9.00 p.m.
Refreshments provided

For more information, please contact
Ruth – contact details on the back page.

This could be fun. She'd give it a try – nothing to lose, after all. She logged on to Amazon and read the reviews of the book – it sounded really good. So she bought it and sent Ruth an email to sign up.

Later on, after a detailed trawl through the many books on alcoholism and sobriety sold on Amazon, Claire chose one which looked like it might suit her.

She clicked the Buy icon and ordered it, paying the premium for next day delivery. She felt light, energised. She was actually doing something positive to change her life. It was ten days until Ash Wednesday, plenty of time to read the book and make the commitment.

After all, it would only be for a few weeks and after that she would be able to have the odd drink when she was out with friends. She would have proved she was not a problem drinker.

She settled down in her favourite armchair with a copy of *Jane Eyre*, which she hadn't read for years, and a glass of her favourite Californian red. After all, she had ten whole days left. She had better make the most of it.

Claire gave Miriam a quick ring during her coffee break on Monday. Miriam was happy to swap her shift. They often did each other this small favour when life got in the way. So that was all right. One step nearer to D-Day.

The first day of the week was often fairly quiet in the small branch library. Thanks to endless local government cut-backs, there were only three members of staff on duty at any one time; today, Claire herself and the two library assistants, Gillian and Celia.

The morning had seen the usual sprinkling of regular library users, who preferred the convenience of being able to walk to the library to change their books or DVDs or CDs, even though their choice was reduced. Claire knew most of them by name, and greeted them cheerfully as they walked in. It was like running a village shop. Everyone stopped for a brief chat as they came in or out, and Claire learned a little more about their lives, marvelling, as ever, at the endless variety of the human condition and getting ideas for her stories from snippets of news and conversation. In between, she dealt with the snail mail and email, accessioned the newspapers and magazines, and helped Gillian unpack the new batch of stock from Central. It was a typical Monday.

At the end of the school day, Claire ran the Homework Club, helping the children to find the books and resources they needed. It was one of her favourite parts of the job – she felt she could make a real difference. The library's computers had a wide range of software suitable for children and she could point them in the right direction.

At five o'clock, she rang the closing bell, and started the complicated process of shutting up shop – closing down the computers, putting the stock the children had used back on the trolley ready for shelving in the morning, pulling down the blinds, and helping

Gillian and Celia to tidy up ready for the next day. Then she locked up, set the alarm, and left.

She could not wait to get home. With any luck, the book would be there. She could spend the evening reading it, and reflect on the pros and cons of making this momentous change in her life.

When she opened the front door, there was the parcel, together with the usual assortment of junk mail and bills. And a small white envelope, addressed in handwriting she didn't recognise. Intrigued, Claire opened it.

It was a greetings card, with a picture of a vibrant daisy pushing its way up through some concrete. 'When you're in a dark place, you sometimes tend to think you've been buried. Perhaps you've been planted. Bloom.'

She opened it.

Dear Claire, I found this amongst my card collection and thought of you. Take it as a sign to Choose Life. May God be with you, Beryl.

What a lovely gesture. She tucked it away in her bag.

After she had fed Baggins, prepared and eaten her own meal, Claire opened the parcel. It was the book. She opened it.

She hadn't got very far, not even to the end of the introduction, before putting the book aside and starting on a list of the pros and cons of continuing to drink. After a few false starts, she came up with:

Reasons to continue to drink:
1. *It helps me to get to sleep at night.*
2. *It helps me to unwind at the end of the day.*
3. *I love the taste and smell of red wine.*
4. *I enjoy drinking socially. If I stop drinking, I won't fit in anymore. Going down to the Red Lion on a Friday is practically the only social life I have these days.*
5. *If I stop drinking, I'll have to face how lonely I am – not sure I'm brave enough right now.*

Reasons to stop drinking:

1. *I'm worried about the effect on my liver – that lower back pain has got to mean something.*
2. *I'm sick and tired of having this thing called alcohol in control of me. I want to get back in control of myself.*
3. *I want to be healthier.*
4. *I'm worried that I'm using it as a crutch, to numb out the pain of being so alone.*
5. *I want to be able to respect myself and my body, to treat myself like a temple, rather than a waste-bin.*

She sat back and read it over. So far, so balanced.

But what she needed was something to tip her into the right direction.

She picked up the book. At the end of the introduction were some questions.

How are you feeling just now? *Fairly crap, actually. The idea of giving up my beloved red wine scares me witless. I love the smell and taste of it so much, how mellow it makes me feel. I'm not sure I can manage without it. Other people seem to manage to moderate – why can't I?*

Are you worried about your drinking? *Yes, damn it. I am.*

Is the amount you drink affecting your health? *I was going to say 'no' to this, but there's no point in lying to myself, I am a bit worried about that lower back pain, and my mouth in the morning as dry as a desert at high noon. In fact, now I come to think about it, I always feel under par in the mornings. Which can't be right.*

Has the amount you drink affected your relationships with other people? *Up to last Friday, I would have said a firm 'no' to that. But after Thursday night's blackout, who knows what Philip and the others are thinking of me? But generally, no.*

28

Do you realise how much money you would save if you stopped drinking? *Yes, I suppose so, but that's not the issue. I guess if I saved all the money I spend on wine, I could afford a really decent holiday next year. Worth a thought, perhaps. Maybe I could even enrol on a Creative Writing course, if I saved up.*

Has losing control become an issue for you? *Oh God, yes! The one thing this last few days has rubbed my nose in is that I am not in control, so far as red wine is concerned. I don't drink before dinner but have to have a couple of glasses in the evening. And that's not good. Not good at all.*

Her mobile rang. It was her best friend, Lucy. They'd been friends ever since Claire and Jack had moved to the village, when they had shared a table with Lucy and Dave, her ex-husband, at the local pub quiz, and hit it off.

'Hi, Claire! How was the conference?'

'Hello, Lucy! Good, thank you. It was great to see Philip and Helen again, and I've picked up some wonderful writing tips. How's things?'

'Not too bad, thanks. Are you going down to the Lion on Friday? We missed you last week – Dawn and I sat there, moaning about our weight and envying you for being somewhere exciting.'

'Yes, of course I'm coming. Looking forward to it. Got to go now, I'm trying to polish my story for the Writers' Group on Wednesday and getting nowhere fast.'

'Oh, OK. See you later, bye.'

Claire rang off and caught her breath. How was Lucy going to take this? That was going to be a difficult conversation. But she had a few days yet.

She fetched a glass and a bottle and settled down. Baggins jumped on to her lap.

'Oh, Baggins,' she sighed, fondling his ears. 'Have you come to help?'

She picked up the book and, pencil in hand, underlined relevant passages as she read. There were a lot of them.

Chapter Five

By 11.15, thanks to her skill at speed-reading, which she had inherited from her lawyer father, Claire had managed to trawl through the whole book. She had underlined many passages, and the book had sprouted tiny pink, yellow, and green Post-its to mark the places she wanted to read again.

She was exhausted, even though she had been sitting all evening. She deserved a hot, soaky bath, and bed without setting the alarm. Not for the first time she blessed the fact that she only worked part-time. Tomorrow was her own, apart from the usual domestic tasks, and the gym – if she could be bothered.

Minutes later, Baggins was shut away for the night and she was lying in a rich froth of lavender-scented bubbles, reading *Jane Eyre*. Her muscles relaxed as she lay there, reading until the water was cool. Once in bed, she read for a few minutes more, then turned off the bedside light.

She wanted to sleep, was desperate to sleep, but her mind was wide-awake, buzzing. The book on quitting had shaken her. Reading it had changed for ever her perceptions of what constituted alcoholism, alcohol dependence and, worryingly, her own relationship with wine.

Maybe. it was because she wasn't used to this self-analysis stuff. When she had received the nudge from God on Sunday morning – was it only yesterday? – it had been a clear message she should quit. But the more she read and the more she thought about quitting drinking, the more she was unwilling, fearful and, yes, resentful.

Part of her dragged at her hand like a recalcitrant toddler, whining 'But I don't wanna!' while the devil sat firmly on her shoulder, insinuating the thought: 'You don't have a drink problem. You don't have to quit altogether. You can moderate – of course you can.'

But this was a big, fat lie. It had taken her a long time to recognise she had a problem, because she rarely had a proper hangover, tending to get tipsy rather than drunk. And she hadn't experienced the nastier side effects – saying or doing things she regretted, vomiting, falling down, or being aggressive. Wine loosened her up – made her bubblier, more vivacious.

She had carefully ignored the warning signs. If she couldn't get her beloved red wine, she drank whatever was around, mainly white wine or rosé, although she *was* partial to the occasional Cinzano Bianco and lemonade. She always finished the bottle. She drank at home, alone. Every morning she woke up feeling dehydrated and under par.

After all, most of her friends drank wine and they certainly didn't have a problem. So obviously she didn't either. Denial can be very strong.

Denial. She had come across a meme on Facebook the other day, which had stopped her in her tracks. It had said: 'DENIAL: Don't Even Notice I Am Lying.' Was that what she had been doing, all these months – lying to herself?

She punched her pillow, then flipped it over to the cool side to get comfortable.

During the years of Jack's illness, wine had been a blessed relief from the daily stresses. Nothing had mattered – apart from Jack. If he was doing well, or had a relatively pain-free day, she drank to celebrate. If he had a bad day, she drank to drown her fears of losing him. Wine had been her friend, her crutch, her support. Surely she deserved a little bit of happiness, in the midst of all this pain and anguish? And now he was gone, and she was still drinking, to numb the pain of life without him. Tears prickled behind her eyelids.

'All right, that's enough!' she told herself sternly. She picked up her phone. Nearly one a.m. She went downstairs for some hot chocolate. Ten minutes later, she was back in bed, dressing gown and all, sipping the thick, milky drink. There had been no sign of Baggins in the kitchen – she supposed he must be out on some jaunt. She envied him. All he had to worry about was eating, sleeping, attending to his human, and patrolling his territory. No responsibilities, no grief. Just eat, sleep, and be fussed.

Maybe the reason she couldn't sleep was because she'd not exercised since a week before the conference. She'd definitely go to the gym in the morning. Then, at bedtime, she'd be tired out.

Drink finished, she snuggled under her duvet, adopted her usual diagonal sleeping posture, and tried the old trick which had always worked for her as a child: counting down from a thousand backwards. By the time she got into the eight-fifties she was asleep.

Claire awoke at 8.30 feeling refreshed and ready for the day.

She dressed in her gym clothes – black capri tights, sports bra, and wicking T-shirt – tied her blond hair back in a sleek ponytail, fed Baggins, had a quick breakfast herself, then drove to the gym.

She chose to do a mixed programme of cardio and weights. Starting off with her customary five minutes on the treadmill to loosen up, she then moved to the cross-trainer, and did a hard twenty minutes. By the end, she was dripping with sweat, her heart pounding in her chest. Then, after her heart rate had returned to normal, she did sit-ups, step-ups and some weights, both upper and lower body, which took up the rest of the hour.

After a shower, she treated herself to a large Americano in the café and went home.

Tuesday was her usual housework day. She washed the kitchen floor, hoovered through, cleaned the bathroom and the en suite, and tidied up.

By lunchtime, the house was spotless, and she was pleasantly tired. After her usual lunch, a wholemeal roll with peanut butter and jam followed by a tub of Greek yoghurt and an apple, she brewed a mug of her favourite herbal tea, peppermint and liquorice, and sat down in the study with her journal and The Book.

She would be systematic – go through the book chapter by chapter, noting down things relevant to her, and questions she needed to answer. But for now she would tackle only the first couple of chapters. The rest of the book was about life after drinking.

The writing style was direct and personal, and it wasn't long before Claire recognised herself in the women described in the Introduction as alcohol-dependent. Such people – and already she knew she was one of them – were usually in denial. They were leading fairly normal lives. In a society that celebrates alcohol, most had tried – and failed – to moderate their drinking.

Oh dear.

They made it sound so easy. As if all you had to do was choose to stop drinking and then . . . stop drinking. But it wasn't that simple. She loved red wine. The smell of it. The taste of it. The effect it had. It was clear she was teetering on the edge of alcohol dependency – if not already in it. Which was not good.

'Maybe,' she told the pages in front of her, 'I could have the odd glass or two at weekends, like Miriam does. I'm so careful about recycling the bottles. Different place each time. The neighbours don't know about all the empties. No one knows.'

Throwing the book across the room, she stood up and stared out the window.

'Will you listen to yourself? And you think you don't have a problem! Good God! You're hiding the bottles from the neighbours!'

Disgusted, she picked up the book, sat down again and turned to Chapter 1, which covered the weeks leading up to the decision to quit. It was like the author was inside her head. All the excuses, all the rationalisations she has made about continuing to drink haunted her.

Then the author talked about the ways she had tried to moderate and how it had always, always failed. The message was coming through, loud and clear. It was time to stop fooling herself, time to look her dependency in the face, time to move on, and start a new, alcohol-free life.

But she couldn't do it alone.

Perhaps she wouldn't have to. She looked up support groups on Facebook and there were a couple which looked friendly and non-judgemental. She'd join them, but not comment, for a while. Until she knew where she was.

For the first time in days, Claire was hopeful about the future. With still more than a week to go before she made the final com-mitment, she was at last seeing that this could be the start of a new phase in her life.

She shut the book, logged on to Facebook on her iPad and had a browse down the posts of the two groups she had chosen

From what she saw, they were good sources of support for people trying to quit drinking. She was going to need an awful lot of that in the weeks ahead.

Chapter Six

A couple of days later, Claire was still drinking – but not so much.

On Wednesday evening, after the Writers' Group meeting, she didn't drink at all. It was difficult to get to sleep but she was determined not to weaken.

Thursday evening, and she was home until Monday. Most Friday evenings, she met her best friend, Lucy, at the Red Lion, where they had a few glasses of wine and caught up on each other's weeks. If she went ahead with this giving-up-booze idea, tomorrow would be the last convivial Friday for a while. She wasn't at all sure that she could be in a pub and not drink.

She poured a glass of wine, settled down at her writing bureau and reached for her journal. The decision now was whether to quit the following Wednesday, the beginning of Lent, or put it off for a while.

Reaching for a pen, she sighed and wrote.

I think I'm getting closer to the decision to quit. I've been thinking about little else for the past few days and have tried to ask God what would be best. I know that I'm in the best place I've been for years and need to capitalise on all the work and heart-searching I've done.

Reasons to quit next Wednesday:
1. I'm more in the right head and heart space than I have ever been.
2. I don't want to be an addict any longer.

3. I would like to lose a few pounds and giving up wine is an easy way of saving calories.
4. The sooner I do it, the better I will feel.
5. I want to be able to respect myself.

But, at the same time, I know that it would be so much easier to drift than to bite this scary bullet. And I know that I'm going to encounter resistance and undermining (whether conscious or not) from some people (like the folk down the Red Lion).

Private or public? This is the other question – do I proclaim that I am going on the wagon because I'm scared to carry on drinking (the shameful truth) or do I pretend that I've just decided to give up for Lent (the face-saving lie)?

I'm truly afraid of people finding out I've been struggling with alcohol (it seems so shameful) and there is still a stigma attached to it, but living a lie is WRONG! At the same time, I don't want to be labelled as an alcoholic because I'm not, and never have been.

I also have the devil sitting on my shoulder, whispering, 'You're not an alcoholic – look, you didn't have any wine last night and you're fine. You can control this. You don't have to give up completely – you know you don't really want to.'

And the little, scared part of me is nodding her head frantically, 'Yeah, that's right! I can control it. I don't need to give up completely.'

Unfortunately, I know myself better than that. With drinking, as with smoking, it's neck or nothing – I can't do half-measures, I can't moderate.

With smoking, it was either fifteen a day or nothing; with drinking, it's half to one bottle of wine in a sitting or nothing. But unlike quitting smoking, when at least there was the alternative of vaping, there doesn't seem to be an alternative for booze. Or at least not one that I'm aware of.

I need to remember that article I came across online on Tuesday, which explained about the brain and body being in the habit of receiving a certain amount of alcohol, so that if you have even one drink, your body/brain will urge you to top up to the accustomed level. Which makes sense.

*So it's a matter of teaching my body and brain new habits and get-
ting them accustomed to not drinking. Knowing all the time that, like
smoking, one will always be one too many.*

God help me – I'm going to need it!

At this point, in some deep-down place, she had made her
choice – she was going to quit next Wednesday.

But she still didn't know how to handle it with her friends –
especially her friends at the Lion.

Then she remembered Geoff. He was an old friend from her running days and had quit smoking as well as alcohol overnight when
he had become a Bahá'i. Before she could change her mind, she
grabbed her mobile and speed-dialled his number

'Hello, Geoff. It's Claire. I was wondering whether I could pop
round and see you, if you're not too busy. I've got something on my
mind and need a sympathetic ear.'

'Hi, Claire. Lovely to hear from you. Yes, of course. I'll put the
kettle on.'

Geoff, a tall thin man with a kind, craggy face and the bluest eyes
Claire had ever seen, made some tea, then showed her into his tiny
front room.

'OK, Claire, tell me all about it.'

And before she knew where she was, she was kneeling on the rug
in front of him, pouring her heart out – how afraid she was of
becoming dependent on alcohol, especially red wine, and how
scared she was of quitting

'I'm not sure I can do this without help. I feel so ashamed. Can
you help me, please?'

Geoff tipped her chin up and looked her in the eye. 'Thank you
for coming to me with this. You're making the right decision. But if
you really want to succeed, you have to do three things: commit
completely, be totally consistent, and make a promise to God. After
that, it's very simple. Choose your quit date – Ash Wednesday, if
that's right for you – make your promise and then that's it.'

He made it sound so easy.

'But it has to be a total commitment,' he said. 'No "I'll see how it goes."'

'But what do I do if someone offers me a drink?'

He smiled.

'It couldn't be easier. You just say, "No thank you, I don't drink." You're an adult, rational being and can choose not to drink. Simple as that.'

He stood up, took her hands, raised her to her feet, and gave her a gentle hug.

As he showed her out, he said, 'After all, if you make a promise to God, you can't break it, can you?'

On the way home, she had a brilliant idea – she would buy herself a ring to wear on the middle finger of her left hand as a constant reminder. She would go into Evesham the next day and find one.

She drove to Evesham and visited all the jewellery shops. The ring had to be gold to go with her wedding and engagement rings. But none were quite what she was after – they were either too flashy, or too expensive.

So she tried the antiques shops. She had nearly given up when she remembered Johnson's Antiques Centre. It was like walking into Aladdin's cave. Everywhere she looked there were glass-fronted cabinets, containing everything from china and silverware to old toys and military memorabilia.

She spotted it after ten minutes. A slim half-eternity ring set with nine different-coloured stones – two purple, two green, two pink, two blue, and one yellow. Now, if only it was the right size!

She went up to the counter at the front of the store and asked whether she could try it on.

Smiling, the elderly lady came out from behind her desk. 'Of course, my dear! Which display case is it in?'

Moments later, the ring was on her finger – it fitted perfectly.

'How much is it, please?' she said, praying it wouldn't be too expensive.

It was only £55. 'I'll have it. Thank you so much – it's perfect!'

Minutes later, she was on her way back to the car, the ring firmly on her finger. The nine stones would stand for the words 'Chose Life' ('Choose Life' was ten letters). This change in her life was now physically on her hand. It was a talisman.

That evening in the Red Lion, Claire and Lucy sat in their usual corner of the snug near the log fire.

Claire held out her hand and showed off the ring. 'Isn't it gorgeous?'

'It's really lovely,' Lucy said. 'Why have you treated yourself – won the lottery?'

'I've decided to quit drinking,' she said quietly. 'I've been hitting the red wine a bit too much lately, especially since Jack passed, and I'm fed up of waking up feeling rubbish. So I've resolved to at least give it up for Lent and see how it goes. The ring is to remind me of my promise.'

Lucy's finely plucked eyebrows shot up. 'Well,' she said, 'that's the last thing I expected. You don't drink that much, do you? Oh, my dear. Don't look so worried! I'm not going to judge you! If you're not happy, then it's the right thing to do. But really? For the whole of Lent?'

Lucy hadn't judged. She hadn't judged! It was so important for Lucy to be on her side. She couldn't go through with this without at least one friend who understood.

She smiled, on the edge of tears. 'Thank you, Lucy. It's so good to have your support. I don't want to make a big thing of it. I'm hoping I'll manage without too many people knowing. I was afraid you might mock me or tease me. I couldn't bear it.'

Lucy nodded. 'How are you going to manage down here? I hope you're not going to stop coming down – I love our Friday evenings together.'

Claire smiled again. 'I've already thought of that. I'm going to drink Becks Blue. At least then it will look like I'm drinking, and no one need know that I'm not.' She sighed. 'It's so ridiculous – why should I have to hide the fact that I'm not drinking alcohol? Anyone would think it was something to be ashamed of! When all I'm doing is trying to look after myself.'

Lucy looked at her. 'You're right. It *is* crazy. But everyone we know drinks and it's going to be really hard on you being the only one who doesn't. Are you sure you need to do this?'

'Yes,' Claire nodded. 'I really do.'

She sipped her drink. 'You know that writing conference I was at last week? Well, I got drunk and made a fool of myself in front of Philip and the others. I couldn't believe how ashamed I was when I found out. I've been doing a lot of thinking about it the past few days. It's the right decision for me. Please don't try to persuade me to change my mind.'

'Up to you. Your decision. Let's leave it at that. I've got your back, whatever happens. But rather you than me. I couldn't do it – I enjoy it far too much.' Lucy shook back her mane of auburn hair and laughed.

And that was it. Dawn arrived at eight o'clock, the third member of their little friendship group.

'Hello, you two!' she said. 'I can't stay long – I've left Jake looking after Mum, and he wants to go into Evesham later.'

'How is she?' Claire said.

'Getting worse, I'm afraid. She's starting to forget how to do simple things, like making herself a hot drink, or turning on the heating. When I got home from shopping the other Saturday, she was sitting there, shivering, because she was so cold.'

'Ah, that's sad. What are you going to do?' Lucy said.

'Oh, I don't know!' Dawn's voice was anguished. 'I *want* to keep her at home with me, but I can't be there all the time to look after her, and the day-care centre's only open during the week. I guess I'm going to have to start looking at care homes.'

Claire gave her a hug. 'I'm so sorry, Dawn. That's really tough.'

Dawn smiled at them both. 'Thanks, you two. You've no idea what a difference it makes, being able to share my worries.'

'That's what friends are for,' Lucy said.

40

'Well, enough of me,' Dawn said. 'How are you? How did the writing conference go, Claire?'

'I was just telling Lucy,' Claire replied. 'It was really good, and I met an old friend, Philip, who I haven't seen for ages.'

The rest of the evening passed quickly, chatting and laughing like the old friends they were.

Claire walked home feeling several tons lighter. She was so relieved Lucy had understood, hadn't tried to dissuade her, had been on her side. But how was she going to explain this to anyone else? She had been lucky with Lucy. The rest of their friends might not be as understanding. They had a strong party culture – their idea of a great night out was to get together at the least excuse: St Valentine's Day, St George's Day, Hallowe'en, anyone's birthday – and drink to excess. Maybe she'd have to duck out of any future gatherings . . .

It was perfectly socially acceptable to admit to being addicted to cigarettes. If you tried to stop, there were lots of support bodies – including the NHS. Nicotine patches, gum, and e-cigarettes were freely available. When she had quit five years ago, everyone had been so supportive.

But publicly admitting to any sort of dependence on alcohol was shameful and definitely carried a stigma. The label 'alcoholic' conjured up visions of people who drank by the bottle rather than the glass, who drank all day, who couldn't hold down a job, who abused their families. None of that applied to her. The label 'smoker' was much less demeaning. Yet both words simply described dependence on, or addiction to, a particular substance.

Claire sighed as she got into bed. There could be some interesting conversations ahead.

Chapter Seven

Claire's Saturday was taken up with food shopping, including what might be her last ever bottles of wine, tidying, and going to the gym.

There had been a big notice in the foyer advertising their next open day, and she wondered whether Lucy would like to give it a try.

She'd been moaning about her weight for ages, but did practically no exercise. She'd mention it to her next time she saw her. It would be something they could share which didn't involve drinking. The problem would be time – Lucy worked for herself as a mobile hair-dresser and was busy six days a week.

In the evening, Claire treated herself to an Indian takeaway, automatically opening one of the bottles of wine to go with it. It wouldn't be for much longer. Might as well enjoy it.

Then she settled down in the lounge, Baggins curled up on her lap, and watched some old episodes of *Upstairs, Downstairs*. She couldn't wait for *Sensible Shoes* to arrive, to give her something new to read.

On Sunday, she went to church, then spent the afternoon at home in the study, devoting part of the time to working on the next assignment for the Writers' Group. This month, it was an historical story. After many false starts, she managed to get the first five hundred words or so down on paper, or at least into a Word document.

Then she moved to the armchair to read Chapter Two of the book again. It was concerned with the process of making the positive commitment to quit, in which the author bravely shared her feelings of doubt and loss when she had stopped drinking.

The author was in the same place Claire was now. It was so good not to be alone. She read on, and began to realise that the early weeks were going to be really tough. But if others could do it, surely she could? And Wednesday would be D-Day – the day when she made a promise to herself and God that she would never drink again.

There would be many occasions in the months ahead, the book said, when the newly sober person would be in stressful situations and sorely tempted to reach for a drink to make the world go away. The author suggested writing her reasons for quitting in the notes section on her phone, so that she could read them any time she was tempted to drink.

It took a while – and more than a few deletions – but, eventually, she came up with six solid reasons to quit drinking on Ash Wednesday.

1. *I want to be back in control of my life.*
2. *I never want to feel the shame I felt at the writing conference ever again.*
3. *I want to find Claire again.*
4. *I want to feel my feelings, not numb them (I think).*
5. *I want to respect myself – to feel good about the choices I'm making.*
6. *I want to look after my body – I deserve it.*

Now she'd always have them with her if she needed a reminder.

But she'd go out in style. She'd invite Lucy for a proper three-course meal – with sherry beforehand, wine during, and Baileys afterwards – and then pour all the remaining alcohol in the house down the sink. Maybe this wasn't what book's author would recommend, but for her, it was a necessary part of the process, a last rite.

She texted Lucy. Minutes later, her phone pinged. *Sounds cool – let's do it! Happy to find a home for any leftovers! What time do you want me? xx*

Awesome! Will 7.30 be OK? Wear your poshest posh frock – I'm going to make this an occasion to remember xx

*

She spent the best part of Tuesday afternoon preparing the meal. Prawn cocktail to start, steak and all the trimmings for the main course, and pineapple cheesecake for the dessert. It was a long time since she had entertained like this – she and Jack had often thrown dinner parties but, since he'd died, she had not had the heart for it.

She was determined to make a thorough job of it and put a clean tablecloth on the rarely used table in the dining room, got out the best dinner service, the EPNS cutlery, and the crystal glasses. The final flourish was a couple of candlesticks in the centre of the table.

Then she went upstairs to get ready. Again, it was months, even years, since she had taken this much trouble to prepare for a social occasion. She tried several dresses on before deciding on her favourite Per Una wrap dress. Red had always suited her. She also put on make-up and perfume. She hardly recognised herself in the mirror – her usual attire outside work these days comprised jeans, top, and cardigan, or gym clothes, and an absolute minimum of make-up, if any at all. But this was an important occasion.

In the kitchen, everything was set to go. The prawn cocktail and the pineapple cheesecake were sitting in the fridge, ready to serve. The mushrooms and onions were chopped. The asparagus was in the steamer, and the buttered steak was under the grill, ready to cook. Seven fifteen. Time for a sherry before Lucy arrived. Then the bell rang.

'Hello, Lucy. Thank you so much for coming – it means the world to me.'

'Don't be daft, Claire! I'm your friend.' Lucy hugged her.

'It's nearly ready. I'll just get the starter out of the fridge, then there'll be a bit of a break while I finish off the main course.'

'Sounds gorgeous! I'm really looking forward to this.'

'Let me pour you a sherry. You like sweet, don't you?'

'Yes, that's great. Thanks.'

They sat in the lounge, sipping sherry, then Claire led the way through to the dining room, and brought in the prawn cocktails. Which they polished off in short order.

'D'you want to come into the kitchen to chat,' Claire said, 'while I finish up the cooking?'

44

Lucy followed her through, and sat at the kitchen table while Claire busied herself.

'I love the smell of frying onions. This is lush, Claire.'

'Thank you! I wanted to make it a really special occasion.'

'You have. It'd normally be a ready meal for me on a Tuesday evening. I'm so tired by the time I get home, I can't often be bothered to cook something proper.'

'I tend to batch cook – I do a recipe that serves four, and then freeze the other three portions and defrost them when I need to. So I only have to cook from scratch a couple of times a week.'

'That's a good idea – I might try that myself. I've bought the latest Slimming World cookbook, and there are some fabulous recipes in there, but I can't be bothered most days. Thanks for the tip.'

'That's what friends are for.' Claire smiled. Lucy was so special. There was no one else she'd rather be sharing this meal with. And now it was ready to serve.

After she had plated it all, they returned to the dining room. 'Would you like some wine?'

'Is the Pope a Catholic?' Lucy grinned. 'Yes, please!'

For a few moments, they tucked in in silence. Everything had turned out perfectly – such a relief.

'This must have taken ages to prepare, Claire. You're so lucky, working only part-time. I didn't finish until six.'

'I know. But you make so many people – including me – feel that bit better about themselves.'

'Aww, that's sweet of you.'

'No, I mean it. A new haircut or perm or colour really lifts my spirits. You're lucky to be able to make a difference to people's lives.'

'I'd never thought of it like that. Cheers, Claire. I'll try to remember that next time I'm run off my feet. By the way, did you hear about Dawn's mum?'

'No, what about her? What's happened now?'

'Such a dreadful thing. Dawn rang me in the week in tears. Apparently, her mum wandered out of the day-care centre when another resident was taken ill, and the staff weren't paying attention.

She was brought back by the police, who spotted her walking in the middle of the road.'

'Oh God! That's dreadful. Poor Dawn! And her poor mum! Thank goodness she wasn't knocked down! She must be furious with the day-care staff.'

'Yeah, she was spitting feathers when I spoke to her. But it looks like push is coming to shove. As you know, Dawn wants to keep her at home, but if she can't trust the day-care staff to look after her mum when she's at work, Dawn said she's going to have to put her in a home. She isn't safe anymore.'

'Ah, that's so sad. It must be such an awful decision to make. I remember how dreadful I felt when Jack moved to the hospice, right at the end. But I couldn't look after him properly any longer. So I kind of know how she must be feeling. I'll give her a ring tomorrow.'

'I'm sure she'd appreciate it. Anyhow, enough of that. What exactly happened at the writing conference?'

Claire smiled. 'It was awesome! I learned so much – how much description to use, and why, how to create convincing characters, and why they have to have setbacks all the time, before achieving their goal.'

'Blimey! Sounds complicated to me. But I didn't mean that. Tell me about the last evening.'

'Oh, Lucy, I don't know what happened! I'm sure I didn't drink any more than I normally do, but Philip said I started talking gibberish and had to be helped to bed. And the terrifying part of it all is that I *don't remember*. I was so frightened when he told me I'd been talking nonsense. I had no memory of it at all. Which is why - tonight.'

'Yeah, I can understand how frightening that must have been. I know you can do this, Claire. You're such a strong woman.'

'I'm not feeling it at the moment. Let's talk about something else.'

'Oh, I'm sorry, hun. Tactless of me. Something else . . . hmm. Have you been watching *The Expanse* on the Amazon Prime?'

'No. What's it about?'

'Oh, it's fabulous! It's a new sci-fi show, set in the far future, and I love the four main characters.

'Sounds good. Maybe I'll give it a try.'

When the main course was finished, Claire cleared the plates and came back with the pineapple cheesecake held high.

Lucy's face lit up. 'Ooh! Your pineapple cheesecake! I haven't eaten that for years.'

Claire cut two generous wedges, then fetched a bottle of Muscat from the fridge. 'My favourite dessert wine.'

'This is a real treat, Claire.'

'I'm so glad you're here to share it with me.'

After they had had seconds, Claire brought out the bottle of Bailey's and poured two generous glasses. She raised hers to Lucy.

'To friendship!'

'To friendship!'

'Right!' Claire said, standing up. 'This is it! This is where I say goodbye to alcohol.'

She went to the drinks cabinet and its collection of half-full bottles. She didn't often drink spirits, but Jack had maintained a selection for guests.

She stopped. Did she really want to do this?

She turned to Lucy, who was watching her from the table. 'Lucy, please help me. I need to do this, but it's so damn hard! I need you to help me.'

She stared at the bottles and back at Lucy. Then she took a deep breath and forced the words out. 'Take anything you want. The rest is going down the sink.'

Lucy came over and gave her a hug.

'Come on, Claire. We can do this. I'll take the Bacardi. Get a tray from the kitchen and we'll take the rest through and chuck it away.'

Trembling, Claire did as she was told.

One by one, the sherry, whisky, brandy, dark rum, advocaat, Cinzano, port, and the rest of the Bailey's went down the sink. Her dripping tears following, mingling with the booze and hot water.

Lucy, standing by her removing corks and bottle tops, said, 'Come on, Claire. You can do this. I'm here. I'm with you.'

'Oh, Lucy! It's so hard. Why can't I moderate like everyone else?'

47

'I don't know, sweetie. But you've decided to do this, so let's get it over with.'

Claire drew her arm across her cheeks to wipe the tears away. Then she sighed the deepest sigh. 'OK. You're right, of course. Hand me the next one.'

Eventually, the job was done. The kitchen stank of booze. But every drop in the house had gone down the drain. Claire got her strong pine disinfectant and cleaned not only the sink, but also the draining board. Then she sprayed the room with air freshener.

She had done it. She had made the commitment. The last rite was over.

Lucy had a final gift for her.

'Give me the empties,' Lucy said. 'I'll get rid of them for you.'

Nearly bursting into tears, Claire said, 'Thank you, my friend. I won't forget.'

After Lucy left, she loaded the dishwasher and went to bed. She'd be hung over in the morning but, at that moment, she didn't care.

Ash Wednesday did not start well – Claire woke up with a pounding headache She squinted at her phone – 7.47. Groaning, she pulled herself out of bed, had a quick shower, dressed, and went downstairs to feed Baggins and fix herself a Recovery drink.

Thirty minutes later, a little more human, she had some breakfast and got herself ready to walk down to St Mary's. The service didn't start until 10.30, so she had plenty of time to pull herself together and clear her head.

It was another cold but sunny day, so she put on her winter coat, scarf, and gloves. There were already a few people there. She exchanged smiles and nods but avoided conversation. She needed to focus on what was ahead and was feeling nervous. She chose a seat near the back of the church.

On the dot of 10.30, Reverend Martin appeared from the vestry, tall and resplendent, the sun filtering through the stained-glass windows picking out the gold in his embroidered stole. He took his place in front of the altar.

'Welcome,' he said, 'to this Ash Wednesday service. Lent is a season of penitence and fasting. By carefully keeping these days, Christians take to heart the call to repentance and the assurance of forgiveness proclaimed in the gospel, and so grow in faith and in devotion to our Lord.'

The readings for the day, one from Joel, one from Matthew, really spoke to her – both talked about the need to do whatever penitence was required in secret. This suited her fine.

In his homily, he said, 'In spite of the penitential language of the liturgy, Lent can be about making a positive commitment *to* something, as well as about giving something up. Rather than a practice of self-denial, it can be an opportunity to spend the season of Lent engaged in a spiritual discipline of deep intention and appreciation of our world, our place in it, and an openness to Grace in our daily lives. It is about choosing Life and choosing it well.'

Claire jumped. There was that call again, the one Beryl had given her.

'Choose Life.'

Now he was making his own confession – he had been struggling with his morning prayer practice.

'They say,' he said, 'that it takes twenty repetitions of a particular action or renunciation to form a new habit, so the forty days of Lent should be ample time to form a fairly solid new spiritual practice.

'In my case, I have decided to commit to the practice of centring prayer, a spiritual practice which I have started innumerable times, but not managed to stick to for more than about a week, before the excuses started. In a way, it is the simplest spiritual practice of all, as it consists of sitting in silence, waiting on God. Just that. Just sitting. Just. Sitting.

'But let me tell you, it is the hardest thing in the world. It is something I really struggle with, because I find it so hard to still my mind. But it is a rich practice, which I commend to you all. You choose a sacred word or short phrase as the symbol of your intention to consent to God's presence and action within, then sit in silence, returning to the sacred word or phrase whenever your mind gets distracted.

'It sounds so easy when I explain it like that, but it isn't, or not for me – my mind is all over the place, and I have to continually refocus. But I'm going to give it a shot, because so many people whose views I respect have talked about the benefits to be derived from this practice.

'So I'm giving it one more try, during Lent this year. I started this morning, and intend to continue until Good Friday, by which time, I hope, I will be starting to get some benefit from it.'

Claire laughed inwardly. Such a relief to hear that even ordained ministers struggled with spiritual practices, with making solid commitments. A rush of affection for Reverend Martin filled her heart. How wonderful that he was willing to share his own vulnerabilities with them, with her.

Then came the ashing ceremony. 'Dear friends in Christ,' he proclaimed. 'I invite you to receive these ashes as a sign of the spirit of penitence with which we shall keep this season of Lent. God our Father, you create us from the dust of the earth: grant that these ashes may be for us a sign of our penitence and a symbol of our mortality; for it is by your grace alone that we receive eternal life in Jesus Christ our Saviour. Amen.'

The small congregation lined up for the ritual, and Claire felt spiritually uplifted as he marked her forehead with the sign of the Cross. As she walked back to her place, she was strengthened and peaceful.

'Dear God,' she prayed, 'help me to go through with this. Give me the strength to commit to giving up drinking. Be with me in the days to come, by your grace. Help me to choose Life. Thank you. In Jesus' name, Amen.'

After the communion and the peace, they shared some refreshments and left.

As Claire walked home, she knew she could do this. With God's help, she could do it! She gave Baggins a quick fuss, fixed herself a packed lunch, then drove to the library.

Miriam greeted her with a smile. 'All well? It's been quietish this morning, but we're expecting a new batch of YA stock this afternoon, so you're going to have a nice busy time! It's going to be fun having Wednesday afternoon off for a change!'

'Oh, crumbs!' Claire said. 'I'd forgotten about that. Oh well, never mind. I wonder when the new Carnegie and Greenaway shortlist titles will be announced – I'm rooting for Malorie Blackman, she's got a title on the long-list.'

'I think it'll be about the middle of March, so a while yet.'

After a little more shop talk, Miriam vanished into the tiny staff-room to pick up her handbag and go home. Claire turned to the day-book to see what she had to do that afternoon. As Miriam seemed to have dealt with most of the incoming mail, Claire hoped the stock would arrive soon, otherwise it would be a struggle to get it unpacked and sorted before the start of Homework Club. If necessary, Celia and Gillian could do the unpacking.

Sure enough, the Library van arrived just after one thirty, which gave them a couple of hours to unpack and shelve the new stock before the children started to arrive.

It was difficult for Claire to keep her mind on her work. She kept thinking about the beautiful ashing ceremony and couldn't wait to get home to read some more posts on those sobriety journey groups. But, somehow, she got through the day and, now, with a sigh of relief, she could go home.

Chapter Eight

Claire fed and fussed Baggins, ate a hurried dinner, the final portion of the chilli con carne she had frozen a couple of weeks before.

She sat down and switched on her laptop. While it was firing up, she got up to get a glass of wine. Then stopped. Of course! She didn't drink wine any more. She'd forgotten. How could she forget so easily?

Slowly, she sat down.

She'd had a good meal and she was still hungry. Naturally. The red wine had always filled that last empty pocket in her stomach. But not now. This was Day 1. The early days were always the most difficult. It would get easier. She knew that.

She squeezed the mouse until her fingers hurt. Onward. Forget the wine. Onward.

She got on to Facebook and settled down. This was why she was here – to stop drinking red wine, not to think even more about it.

She had decided to create a duplicate Facebook account under a pseudonym, to preserve her anonymity and had come up with a brilliant new ID for herself: Lent Lily

As she browsed through the posts, she was amazed by the depth of sharing that went on, by the courage and vulnerability of the members. And they all seemed to be very supportive of each other.

This was going to be a place where she could be safely vulnerable, hidden behind her Lent Lily ID. There were as many reasons for quitting as there were group members – some had been long-term alcoholics, but the majority seemed to be like her – verging on the brink of alcohol dependency and trying to get out in time. Which was heartening. There also seemed to be no judgement for lapses. Claire was determined to stick to her commitment but was glad to see that she wouldn't be condemned if she had a wobble. And behind the safe anonymity of the computer keyboard, she could choose how much she wanted to share about her journey.

She took a deep breath and typed her first post:

Hello, I'm Lent Lily. This is my first sober day for many months, and I've got a feeling I'm going to need a lot of support. So glad to have found this group! Looking forward to getting to know you all.

That was enough sharing at present, so she logged out. She'd log in again later to see whether there had been any responses.

She made herself a cup of herbal tea, grabbed a packet of cheese and onion crisps and curled up in the lounge to carry on reading the book, which she had been amused to see described as 'quit lit' by group members.

Chapter Three covered the first few weeks of not drinking. The author was obviously trying to encourage people to stay on track in the early difficult days, so bigged up the benefits – no shameful incidents, better sleep, a clear head.

That sounded good. But then, somewhat diluting her message, she mentioned how difficult the early days could be, and how newly sober people would find it difficult to manage without their usual crutch.

Too right. She hadn't realised how dependent she was becoming. It was only half past eight and if she couldn't have a glass of wine, all she wanted was to go to bed.

She laughed out loud at the final section of the chapter, which warned of the perils of boredom and suggested various methods of distracting yourself.

Distraction. What could she do? Bingo! Claire put her bookmark back in the book and went upstairs to Skype her parents, as she always did on the first of the month. After which she'd run a Radox bubble bath and have an early night.

This ritual of the monthly conversation via Skype was the only real contact she had with her parents these days – they were getting too old to manage the long flight back to the UK.

Not for the first time, she wished that they hadn't decided to go back to New Zealand. But her mother's parents had still been alive then and needed her to look after them. So they had bought one-way tickets to Wellington, packed up, and left their daughter, safely married and happy, as they had thought. When Jack died, her father had offered to fly over for the funeral, but Claire had demurred, knowing how hard it would be for him, at his age, to take such a long flight. So she hadn't seen them in the flesh for years, not since she and Jack had gone out there for a visit.

Now she felt she didn't really know them. She kept in regular touch with her father via email (her mother wouldn't go near it) and Skyped them every month.

More importantly, they didn't really know her. They had no idea that she had taken Jack's death so hard, nor about her drinking. She had closed herself off from the world, which had included her own parents.

'Morning, Mum, morning, Dad.'

'Good evening, Claire,' her father said. This recognition of the differences in the time zones was part of the ritual. She Skyped them at nine p.m. her time, eight a.m. theirs. They had always been early risers.

'How are you, daughter?' her mother asked. 'You look tired.'

'I'm fine, thanks, Mum. Yes, I'm really good. I went to a writing conference a couple of weeks ago, and met up with Philip again, after all this time. It was such fun.'

'Who is Philip?' her mother said.

'Oh, sorry, I suppose there's no reason for you to remember . . . Philip house-shared with Jack and me when we were at uni. He lives in Bath.'

'Are you writing anything at the moment, Claire?' her father said.

'Just the short stories for Writers' Group, but I'm hoping to start re-hashing my novel soon. I started it when Jack was ill but didn't get very far.'

'No, I don't expect you did,' her mother said softly. 'That's a good idea. What's it about?'

'It's about a young travel writer who visits various places. I'm really not sure where I'm going with it.'

After a few minutes' more conversation – her parents were glad summer was nearly over, as the heat had been very trying – Claire rang off.

Then she logged back on to Facebook, to see whether anyone had replied to her post. To her surprise, there were three comments welcoming her and congratulating her on making this choice. She posted a quick 'thank you', then had her bath. After which, she shut Baggins in the kitchen and went to bed with a mug of hot chocolate.

Hours later, she was not so sure quitting booze was the right decision. She tossed and turned, but could not get to sleep. She was waiting for the better sleep promised by the book to kick in and it certainly wasn't happening tonight. Maybe this was part of the withdrawal. After all, her body was used to being sedated by wine and dropped easily into a deep sleep.

Worn out but wide awake, she put on her dressing gown and fluffy slippers and padded through to the study. She logged on to Facebook and posted:

Just coming to the end of my first day of sobriety. It's 1.30 am, and I CANNOT sleep. Please could somebody a) reassure me that this is normal at this stage, and b) give me some hints and tips around how to get some sleep. I'm shattered, and I've got work in the morning. Thanks. Lent Lily.

Straight away somebody from the US pinged back:

Hello, LL. Sorry to hear you're not sleeping. Yes, it is usual at this stage – it will take your body a couple of weeks to make the adjustment to not drinking. But it *will* happen, I promise! In the meantime,

make yourself a hot, milky drink, drink it slowly, and then try to relax
your body, muscle by muscle. Good luck!

Claire posted her thanks and logged out. She went downstairs, made herself another milky hot chocolate, helped herself to a couple of biscuits for good measure, and trailed back up the stairs to bed. She hopped into bed, still in her dressing gown, and sipped the hot chocolate. One of the biscuits broke, and she brushed the crumbs onto the floor. She'd have to clear it up tomorrow. But she was so tired. She put the mug down on her bedside table, took off her dressing gown, and snuggled under the duvet. Starting with her feet, she first tensed, then relaxed, all the muscle groups she had control of.

A few minutes later, she was fast asleep. Her first day of sobriety was over.

The next couple of days were much the same.

Thursday wasn't too bad. At least until the evening, as she had been at work and too busy to think about wine. And *Sensible Shoes* had arrived, so she spent the evening curled up in the lounge, Baggins by her side, reading it. It was so good.

But Friday was hard – she went to the gym, did the weekend shop, and cleaned the house to within an inch of its life, all in an effort to keep busy, to distract herself.

Then came Friday evening – when she was accustomed to meeting Lucy and Dawn at the Red Lion. But she didn't feel up to it, not yet.

She posted in the group:

Hello! I'm on Day 3 AF, and on Friday evenings I usually meet my
best friend down at our local pub. I'm not sure how well I'm going to
deal with being around alcohol . . . any advice please?

Several responses soon came through:

If you're set on going to the pub, I'd suggest buying an AF drink, such
as Beck's Blue or Eisberg, and not staying very long. Because the

longer you're around booze, the easier it will be to succumb to temptation. Good luck!

LL: I wouldn't go anywhere near a pub at this early stage of your sobriety journey. Your body is still craving alcohol, and it would be only too easy to give in. Stay at home and apologise to your friend.

Hello LL. If I were you, I would be inclined to avoid pubs and clubs at this stage in your sobriety journey. It is still very early days, and the Wine Witch is bound to be on your shoulder, tempting you to drink. Why not get in touch with your friend, and invite her round to your house instead? If she is a true best friend, she won't mind the change of venue. That way, you can still have your weekly catch-up, without being tempted. But if you do decide to risk the pub, make sure that they sell an AF drink you will enjoy, and don't stay for very long.

Good advice. Claire texted:

Hi Lucy. I'm on Day 3 of my AF journey and, man, is it hard! I was wondering whether you would mind coming round to my house this evening instead of meeting down the Red Lion. Let me know, xx

A few minutes later, Lucy replied:

I thought you weren't going to give up coming down the Lion? I'm sorry, but I've arranged to see Dawn down there at 8 o'clock, I don't mind popping in to yours first . . . hope's that's OK. xx

Shit! She couldn't go down the pub tonight. She couldn't. Lucy was supposed to understand.

Close to tears, she started a bitter, scathing reply. And stopped. Lucy had been so kind and understanding on Tuesday, even holding her hand. A tear dropped down her cheek when she remembered she *had* said she wouldn't be stopping going down the Lion. She had let Lucy down.

But all that was before going without alcohol for three days. Without a large glass of red wine – the smell of it, the taste of it, how chilled it would make her feel. Surely one glass wouldn't do any harm?

She looked down at her left hand, at the glittering Chose Life ring on her middle finger. Damn it! She couldn't give in that easily!

She took a few deep breaths and texted:

I'm just not sure I could cope with being around booze just yet. Look forward to seeing you about 7? xx

Then she logged back on to Facebook, and posted:

God, I'm feeling so fed up! My best friend has arranged to meet someone else (a mutual friend) down the pub at 8, but she's going to drop round to mine for an hour beforehand. I'm trying to feel grateful but am really feeling totally pissed off. I would so love to be down there with them, drinking a large glass of red, just chilling out on a Friday. Help me, please!

Back came the response:

Hello LL. It might help if you play the movie to the end. Yes, the evening might start with just chilling out on a Friday, but is that how it would end? Imagine yourself getting steadily drunker, and more out of control. Imagine how shite you would feel the following morning. Imagine how fed up with yourself you would feel for having lapsed. It really, truly isn't worth it. We've all been through this, and it just doesn't pan out, in the end. You Can Do This! Stay strong and log back on when your best friend has gone. We are here for you!

Smiling through her tears, Claire typed:

Thank you so much. I know you're right. Will be back later.

She washed her face, then went downstairs to wait.

Lucy rolled up at about ten past seven and sidled in. When she got to the kitchen, she turned round and faced her friend.

'I'm sorry, Claire,' she said. 'I don't understand. I thought nothing was going to change. But now you're ducking out of coming down the Lion altogether. What gives?'

'I'm sorry too, Lucy' Claire sighed. 'I'm finding it very hard to go without wine, much harder than I thought it would be. I guess I hadn't realised what a hold it had on me. I don't feel ready to be around other people drinking yet. Maybe we could meet up at the Costa in Evesham on a Saturday morning for the next while? I definitely don't want to miss out on our weekly catch-ups, but I can't be down the pub at the moment.'

Lucy shrugged. 'OK, if that's how you feel. I'm going to miss you down there, but if you really feel that this is what you need to do, we've been friends too long for me to argue the toss. I think I've got a gap in my Saturday appointments at about eleven – would that do?'

Claire hugged her friend. 'Thank you so much! I am so very grateful. I'm not sure I could have borne it if you had abandoned me.'

Lucy smiled, brown eyes twinkling. 'As if I would! Don't be such a worry-wart, Claire! Now, let's have that coffee, then I must be off.'

After she left, Claire logged back on to Facebook:

Well, thank God for that! It was OK! I'm meeting her in Costa tomorrow morning for a coffee and cake. And now I'm heading upstairs for a long, hot bath, and an early night. Thank you, everyone.

She had passed an important test. She had been tempted and she had not fallen. She could do this.

Chapter Nine

After another uneasy night, Claire slept in late and had to hustle to reach the Costa in Bridge Street in time. Lucy was waiting in the queue. After a swift hug, she said, 'What would you like, Lu? This is my treat.'

Lucy decided on a medium black Americano and a lemon muffin. Then Claire suggested that Lucy bag a table for them both, while she waited in line. A few minutes later, she wove her way through the crowded café to where her friend was sitting.

At first, she didn't know what to say. Maybe Lucy was waiting for her to apologise for the previous evening, but Claire was damned if she knew why. Anyone would think she had done something wrong. That was ridiculous!

She smiled. 'How was the Lion?'

'You were missed. I wasn't sure whether you wanted anyone else to know that you've quit drinking, so when people asked, I said you weren't feeling well. Dawn and I had a good natter, but she couldn't stay long. It wasn't the same without you.'

'Thank you. I'll explain to folk when I'm ready, but you were absolutely right not to mention it. I'm sorry you had to lie for me. Hopefully by next week, I'll be up to coming along and having a Beck's Blue. After all, I will have been AF for ten whole days by then.'

'Ten *whole* days?' Lucy said. 'Is it really that much of a challenge? Do you want to talk about it?'

'It's not really much of a story,' she nodded. 'I'm finding it harder than I expected and am a bit dismayed to discover how much I'm missing it. It's a bit like being on a strict diet – you know what that feels like, you're ravenous the whole time. Talking of which, how's Slimming World going?'

'Not bad – I lost two whole pounds this week!' Lucy grinned. Since she had got divorced from Dave five years ago, she had become obsessed with her weight, desperately trying to get back to the size 10 she had been in the early years of her marriage. But she also loved sweet treats – hence the muffin with the black coffee – and was finding it an uphill struggle. Two pounds in a week was excellent.

'Oh, well done you! That's great. Which reminds me, I know you're really busy with work and all, but I was wondering whether you felt like coming along to my gym on the eighteenth – they're having an open day. You've always said you fancied giving it a go.'

'I'll have to check my appointments book. Do you really think it could make a difference? I'd do anything to speed the process up. But I'm really unfit – what if they laugh at me?'

'They won't. There are people of all shapes and sizes in there, including some seriously overweight ones – you'll look like a sylph besides some of them.'

'OK, I'll check the book and let you know – could be fun!'

They chatted for a while longer, then Lucy had to go, as she had a cut and colour booked in at twelve.

Claire got home half an hour later and ate her usual Saturday lunch of a carton of Covent Garden soup – this week, her favourite carrot and butternut squash – and a part-baked roll, warm from the oven, slathered with butter. Delicious.

While she was washing up, her phone pinged. To her surprise, it was a text from Philip.

Hey Claire! How's the great novel coming along? I hope you'll let me see it as it unfolds. I've been working away on mine. Talk to you soon x

Oh my! She hadn't done any creative writing since Sunday afternoon. Most of her writing for the past week had been journaling about her relationship with red wine, and her resolve to quit. But that had been a vital part of the process.

Now she had something solid to distract her – she would spend the rest of the weekend finishing the assignment. Then she'd re-read the novel, as far as it had gone, before working out where she wanted to go next with it. And finish reading *Sensible Shoes*.

Scooping Baggins up in her arms, she gave him a quick hug and kiss. 'I can do this, Baggins! I really can!'

Once in her study, she re-read what she had written so far of the assignment, editing as she went along. Then she set to work. She was so engrossed that she was surprised when Baggins jumped up on the desk between her and her laptop and demanded some attention. She looked at her watch. It was five past five.

'OK, I know. It's teatime. I'm coming.'

When she got up from her desk, she was stiff from sitting in one position for so long. She stretched, then went to feed Baggins, nearly falling over him as he slipped between her legs and skipped down the stairs ahead of her.

Cat fed, she brewed a cup of tea, then remembered she hadn't answered Philip's text.

Hello Philip! I was so grateful to get your text. It reminded me I haven't done any creative writing since last Sunday, and I've just spent the last few hours up in the study, finishing off my next assignment for the Writers' Group. I'm really enjoying getting back into it. Think I'm going to spend Sunday with the novel. How is yours going? Love Claire x

His reply came back a few minutes later:

That's good to hear! Mine's going fine – I've got all my suspects lined up, each with a suitable motive, but I've no idea which one did it yet! How are you otherwise? I was quite worried about you at the end of the conference – it was so unlike you to be that drunk. Tell me to mind my own business if you think I'm being nosy, but we've been friends for a very long time, and I care about you! Hugs, x

Claire's eyes misted over. He was so kind, so caring. She didn't know what was wrong with her these days – any small act of kindness reduced her to tears.

Taking a deep breath, she looked up Philip's number in her contacts and touched the little icon to call him.

'Hey, Claire! How lovely to hear your voice! How are you, my dear?' His voice sounded soft and warm.

'Hello, Philip. I'm fine . . . No, I'm not really . . . In fact, I'm not fine at all. Quite the opposite. Which is why I've phoned, not texted. I need you to understand.' Please, God, don't let me cry. 'This is going to be difficult to explain. Please just listen and try not to judge.'

'You know I wouldn't do that. What's up? Can I help?'

'It's about the drinking,' Claire blurted out. 'You know, when I was drunk at the conference, and you all found it so funny.'

'Oh, Claire. We weren't laughing *at* you, only *with* you,' Philip said.

'Well, it wasn't funny to me. I was devastated. I've rarely lost control like that before, in front of people whose good opinion I care about. I was so ashamed! In fact, I've been able to think about little else since. So I've decided to quit drinking altogether. I can't risk anything like that happening again, I can't.'

'Oh, sweetheart, we weren't judging you – we thought you'd had one too many. It wasn't a big deal – everyone screws up occasionally.' He paused. 'But it's more than that, isn't it?'

'It started to be a real problem when Jack became ill,' she said. 'Until then, we had often shared a bottle of wine after work, but not every day. No more than most people do.' She hated the apologetic, pleading tone which was coming into her voice.

'But after the diagnosis, when everything went to hell in a handbasket, I started to drink more, and more often. I was in such a dark place. The endless rounds of treatment, our hopes being raised and dashed, raised and dashed. Having to deal with everything, having to be the strong one, the cheerful one. I guess it took its toll, and I found that I needed a drink in the evenings to relax. There, I've said it, I *needed* a drink. Then after Jack died, there didn't seem any point in stopping. For weeks after the funeral, I would drink myself to sleep every night. I needed to numb the pain and wine seemed to be the best way of doing it.'

'I'm so sorry, Claire' he said. 'I hadn't realised it had hit you so hard, or that you felt so low. You should have phoned me – I wouldn't have minded.'

'I know,' she sighed. 'I felt if I hung on to myself, pulling it all in, tighter and tighter, I could somehow bull through it all. But I couldn't. I failed. So I hit the wine instead. It seemed to help – to make the world go away, at least for a while. It wasn't until the other week, when I made such a monumental fool of myself, that I woke up to the fact that things were getting out of hand.'

'So what happens now? Are you doing anything about it?'

'Well, yes, I am – I have. I went to the Ash Wednesday service at St Mary's in the village, you know, the church where Jack is buried? I realised the Sunday after the conference that I would need to make a real commitment to this, for it to have any chance of succeeding. And I spoke to Geoff, my Bahá'i friend from running. When he became a Bahá'i– they're not allowed to drink or smoke, so he just made a promise to God, and that was it. He told me, "If you've made a promise to God, you can't break it, can you?" So that's what I did, made a promise to God and myself. But I hadn't realised I'd find it so hard.'

'Wow! That's quite something. I take my hat off to you, Claire, I really do. And you've not had a drink since Ash Wednesday – that's, what? Four days? How are you coping?'

She told him about the sobriety self-help book she'd bought and about the group she'd joined. 'They are such lovely people! I can log on there any time, day or night, and there's always someone on hand to answer my questions or bolster my resolve. I've got the app on my phone, so I can log on even if I'm out somewhere. It's such a help to know there's a vast community of other people who are going through, or have gone through, the same struggles that I am. Some of them have been AF for years!'

'AF?'

'It's a shorthand way of saying "alcohol-free". The group's been going for a few years now, and they've got members from all over the world. I was gobsmacked – who would have thought that so many people struggle with drinking?'

'You're right there – I'm surprised too! But you're getting real support from them? That's good to hear. Is there anything I can do to help?'

'Thank you so much! I was so afraid you would judge me, you'd think I was an alcoholic or something. But I'm not, I'm really not.'

'Claire, honey. It's OK, I know you're not. You're a woman who's gone through hell these last years, and are now coming out of it. Why would I judge you? I respect you far too much for that.'

And at that – at last – her tears fell.

'Sweetie, don't cry, don't cry. It's OK, I do understand. Ring off, make yourself a cup of tea, then get back to that novel! I'm expecting great things of you. But if you need me any time, I'm here. Pick up the phone.'

Filled with gratitude, Claire rang off. He had been so kind, so very understanding. She was so blessed to have such a friend. But she was also exhausted. She stumbled to her feet and went to make herself a cup of tea. It was all she could do.

Chapter Ten

After lunch next day, Claire retrieved the tattered pages of her novel from the bureau. She curled up in the study's comfortable high-backed armchair covered in pale green brocade and started to read.

Her heroine, Dani, was a young, single woman with a yen for travelling to exotic destinations. This choice had been quite deliberate – Claire had wanted to write about something different from her own sad experiences. So she had made Dani a travel writer and had enjoyed googling for information about faraway places.

But reading it now was a shock. It was so lightweight, so facile, so unaware of the darkness lurking at the edges of human existence, ready to pounce when the chance arose.

She threw the pages down in disgust. How could she ever have thought it had been worth all that time and energy? She couldn't believe anyone could skate through life so blissfully unaware of anything outside her own concerns. No, she was going to have to abandon it and start all over again. What on earth made her think she could ever be a writer?

But she couldn't quite bring herself to throw it all away. She had spent so long on it while Jack had snoozed on the sofa, not even having the energy to watch TV. It was part of their last precious years together. She couldn't give up on it. Not all of it.

What could she salvage? She quite liked Dani, but the character needed a complete overhaul to make her interesting to anyone else.

Then she remembered some advice from the conference – that your characters had to come up against some kind of conflict, to enable them to develop and grow as people. What could she embroil Dani in? A meeting with Mr Wrong would be the obvious solution, but was so clichéd.

She would get her involved with a religious cult. That could be fun. One that was sweetness and light from the outside but in reality had an all-powerful leader who brainwashed the cult's members.

Excited, she moved over to the desk, logged on, and started to do some research. The first thing was where Dani would be when this happened – somewhere plausible. No use setting it too near the UK, as her friends and parents would come to the rescue.

After some poking around, she concluded the United States would be ideal, and found a weird religion that she thought would appeal to someone like Dani. She looked on their website and saw that the way in was through a personality test, something Dani could be likely to do for fun.

Then she began to have doubts. She found the whole notion of religious cults quite scary and wasn't sure how powerful the cult leaders were. Was this sort of research was a good idea, anyway – what if *she* got sucked in? Maybe she should ask someone for advice?

Duncan, the leader of the Writers' Group, would help. He was a published author and editor. She emailed him:

I've just been re-reading the novel I started a while back and have realised that it needs to be re-written backwards, to be any good. I've come up with the idea of getting my heroine involved with the one of those fringe religious cults, but am wondering whether I could end up getting into trouble. What do you think?

A few minutes later, he replied:

It sounds like a good plot line, with great possibilities, but I would caution you to be very careful. Your research will have to be immaculate, because people like that sue at the drop of a hat for defamation. Let's talk about it when we next meet.

67

She couldn't immediately think of any other, less dangerous, ideas. Maybe she wasn't up for it. She was hopeless. Why did she ever think she could be a writer? She'd wasted the best part of the day on this and got precisely nowhere. God, she could use a drink!

There it was again. Her first and only reaction to the slightest stress.

Have a drink.

She slammed the laptop's lid down.

Can't think of an idea for a novel within five minutes so have a drink! One tiny problem and she was ready to head down to the Co-op and buy a bottle of red. She was better than that. The key was, as she very well knew, to distract herself.

Get a grip. There must be something she could do that doesn't involve booze.

The gym. She'd go to the gym.

Two hours later, having given her body an hour of hard exercise, she was back home. She had pushed herself to her limits and her muscles were protesting. But that was better than being halfway through a bottle of red.

She sighed, got herself and Baggins some dinner, then walked into the lounge to see whether there was anything good on the TV, or failing that, a DVD she hadn't watched recently. Her eyes fell on Jack's easy chair, still sitting in its corner.

'Oh Jack, Jack!' she wailed. 'Why did you have to die? Why did you have to leave me? I feel so alone! I can't do this by myself, I can't cope without you.'

Abruptly the tight pain in her chest burst and she slumped to the floor, tears flooding down her face. She wept and wept – for herself, for Jack, for what might have been. She hadn't allowed herself to cry for so long, and now she couldn't stop. A minute or so later, her hair was stroked. She looked up. It was Baggins rubbing his head against hers.

'Oh, Baggins!' she cried, scooping him up in her arms. 'Whatever would I do without you? You are such a comfort!'

She got up on to the sofa, still crooning over her beloved cat. He curled himself up on her lap, purring deep in his chest. She stroked his fur over and over again.

'Thank you, my lovely', she whispered. 'I love you so much.'

The following Tuesday, her regular spiritual direction session with Beryl started in its usual way – in Beryl's peaceful study, with the lighting of a candle, and a few minutes of silence. Claire loved this part – it helped her to feel centred and closer to God. When the chime sounded to close the silence, she took a deep breath.

'Well, I've done it!' she said. 'I've quit drinking. I went to the Ash Wednesday service at St Mary's and promised God I would stop. And I've bought myself this ring' – holding out her left hand – 'to help me stay on track. And thank you for the card, I'm carrying it in my bag as a talisman.

'But God, I never expected it to be so hard! I can't think about anything else. Which is bizarre. When I was drinking, I never thought about it at all, except to look forward to the evening. But, now, it's on my mind all the time. I'm so scared I'm going crazy, or something. It's taking every ounce of willpower I've got not to go out and buy a bottle of wine. It's frightening me, how much I'm missing it. I know I've promised God not to drink again, and I don't want to, but even with a Facebook sobriety group for support, I'm finding it so hard.'

'Sobriety group?'

'It's this brilliant secret group on Facebook, with thousands of people, just like me, all struggling to stop drinking. I'm finding it a real help, being able to log on whenever I feel desperate . . . But I wish I didn't *feel* desperate quite so often. Surely I should have got over it by now?

'Wherever I go, I'm surrounded with booze – adverts, aisles and aisles of the stuff in the supermarket, everywhere. I haven't dared to go down the pub . . . I'm sorry. The shame is hard to bear.'

'Shame? Why on earth should you feel shame, Claire? Do you think God would be ashamed of you?'

Claire was silent for a few moments. 'I guess not. I suppose He'd be pleased that I'm doing something about this and not just letting it drift.' Another pause. 'But then why *do* I feel so ashamed? It feels like I've got a guilty secret, which I can't share with anybody, because if I did, they'd revile me, despise me, not want to know me.'

'Think about the Gospel stories,' Beryl said. 'Can you think of any time when Jesus reviled or despised anyone in need, or turned His back on them? He came to help us, Claire, and can still help us, if we only ask.' Beryl smiled. 'Have you taken this to God?'

'No, I haven't,' she admitted, looking down. 'Not since the Ash Wednesday service, when I made the promise. I didn't even go to church on Sunday. I didn't want Reverend Martin to ask any questions. You see, I can't even share it with him! I know it's ridiculous, but I want to be a bit more secure in my sobriety before I let anyone know.'

Beryl nodded. 'Try taking it to God in prayer. He will always listen to you, always understand. He *is* Love, and will always help us, if we ask. How have you been otherwise?'

Claire laughed. 'There hardly seems to have been an otherwise,' she said. 'I've tried to get on with my life, work's been OK, and I've been trying to do some writing. Then on Sunday night, I thought I'd relax with a film, and found myself in bits on the floor. I was missing Jack so much, I couldn't stand it. I haven't cried so much for months. Why did he have to die and leave me alone? Why?'

'I know,' Beryl said. 'When we lose someone special, the grief never really goes, it can rise up and seize us at unexpected moments. There is nothing wrong in feeling this – it's natural for you to miss Jack. I know how dear he was to you. Can you believe me when I say that you have to go through this in order to truly live again? It will pass. Eventually. But you will never stop missing him. That is the nature of great love and you two shared great love. Don't be hard on yourself. Cry when you need to, pray to God, and then choose Life. You know that Jack wouldn't have wanted anything else for you.'

'OK, I'll try. Thank you. But I'm fed up of being such a wet mess. Every little kindness, every memory, sets me off.'

'That's to be expected,' Beryl said, nodding again. 'For months now, you've been numbing your emotions with wine. Now you're not drinking, it's only natural all these feelings are coming to the surface. Don't try to suppress them – it's doing you a world of good to let them out. It *will* pass. Just give time, and God, a chance. He's always with you, even when you feel lost to yourself.'

She paused, then said, 'I'm so proud of you, Claire. You've made a hard decision, and you're sticking with it, despite the difficulties. I'm not going to pretend it's all going to be plain sailing from here on in. It's not. There are going to be days when you would do anything for a drink. But you've made the right choice. Keep logging on to that Facebook group and call me if you need to. And take it to God, who can help you more than anyone else. How would you like me to pray for you?'

After a few seconds' thought, Claire said, 'I'm going to need courage and determination to get through these next few weeks. Can you pray for those, please?'

'Of course.' Beryl stood up and gave her a hug. 'You can do this, Claire, I know you can. See you next month.'

Chapter Eleven

The first meeting of the Spirituality Book Club was two days later. Claire had loved *Sensible Shoes* and was looking forward to sharing her thoughts about it with other people.

When she arrived, Ruth greeted her warmly. 'Hello, Claire! Good to see you. How's everything going?'

'Fine, thank you,' Claire replied. 'This was a really good idea of yours, Ruth. I loved *Sensible Shoes*. How many folk are coming?'

'I'm expecting eight. I put it on Meetup, but you can never tell whether the people who say they'll be coming actually will be.'

'Can I help you set up?' Claire said.

'If you wouldn't mind putting the biscuits out on a plate, that would help,' Ruth said. 'I've already put the chairs out, got the mugs, and boiled the kettle.'

By seven o'clock, seven people had arrived, including Claire and Ruth. Claire recognised a couple of them from church, but the others were strangers. Once they had all had a hot drink, Ruth opened the meeting.

'Welcome to St Mary's Spirituality Book Club. As you know, we'll be meeting every month, and sharing our thoughts about the book of the month. We'll start by lighting a candle and some opening devotions, followed by a check-in, so that we can all get to know each other a little. This first session is going to be a bit different to the rest, because after we've talked about *Sensible Shoes,* I'm going to give you all the chance to nominate a book for us to discuss at future meetings. We'll have a coffee break halfway through.'

She lit the candle, then offered a brief prayer. 'Loving God, we are meeting together here, for the first time. May we grow in friendship and trust, and may our sharing enrich our lives. In Jesus' name, Amen.

'Welcome!' she said again. 'Let's start our sharing by going round the circle, saying who we are, where we're from, and what our hopes for this Book Club are. I'll start. My name's Ruth, I'm from Pershore, and I'm hoping this Book Club will offer all of us the chance to go a little deeper in our Christian faith.'

Claire listened as the others introduced themselves. She was attracted by one woman she didn't know, who said: 'I'm Julie. I'm from Evesham, and I'm here because Ruth told me about this group in our yoga class. I'm more of a seeker than a regular Christian, but I'm hoping to learn more about Christianity by coming here.'

Then it was Claire's turn. 'I'm Claire. I live here, in the village, and I'm hoping this group will help me to re-connect with my faith.'

'So,' Ruth said when the check-in was over, 'what did everyone think of *Sensible Shoes*?'

'I absolutely loved it,' Claire said. 'But we could spend a whole year going through it! There's so much in it – the different spiritual practices, the growth of the four main characters, everything! I've read it once, but I want to read it again, more slowly, trying to absorb more of the deeper stuff.'

Pat, one of the older women from the congregation, chimed in, 'Yes, it was a good choice to start us off. But I found it a bit too American for my taste. And I wasn't expecting a fiction book.'

'What were you expecting, Pat?' Ruth said.

'Something more serious, with some theological meat in it,' Pat said.

'Oh! But I thought it had plenty of that,' Claire said. 'What with all the Gospel readings and Psalms.'

'What did anyone else think?' Ruth asked, chipping in quickly, to avoid a confrontation.

'I found it quite challenging,' Julie said quietly. 'As I said, I'm not a regular Christian. But by the time I reached the end of it, I found I was longing for a deeper connection with the Divine.'

73

Claire admired her bravery. She wouldn't have been able to make herself that vulnerable, not in front of strangers. She'd like to know Julie better. Then her attention returned to the conversation. Most of the group had found the book uplifting and not a little challenging.

By the end of the evening, each person had named a book they would like to share with the rest of the group.

'Thank you all for coming,' Ruth said. 'I'll send the list of books round by email tomorrow. Our next meeting will be on the thirteenth of April, at seven o'clock.'

Claire walked home slowly. It had been a rich evening. She was looking forward to the next one.

In spite of her best resolve, Claire shied away from going to the Red Lion on Friday evening. When she texted Lucy to let her know, her reply was disappointing:

Sorry you're not going to be there. Dawn and I had planned a nice get-together, but I guess we'll have to do it on our own. Hope you come back soon x

Sorry hun, Can't do it this week. Maybe next Friday. Hope you and Dawn have a good time. x

Sunday morning, she went to church, as Beryl had advised, but didn't get much from the service. The first anniversary of Jack's death was fast approaching – he had passed away on 15 March, her own personal Ides of March. She would never forget it, not if she lived to be a hundred.

The last couple of weeks of his life had been spent in the local hospice, when the care he needed had finally got beyond her. Looking back now, Claire saw it as a brief interlude of peace before the devastation of his death.

He had been on morphine for the pain, but had had intervals of wakeful lucidity during which she had lain beside him on the narrow bed, holding his hand. They had talked softly of their love for each other, of past happy times – and she now treasured these memories. The hospice staff had been wonderful – caring and kind, but unobtrusive, giving them the space they needed to say goodbye.

Now she was wondering whether she could bear to face her grief sober, without a drink or three to numb the pain. Every time she thought about Jack, about how empty her life was without him, visions of red wine floated across her imagination.

Drink me, and you'll feel better. Drink me, and your pain will go away. Drink me. Drink me. Drink me.

Some months earlier, Beryl had introduced her to Elisabeth Kübler-Ross's five stages of grief – denial, anger, bargaining, depression, acceptance – to help her understand and deal with her maelstrom of feelings.

The emotional rollercoaster had been nightmarish, and that was when she was numbing herself with red wine. Now she was as raw as a peeled onion, enduring each succeeding emotion clearly and deeply. Denial was no longer possible, her bargaining with God was over, but anger and depression were constant companions, lurking in the wings of her life, calling for her attention. She was so angry with God for turning her life into an empty husk.

No wonder she had found the church service uninspiring.

Wearily, she wondered whether she would ever feel happy, feel whole, again. Jack's death had left such a hole in her life. She wasn't sure she could cope without him. She continued to exist – to go to work, to shop for food, to feed herself and Baggins, to go through the motions of living.

She was so stuck in her grief – acceptance of Jack's death was a million miles away. She could not foresee a time when she would not feel angry with him for leaving her, or angry with God for taking him away. She longed to feel his arms around her, his voice in her ears, speaking words of comfort and love.

But it wasn't going to happen. She scrubbed at her cheeks, brushing away the insistent tears that just kept falling. This was ridiculous.

She could cry for ever and it still wouldn't bring him back. How she needed a drink! Surely just one wouldn't hurt?

She was on the verge of grabbing her car keys and driving down to the shop for a bottle, when she caught sight of her Chose Life ring.

'Shit! I can't give up! I've got to get through this somehow.'

So instead, she logged on once more to Facebook, and posted:

Feeling very wobbly. It's coming up to the first anniversary of my husband's death, and I'm feeling so very down. The need for a drink, to make the pain go away, is very strong. I can't do this on my own. Please could somebody help me? LL

Almost straight away, replies came:

So very sorry for your loss. That's a tough one. But drinking won't make the pain go away; in the end it will only add to it. You will not only be feeling the grief from your DH's passing, you will also be feeling the shame for having had a drink. Be strong, dear LL. Xx

I'm really sorry to hear this. Have you heard of HALT? It's a mnemonic you can use to check why you feel you need a drink. Ask yourself if you're feeling Hungry, Angry, Lonely, or Tired? Because these are strong triggers for the craving. Try to distract yourself – have something sweet to eat, run yourself a nice bubble bath, phone a friend, and the craving will pass. You're doing so well – nearly two weeks AF! Don't give in now! Don't let the Wine Witch win – she is not your friend! Xxx

But the most helpful response:

Oh, LL! I so feel for you. I lost my DH four years ago, and can remember the emptiness, the devastation. I too wanted to drink to numb the pain, and did, for a while. But it doesn't work! It only adds shame to the rest of the negative shit you're feeling. In the end, I had to face up to life without him, and without drink. It's still hard, and will always be hard, I think, but I am so much stronger in myself, being able to face it sober. The edge will come off the pain, you will get used to it in the end, hard though that is to believe now. Much love to you, dear LL. Xx

She posted:

Thank you all so much. OK, I'll try. I'll try to remember HALT – that's really useful! And thank you for the reminder that the worst will pass. I know that's true. LL xx

Sharing her pain with sympathetic strangers made her feel a bit better, less alone.

Sighing, she went downstairs, fixed a meal for herself and Baggins, then went upstairs again and, as her online friend suggested, ran a nice bubble bath. Another crisis averted, and she had somehow got through it, without a drink. But she had so far to go.

Chapter Twelve

Some weeks before, Claire had decided to spend the anniversary of Jack's death at home by herself, in case she was overwhelmed by her grief. But now, with nearly two weeks of sobriety under her belt, spending a whole day – that day, of all days – on her own would be an excuse to drown her sorrows in a bottle.

Instead, she'd go out for the day. Up to London, maybe. She powered up her laptop, intending to find a museum or art gallery to visit. But then she got distracted by Facebook – as usual – and was idly scrolling down her news feed when a message pinged up. It was from Philip:

Hey Claire, saw you were on here, which saves me a text. I've got this coming Wednesday off work, and there's an exhibition about modernist photography at the Tate Modern, which I'm planning to visit, and I wondered whether you'd like to join me? I remembered we had talked about photography at the conference. Let me know soon, as I'll have to book tickets. x

For a moment, she gazed off blankly into space. Oh, my God. How could he know? This is just too weird!

Maybe it was just a coincidence. A very good coincidence. Quickly she messaged back:

Philip, that sounds great. I'd love to spend the day with you, and the exhibition sounds fascinating. Shall we meet up at Paddington? What time? Thanks for thinking of me, x

Her train was a stopper – it took an hour to get to Oxford, and nearly another to get to Paddington, so she was glad she had thought to bring her Kindle. When the train drew into the station at 10.57, on time, she hurried down the platform towards their meeting point outside Boots. Philip was already there, in his usual jeans, shirt, jumper and leather jacket ensemble.

His face lit up when he saw her. 'Claire! It's wonderful to see you!' He reached out and folded her into a big bear hug. The smell of his leather jacket was wonderful. She pulled back and smiled into his grey eyes, surrounded by laughter lines.

'It's lovely to see you, too!' she said.

After a twenty-minute tube journey, they were walking in the late morning sunshine on their way to the art gallery.

'Let's have a coffee first,' Philip said. 'I don't know about you, but I'm thirsty after all that travelling.'

They went to the Boiler House Espresso Bar and enjoyed cups of coffee and some very rich cakes. Then they headed for the exhibition.

The tickets had been quite pricey, but they agreed they would be worth every penny.

They stopped in front of a photograph of a metal tower, viewed from the bottom.

'I love this viewpoint,' Philip said. 'It shows off its symmetry in so many different ways. I bet it's Russian.' He read the title, *Shukov Tower,* by Aleksandr Rodchenko. 'Right again! Russian it is.'

'OK, clever clogs. How could you tell?'

'I'm not sure. I think it's how it seems to glorify human achievement – you know, onward and upward forever.'

'Hmm. I see what you mean. It is spectacular. I wonder whether it's still standing?'

'Hang on, I'll check on my phone.' He googled Shukov Tower. 'Yes, it is, but it nearly wasn't.'

'What on earth do you mean?'

'It says here that the Russian State Committee for Television and Radio Broadcasting wanted to demolish it in 2014, but it's

79

been saved by Moscow City Council, who put a preservation order on it.'

'However did we manage in the days before Google?' Claire laughed.

'You're right there. I suppose people had to save their curiosity for the next visit to the public library.'

The next section of the exhibition was devoted to portraits.

'Oh, look at this one!'

Claire pointed to a photograph of a woman's head and shoulders.

'I can't stop looking at this,' she said. 'What a face! It's so clever, the way her body's draped in white, and her head is bandaged. So you can't help focusing on her face. It's so symmetrical, almost unreal – two pencil-thin brows, two compelling, beautifully made-up eyes, a long, straight nose, and that immaculately shaped tight rosebud of a mouth. She looks perfect, almost creepily so. But the photographer's made her look so fierce, too. And look at that mask she's holding – I've no idea what that's supposed to symbolise.'

'I see what you mean. I'm not sure I'd want to spend much time alone with her!' Philip grinned. 'Who's it by?'

Claire peered at the title. 'Adolph de Meyer. And it's called *For Elizabeth Arden (the Wax Head)*. Now I'm really confused! I'm not at all sure I understand it, but wow! Those eyes! I wonder who she was – it doesn't say.'

'I guess we'll never know. There are some amazing portraits in here, aren't there?'

'Oh, yes! Thank you so much for suggesting this – it's fascinating.'

He hugged her. 'It's lovely to be sharing it with you.'

Then Philip stopped in front of a photograph of a young man with a shocked expression on his face, whose mirror image seemed to be holding a section of his own left arm in his right hand, sliced out below his shoulder..

'Oh my!' he said. 'This one's weird. No wonder he looks shocked. Look at the place where the slice of his arm's been taken from. It looks more like marble than flesh – it reminds me of one of those

Greek or Roman armless statues. And the rest of the arm seems to be floating in space. What's it called? *Humanly Impossible (Self Portrait)* by Herbert Bayer. And wow – it was taken in 1932. I didn't realise that stuff like this was even possible without Photoshop. I wonder how he did it?'

'Ugh! I think it's horrible. Can you imagine having that on the wall at home?'

'I suppose not. But it's so clever. I can't work out how it was done.'

'You're right. It is clever. But not nice, not nice at all.' She shivered, and moved off.

When Philip caught her up, she was looking at Dorothea Lange's *Migrant Mother*, spellbound by the sadness in her eyes as she gazed into the distance, combined with the strength of her stance as she comforted her two young children.

'What she must have gone through. But to survive it all with such grace and dignity . . .'

'You're right,' Philip said. 'It is such an amazing photo. She looks so sad, but not at all defeated.'

'That's it! That's what I mean. She seems to have got through everything with her soul intact.' She paused. 'I almost envy her.'

'Claire,' he said, gently. 'What's wrong?'

'Oh, nothing,' she said, not looking at him. 'Well, if you must know, today is the first anniversary of Jack's death. I feel so very sad and alone, and I've lost any strength I had. It went missing when Jack died.'

'I'm so sorry,' he said, putting his arm around her shoulders. 'I hadn't realised it was today. Firsts are so hard. I know it's impossible for you to believe, but it *will* get easier as time goes by. Don't doubt yourself so fiercely – you are one of the strongest women I know. You *do* have inner strength. Look at the way you've kept going these last twelve months. I remember how grim I felt in the first months after Angie passed.'

'Oh God!' Claire gasped. 'I'm so sorry. I'd forgotten we're in the same boat. No wonder you understand. Thank you. But,' she added, pulling away, 'at least you've got Chas – I don't have anyone.'

'It's been six years,' he sighed, 'and I've more or less come to terms with it. And having Chas *has* made a difference, after all, he's part of Angie and part of me . . . But he's away at uni, so it's just me.' He smiled at her. 'Billy No-mates.'

'It's so hard! My friends *try* to include me, but I can tell they feel awkward. They don't know what to say. I wish they could understand seeing them happy doesn't make me unhappy – somehow, their being happy honours my past happiness. Does that make sense?'

He nodded. 'You're right. That's how I feel too. But most people don't encounter this grief so young, so they don't know how to react. I'm so glad we can share this. You know you can ring me, any time?'

She smiled at him. 'Thanks, that means a lot.'

'Any time,' he repeated. He hugged her again. 'Come on, woman! We've got the rest of this exhibition to get through, then the whole day to enjoy.'

After the Tate, they wandered around Covent Garden market and sat in the basement café listening to a talented string trio. Then they had a good look around the stalls, where Claire was attracted by some beautiful silver jewellery.

There was one particular bracelet she loved, a row of tiny silver daisies linked together, with every other daisy enamelled in delicate white and gold. It was exquisite. When she pointed it out to Philip, he promptly bought it for her as a memento of a lovely day out.

She reached up and kissed him. She had intended it as a simple thank you and was not prepared for the reaction of her body. As her lips met his, she felt the heat, and drew back with a gasp. Then somehow, their arms were around each other, and she was being kissed, thoroughly and expertly.

And it was right. And she felt so safe.

When they drew apart, Philip grinned at her. 'I've been wanting to do that all day. I hope you don't mind.'

'No, not at all.'

After dining in a bijou restaurant off Covent Garden, they were back at Paddington by quarter to seven. Philip had a seat booked on the seven o'clock train back to Bath. Claire had allowed herself the luxury of an open return, and her next train was due at 19:22.

They enjoyed a hasty coffee and made tentative plans to meet up again the following weekend, but nothing was fixed. Philip's job as a social worker meant it was difficult for him to plan in advance because, at any time, one of his clients might need him.

'I should know how things are going to pan out by the middle of next week,' he said. 'I'll give you a ring then. Thank you for a wonderful day – I've really enjoyed it.'

'Me too! You can't know what it's meant to me, not having to spend this day, of all days, alone. Thank you so much.'

'All part of the service.' He smiled at her, his grey eyes twinkling. 'It's been special for me too.'

They shared a final, tight hug at the ticket barrier and then he was gone.

Her journey home passed in a dream. Gazing out of the train window, her mind in a turmoil, she was reminded of Celia Johnson in *Brief Encounter*, right down to the vague feelings of guilt. Which was ridiculous, because she knew Jack would have been happy for her.

But mostly, she was happy. She still had to pinch herself. Of all the outcomes she had expected, this was the least likely. She had always been fond of Philip, but he'd had Angie and she had been madly in love with Jack. Who would have thought, after all these years, they would feel this way towards each other?

When the train finally reached Evesham, she trudged up the slope towards her car, slung her bag on the back seat, and drove home.

Twenty minutes later, home, she fed a very hungry Baggins, gave him an apologetic fuss and, after a quick bath, went to bed. But she couldn't rest. Too much had happened, her mind was racing. So, after twenty minutes of tossing and turning, she accepted sleep was not going to come.

She went downstairs and made herself a hot chocolate – so proud she had got through the day without alcohol – then collected her journal and biro and went back to bed.

I cannot quite believe this day. This time last year, I was in hell. Jack had died in the early afternoon, and I can remember coming home from the hospice, almost too numb and in shock to feel anything. Then I walked in the door, saw his coat hanging on the rack and burst into floods of tears, which lasted for hours.

Each time I managed to stop, wash my face and calm down a bit, another memory would start it all off again. I don't think I have ever cried so much in one day. I never want to be that miserable again.

And now it's a year later. I'd booked the day off work, to be alone with my memories, knowing it would be hard to stop thinking of him today and not wanting to make a fool of myself in public. I still miss him so much – his smile, the feel of his arms around me, the wonderful meals he used to cook (at least before he got so ill). Even his dreadful jokes, which were rarely funny. I would kill to hear him tell another one of those; just to be with him again, on an ordinary Saturday – doing the weekend shop together, arguing about how we wanted to spend the evening. Just being together. Like most people, when I had it, I took it all for granted. Now I've lost him, I would do anything to go back and deeply appreciate every last day, every last moment.

She paused to wipe away the tears and blow her nose.

I'd booked this day off, expecting to spend it sad and alone. Then to get that FB message from Philip, which led to today . . .

I'm still pinching myself, TBH. I've always been fond of Philip, right since college days. But he had Angie, and I had Jack, so we were always good friends. So when he suggested going to the Radical Eye together, I was so grateful that I wouldn't be alone, today of all days.

Oh, it's been such a gorgeous day! Right from the first hug at Paddington, I haven't enjoyed myself so much for yonks, not since way before Jack died, really. It makes me feel quite disloyal to his memory, especially today.

What on earth was I thinking of, spending this first anniversary of his passing with another man?

But no, that's ridiculous. I know Jack wouldn't have wanted me to spend the day alone and in sorrow. Which was why I accepted the invitation in the first place. So I wouldn't have to. Especially as I'm damn sure I'd have ended up drinking, to drown my sorrows and make the memories go away.

And then this. Oh my. It's been such a gorgeous day. When I kissed him, I only meant it as a thank you. But somehow, it turned into more than that. I haven't felt so aroused for years. My whole body reacted, not just my lips. If we hadn't been out in public, goodness knows where it could have led to.

It was so wonderful to be held that way again, to feel safe, to feel special, to feel loved. And then my beautiful bracelet – such a lovely gesture.

I wonder whether this will lead to anything? I'm not sure I'm ready for another relationship yet, but on the other hand, today was wonderful. It was so very, very nice not to be alone, to be sharing something special with someone special. Maybe I've struck lucky...

Come back down, Claire. You've had a wonderful day, but don't read too much into it. Take it as it comes. It's time to sleep now.

She sighed. It was late, she had work in the morning. Time to go to sleep. She closed her journal, snuggled down, closed her eyes.

85

Chapter Thirteen

Tired, Claire got through work on auto-pilot, buoyed by the occasional text from Philip. The Carnegie shortlist was out and, although Malorie Blackman hadn't made the cut, the titles were fascinating. She was looking forward to reading them and judging for herself. The next day, Friday, in need of a good workout, she went to the gym.

Afterwards, she drove to the supermarket to do the weekend shop. They were doing a special wine promotion, and as soon as she walked through the automatic doors, the display hit her in the face. Wine Festival – Special Offers.

She was seized by a longing to browse the aisle and pick out her favourites – Merlot, Shiraz, Cabernet Sauvignon . . . It took a Herculean effort to walk past, to choose not to stop. The wine was calling to her, her body was longing for it. She could smell it, that wonderful, complicated bouquet of red wine.

She stopped, closed her eyes, fingered her Chose Life ring. Come on. You can do this. You Can Do This.

She ducked into the shampoo aisle, out of sight of the wine, and fished out her phone. Fingers shaking, she logged on to the Facebook group.

Help! I'm in the supermarket, and they've got a Wine Festival going on, and I'm really struggling. The temptation is horrendous.

Back came the response:

*Does your supermarket have a café? Dump your trolley and have a
coffee and cake – being hungry makes the craving worse. Remember,
every time you resist her, the Wine Witch gets weaker. You can do
this! Xx*

Thank God for online friends who understood!

She did as her kind friend had advised and treated herself to an
Americano and a large slab of carrot cake, then went back in through
the clothing section, avoiding the wine.

She had averted the crisis for now but was far from out of the
woods. She went through the rest of the store like a dose of salts,
then drove home.

She was shaken. Surely, after two weeks, the worst should be over?
Clearly not. Would there ever be a time when she could walk past a
display of wine without having to call for help, without having to
run away, without shaking with fear?

Then she remembered the book. She hadn't looked at it for days.
Maybe it would have some helpful advice. She fetched it down and
read it over lunch.

She remembered reading something about neurological re-wiring
in the first couple of chapters. Ah, here it was! About the necessity of
allowing time for your brain to learn the new habit of not drinking.
First of all, you had to make a commitment to sobriety.

She looked down at her Chose Life ring and smiled. She'd done
that. But could she keep it up?

The author went on to say that the early weeks and months
would be challenging, offering many temptations to drink, when
you would come so close to picking a bottle off the shelves when
shopping.

She sighed. This was her to a T. This morning's encounter with
the wine display had proved that she was still a long way from being
over the worst.

But at least what she was feeling was normal – or at least normal
for newly sober people who were once alcohol-dependent. As she

continued to read, first the book, then some of the stories on the Facebook group, she was reassured – so many wonderful, strong people had gone through what she was going through and had stayed the course.

All the same, she wasn't looking forward to the evening. She had promised Lucy to meet down the Lion for their usual Friday catch-up. She gave herself permission to stay for as little or as long as she was comfortable. There would be no shame in walking out after one drink, if it was too hard. And she'd get there a bit later than usual, so Lucy would already be there. That way, she could make the most of seeing her, while staying for the minimum possible time.

So she walked down a little after 7.30, and sure enough, Lucy was there. Claire smiled at her, then went up to the bar. 'Becks Blue, please, Fred.'

'That's a change from your usual, isn't it, Claire?'

She was prepared. 'Yeah, I'm giving it up for Lent.'

To her intense relief, he made no further comment on her choice, just asking whether she wanted it in a glass or a bottle.

'Glass, please.' Hah! Sucks to you, Wine Witch! I'm in the pub, drinking Becks Blue. And you can fuck off back to where you came from!

'Hello, Lucy. How's your week been?'

'Not too bad, thanks. Work's been crazy – I've had to work late every evening. But I've lost another pound and a half at Slimming World, so that's good.'

'Yay! Excellent news. I thought you were looking svelte.'

'Aw, thanks for noticing. How about you?'

'I seem to be eating for England at the moment. I suppose it's because I'm not drinking anymore.'

'How's it going, Claire? This not-drinking thing? You seem to be managing fine. Are you really planning to quit for good?'

How much should she share? Lucy had been so good to her, not only these past few weeks, but for all the years of their friendship. Better tell the truth.

'It's been bloody difficult, to be honest. I hadn't realised how dependent I was, and I'm still getting cravings. It's like giving up smoking – your body's used to a certain amount of alcohol and tries all sorts of skulduggery to persuade you to drink again. But I've joined a secret Facebook group for people who are trying to quit, and it is brilliant – I can log on there any time for advice and support. And here I am, drinking Becks Blue, trying not to reach for your wine, which smells absolutely fantastic!'

'God, I'm sorry, Claire,' Lucy replied, moving her glass away. 'I'd no idea it was that bad. I really admire what you're doing – more than two weeks now, isn't it? But are you sure it's necessary? I mean, you aren't an alcoholic, are you?'

Whoa! Didn't see that one coming! 'No,' she said. 'I'm not, and never have been. But I *was* having an unhealthy relationship with red wine, drinking every night, and I just need to knock it on the head while I still can. So that I don't end up as an alcoholic.'

Just then, Dawn arrived. Saved by the bell.

'Hello, Claire, hello, Lucy. Sorry I'm late,' she said.

'No worries,' Claire said. 'We've not been here that long.'

'What are you drinking, Claire? I didn't think you were a lager girl!' Dawn said.

Oh crap. Was she ready to tell her? Yes. Deep breath.

'Actually, I've decided to give it up for Lent. This is Beck's Blue,' she said, in as casual a tone as she could manage.

'Oh, good for you! What brought that on?' Dawn said.

'I thought I needed a break from it, that's all.' Claire paused, then said quietly, 'To be truthful, I was drinking a bit too much red wine, so I've quit for Lent, to prove to myself that I can.'

'Oh, God. I'm sorry, Claire. I didn't realise,' Dawn said.

'It's no big deal,' Claire lied, carefully not catching Lucy's eye. 'It's been a tough couple of weeks, but I'm getting used to it now.' She changed the subject. 'Anyway, enough about me. How are you? And how are your mum and Jake?'

'Jake's fine – his A level mocks went well, so he's on the final straight now. I can't believe he'll be heading off to university in the autumn.'

89

'That's good to hear,' Lucy said. 'How about your mum?'

Dawn's face changed. 'I've started to look at care homes,' she said. 'I absolutely hate the whole idea of putting her in one, but I just can't risk having her at home alone any longer. She's a danger to herself these days – not often, but enough to worry me. And Jake and I can't be around the whole time, every evening and weekend. Especially as he won't be around at all after September.'

'That's tough,' Claire said, giving Dawn a hug. 'But I think you're doing the right thing.'

'Am I, though?' Dawn said. 'She looked after me when I was a child. Why can't I look after her now? It's so hard. I feel like I'm betraying her.'

'No, you're not,' Lucy said. 'It's just got too much for you. You mustn't blame yourself, Dawn.'

'Absolutely not,' Claire agreed. 'No one could have taken better care of her than you have, Dawn.'

'Thanks, you two,' Dawn said. 'That helps more than you know.'

After a while, Claire finished her drink, smiled at them both, then stood up. 'Time for an early night. Lucy, I'll see you for our gym session tomorrow – pick you up at ten thirty?'

Then she gave her friends a hug and walked out. She had done it. She had gone to the pub and not drunk. Exultantly, she punched the air.

Chapter Fourteen

When she got to the Writers' Group, Duncan, the group's leader, was already in the room, setting up. As she helped him put the chairs out, she said, 'Duncan, if you've got a moment afterwards, I'd be grateful if we could talk for a few minutes about my religious cult idea.'

For a moment, he looked puzzled. 'Oh, yes, I remember. You want to involve your heroine in a cult! Yes, of course. Let's have a word afterwards.'

Then the others started to stream in, and she put the idea to the back of her mind. The theme for the month was 'Rising to the challenge' so she had written about the time she had trained for and run the London Marathon ten years earlier. It had all the elements required: a definite challenge, some obstacles along the way and final victory. She preferred writing about things she had experienced first-hand – it was so much easier than having to do research.

She was in awe of the talents of her fellow writers. There were some very experienced ones in the group, who had published real books, and they always contributed marvellous pieces, which made her own efforts seem amateurish in comparison.

But she was finding her own voice and, over the months, comments had become more positive. Last month, Duncan had even said that her writing was coming on by leaps and bounds. She settled down to listen to the contributions of the others.

It was fascinating to hear how the same assignment could be

interpreted in so many different ways. One member shared a story about Robert the Bruce and how he had risen to the challenge of fighting against the English, following earlier defeats in battle. It was immaculately written, with just enough Scottish words to give it an authentic flavour. She had obviously done her research – how did she find the time? Another wrote about the challenge of raising a child with Down's Syndrome, which left Claire teary-eyed. A third shared their weight-loss journey, turned into fiction. Each story was so different, but each was moving in its own way.

Each story was critiqued by the rest of the group and Claire found their insights so useful. She'd been a member of this group for two years now and had learned a lot from the others – starting *in media res*, not wasting words, making the characters distinct and memorable, among other things.

When it came to her turn to read, she took a deep breath and read steadily. To her joy, their comments were mostly complimentary, not only about the writing, but about the fact that she had actually run a marathon. She smiled in relief.

When the meeting was finished and the other members had left, Duncan came over. 'All right, Claire. What's this idea of yours?'

'I read somewhere,' she said, 'you have to involve your main character in some kind of conflict, so they can grow and develop, and the idea of embroiling her in a religious cult popped into my head. I had thought of making her meet Mr Wrong, but that seems so clichéd. But now I'm dithering. It will take a lot of research and I'm not sure I know enough about the effects of such things. What do you think?'

After a few seconds' thought, Duncan said, 'It *could* work very well, but, as you say, it would involve a lot of research. There are so many other ways you can put obstacles in your character's way. You say she's a travel writer? You could lose her in a jungle or have her stray into a war zone, or get involved with a desperate human rights situation – any number of things. All of which would have an impact on her character.' He smiled. 'Give it some thought and let me know how it goes. You know I'm always here for advice.'

'Thank you so much, Duncan! I'm really grateful. You've given me a lot to think about.'

'Was there anything else?'

'No, that was all, thank you.'

'Then I'll see you next month. I'm expecting great things of this novel of yours. When you're ready to show it to someone, I'd be happy to cast an eye over it – my editing rates are very reasonable.' He smiled.

She smiled back. 'Thank you. I'll bear that in mind, if I ever get that far.'

'You will. I have every confidence in you. See you next month.'

Claire was hardly conscious of driving home. Her mind was full of ideas for Dani – any of the suggestions Duncan had made seemed so much better than her original thought. She couldn't wait to start. But she knew she wouldn't have a chance to do any serious writing until Friday and then Sunday. She had work the next day and was meeting Philip on Saturday.

She had her usual bath and prepared for sleep. But her mind was buzzing. It was no good – she was going to have to get up and write it all down. She swung her legs out of bed, put on her dressing gown and slippers, and went to the study. Once there, the ideas started to flow.

Duncan's given me lots of suggestions about how to grow Dani:
1. *To lose her in a jungle (or desert, or even big city?)*
2. *Have her stray into a war zone – oh my, that would be a tough one to research. But perhaps she could be checking out Israel, and Christian-based tours, and head over to Bethlehem? Hmmm, that's got some mileage.*
3. *Get her involved in a desperate human rights situation – not quite sure what he meant about that – perhaps going to a developing country and seeing some dreadful things, and being moved to help?*

Or . . . I wonder if she could be doing a series of articles about pilgrimages? Let's think, how many pilgrimage sites do I know anything about:

1. *Canterbury*
2. *Jerusalem (of course) which could fit in with Duncan's idea . . .*
3. *The Camino to Santiago de Compostela – I've read that it's a gorgeous walk, and she could meet all sorts of interesting people along the way . . .*
4. *Oberammergau – I could write about that from first-hand experience, from when Jack and I went in 1990 . . .*
5. *Lindisfarne and Iona*
6. *Glastonbury*
7. *Dharamsala*

Then if I wanted something a bit different, I could include Ground Zero in New York and the wonderful War Memorials. Oh, and Ellis Island. This is beginning to sound like a distinct possibility. I can't wait to do something about it.

She looked at her phone. Nearly eleven o'clock. Turning off the desk light, she went back to her room, fell into bed and was asleep in minutes.

After a tough day at work – Celia had been off sick, so she and Gillian had to manage alone, and the Homework Club had been heaving – Claire was glad to reach home. To her joy, the next Spirituality Book Club book had arrived – Ruth's choice. She knew that Ruth was interested in Celtic spirituality, so the title was not a surprise: *Water from an Ancient Well: Celtic Spirituality for Modern Life* by Kenneth McIntosh. She ran her eye down the list of contents and saw the chapter heading *Uncharted Seas: Life's Pilgrimage.* This could be useful . . .

After dinner, she settled down to read. Each chapter was a lovely mixture of stories of Celtic saints and martyrs, together with some history and theology and, finally, suggestions for applying Celtic spiritual practices to contemporary living. The writing style was easy to follow, yet deeply devotional. Could Christianity be like this? Could her life be like this? A spiritual journey into relationship with God?

Halfway through, she put her bookmark back in, and moved to her desk to do some journaling.

I've never come across this sort of Christianity before. It seems to be so different to what I'm used to — so much less structured, so much more devotional. I love the idea of incorporating some of the spiritual practices he mentions into my life — trying to recognise God's presence in the ordinary events and connections of my days, and having a daily time of stillness and reflection. I can't wait to see what the rest of the book says — the last chapter's about pilgrimage, so it could be really handy for writing about Dani too.

I think I'm going to start doing a morning sit, tomorrow. That's what Reverend Martin called it, at the Ash Wednesday service. And he said he found it really difficult. Oh well, I can but try.

It'll mean getting up half an hour earlier, but that shouldn't be too difficult. I've always been a lark rather than an owl. And I can use my phone as a timer.

It was getting late. If she was going to get up early tomorrow, she'd better try to get some sleep.

Next morning, after her alarm went off, she splashed her face with cold water to wake herself up, then went through to the study. She lit a candle, set her phone's timer to twenty minutes, then re-read the instructions in the book. It sounded very simple — it was about sitting still, in silence, and listening to God. How hard could it be? She touched the start button on the timer, and settled in her chair, feet flat on the floor, back straight. Took a few deep breaths then closed her eyes.

Immediately her mind was filled with thoughts, all competing for her attention. How on earth was she supposed to stop thinking? Concentrate on the breath . . . She tried that . . . A bird, outside the window, welcoming the morning with its song . . . Follow the breath . . . Must get some writing done today — it'll be my last chance until Sunday. And there's the rest of the book to read . . . Follow the breath . . . Why can't I do this? Oh, it's hopeless . . . Follow the breath. And on, and on.

It was no good. Every time she tried to follow her breath, as instructed, her mind chattered and whooped like a barrel-load of monkeys. This was ridiculous.

She gave up, opened her eyes. Have a shower, then do some research. There must be easier ways than this.

After breakfast, she went on to Facebook and posted:

Facebook Hive Mind: does anyone know any good meditation apps? I'm trying to meditate in the mornings and cannot quieten my mind.

One friend commented, *Have you tried Headspace? You can get it free for a month. I've found it really useful.*

Another wrote, *There's an app called Insight Timer – you can set it for different times and different sounds – again, it's free.*

She posted: *Thank you! I'll give them both a try.* She downloaded both onto her phone. She'd give them a go tomorrow. Now it was time to write. She'd have the whole day to rough out her new idea for Dani. She made herself a mug of coffee and climbed the stairs.

By lunchtime she had the beginnings of a headache. She'd go for a walk, clear her head. It was a grey, uninviting day outside, but she'd feel better for it. She wrapped up warm and set off on a brisk walk round the village. Forty minutes later she was back indoors, but not inclined to do any more writing. She'd read the rest of the Celtic spirituality book, then go down to the Lion to meet Lucy and Dawn.

The last chapter of the book had some wonderful suggestions for pilgrimage destinations, so Claire added them to her list for Dani. How weird that Ruth had suggested this book, just as the idea of sending Dani off on pilgrimages had come. Or maybe it was grace . . . She sent up a quick prayer of thanks, in case.

Lucy was already there when Claire got to the Lion. Claire got herself a Beck's Blue, then joined her friend.

'Hello, Lucy, how's your week been?'

'Mm, so-so. I've had a really busy week at work, but Slimming World was a disaster. Not only have I not lost any weight, I've put on a pound!'

'Oh, dear. I'm sorry to hear that. Any idea why?'

'Well,' Lucy said, looking sidelong at her friend, 'it *might* have something to do with the large bar of chocolate I ate on Tuesday evening. It jumped off the shelf in the supermarket and into my trolley. And Slimming World was on Wednesday evening.'

'Oops! Never mind, don't give up. You've been good since then, haven't you?'

'Yes, I really have. But I'm getting so fed up – I just can't seem to lose the last ten pounds.'

'You've done really well up to now – how much have you lost so far?'

'A stone and a half. But I'm stuck now.'

'Maybe this is the weight you should be – you know, your natural weight? You look pretty good to me.'

'D'you really think so? I'd love to stop now, but I'm afraid that if I don't hit my target weight, it'll all come back on.'

'Are you managing to get to the gym regularly? That should help to keep you from gaining it back.'

'I've been going twice a week, but it's so hard to fit it in, on top of everything else.'

'Yes, I can understand that. It's much easier for me, being part-time. But stick with it, Lu. It helps me to stay on track, weight-wise.'

Lucy sighed deeply as she looked at Claire. '*You* don't need to worry, Claire. You've got a gorgeous figure.'

'Aw, thanks, hun.' Claire blushed. 'But I can assure you that I wouldn't have, if I didn't work out regularly.'

'OK, I'll give it a go.'

'That's my girl!'

Chapter Fifteen

While Claire had managed to avoid drinking on the Friday evening, she still suffered what her favourite author Brené Brown called a 'vulnerability hangover' that weekend, which was as bad, if not worse, than a real one.

The planned meetup – she scarcely dared call it a date – with Philip hadn't come off. He texted late on Friday evening just after she got back from the Red Lion:

Hey, Claire, I'm so sorry – I can't make it this weekend – as I half suspected, one of my work cases has gone critical. I'll be in touch soon. xx

Although most of her brain believed this text implicitly, the other part was saying, 'See. You've made a fool of yourself. He was just being kind.'

Then she would long for a glass of red wine to ease the pain of rejection.

But she somehow managed to keep her sobriety promise, by reading back through her journal entries, going to the gym and generally keeping herself busy, to avoid feeling – well – anything. Any time she stopped, she wobbled, logging on to the sobriety group with increasing regularity and desperation. Without their support, she would have succumbed to temptation.

She went to church on the Sunday morning, to be out of harm's way for a couple of hours, and to ask Ruth's advice about sitting, which wasn't getting any easier.

'I'm loving *Water from an Ancient Well* so much,' she said. 'It's really speaking to me.'

'I'm so glad,' Ruth smiled. 'It's one of my favourite books about Celtic spirituality.'

'But I'm really struggling with trying to sit quietly,' Claire said. 'My mind's all over the place – the very opposite of quiet and still. How on earth do you manage it?'

Ruth laughed. 'I don't!' she said, 'or at least not always. They don't call this stuff spiritual *practice* for nothing. I can remember when I first started centring prayer, I found it incredibly difficult. And there are still some mornings when I get very little benefit from it. So don't be disheartened, Claire. Keep on doing it faithfully and your mind *will* quieten.'

'Thanks, Ruth. I was beginning to think there was something wrong with me.'

'Not at all. It's not an easy practice, but it's a very rewarding one.'

Philip finally rang the following Tuesday evening.

'Claire? I'm so sorry about last weekend. I've spent the last three days on standby, in case I was needed to make sure that correct procedures were followed for my clients. But it's all been sorted now – the children have been placed with one of our regular foster parents, so they should be safe enough. It's one of the hardest parts of the job, splitting families up. At least the kids are all together – for now, at least.' His voice changed. 'Are we on for this weekend? I'd really love to see you.'

The tight knot in her stomach began to unwind. 'Philip! I'm so pleased to hear from you. I'm glad those children are safe. They're lucky to have you to look after them. And yes, I'd love to meet up this weekend. Where shall we go?'

'Thank you for understanding . . . I was wondering about Bourton-on-the-Water . . . it's not too far from you, and I haven't been there for years. What do you think?'

'That sounds lovely! We could go to the Model Village – I haven't been there since I was a small girl. And there's the Cotswold Perfumery, and the Motor Museum too, if you like.'

'Ah, that's good. I'd like to go to Birdland as well. Sounds like we've got the makings of a great day out! Where shall we meet?'

They arranged to meet at the big car park on the Burford Road at the edge of the village, at 10.30 the following Saturday morning. When they rang off, she danced a little jig of delight – she was going to see him again!

Claire awoke early on Saturday and dressed with care in her Karen Millen jeans, her favourite turquoise jumper, her North Face fleece, and black boots.

She drove through Broadway and Stow, reaching Bourton-on-the-Water at 10.15. She found the car park easily, paid for an all-day ticket and settled down to wait for Philip. She had a momentary panic when she realised that they hadn't arranged a specific meeting place in the car park, so decided to wait by the gate, as she didn't know what his car looked like.

But she needn't have worried. He found her at just before half past and swept her into a big hug. 'You look good enough to eat! Let's go.'

Once more, she was startled by the intensity of her feelings. She felt so happy, just being with him. She tucked her hand through his arm, as they walked into the village.

'What shall we do first?' he said.

'I'd really love to go to the Model Village before it gets too busy.'

Claire was instantly enchanted, remembering a visit there with her parents as a small girl. She remembered how wonderful it had been to kneel and look inside all the little houses, marvelling at the fact that this was a village-inside-a-village. There was also a new exhibition inside the Village, of exquisitely detailed miniature scenes and room-sets. Everything was so tiny and so perfect.

After coffee, they turned down Victoria Street to find the Cotswold Perfumery. It was deliciously fragrant, and Claire treated Philip to some Oberon aftershave. The Perfumery also offered tours of the factory, which was new to her, but unfortunately, they had to be booked in advance. They promised themselves they'd come back another time.

By now they were hungry, so they wandered back to the High Street to find somewhere to eat, eventually settling on the Chestnut Tree Tea Rooms, where they enjoyed some homemade vichyssoise with half a fresh baguette.

'Where to next?' Philip said.

'Up to you. I honestly don't mind. We could go to the Motor Museum, or just have a wander. I think it would make sense to leave Birdland to the end, because it's right near the car park.'

'Let's go to the Motor Museum. I haven't been there for years and really enjoyed it last time. Are you sure you don't mind?'

'Of course not. We've already done the things I wanted to do, so now it's your turn!'

They crossed one of the little bridges over the River Windrush and walked into the Museum. To Claire's surprise, she quite enjoyed it. The cars didn't excite her, but there was so much more to see – all the old signs, and posters, and other bits of motoring memorabilia. It was really well done.

Coming out into a fine drizzle, they decided to pop in to Birdland before calling it a day. Although the rain took the edge off their enjoyment, they both found Birdland enchanting – it was such a rare joy to see flamingos and ostriches, parrots and penguins, as well as the less exotic species. They agreed it had been the highlight of the day.

Then they walked back to the car park.

'This has been such a lovely day,' Claire said. 'Would you like to come back for dinner?'

'Are you sure?' His face lit up. 'Lovely!'

'I've got plenty of food in. I'm sure I can put something together.'

He squeezed her hand. 'Then let's go.'

What was she thinking? Did she really invite him back?

But it was done now.

In her rear-view mirror, she could see Philip's red Skoda.

Time for some quick thinking. The dinner part was fine. She'd done another lot of batch cooking the previous day and had several portions of lamb and spinach risotto in the freezer.

It was what happened afterwards.

No, it wasn't. This was Philip, not some woman-eating gargoyle she hardly knew. She'd known him for years. He'll respect 'no' if it comes to it. Stop panicking! Breathe!

On the other hand, she might not want to say no.

Best to see what happened. Go with the flow.

In the end, that was all she *could* do. Go with the flow.

When they got back to the house, she said, hoping she didn't sound nervous, 'Come on in! I've just got to feed Baggins, then get the food out of the freezer, and put the kettle on. It shouldn't take too long.'

'Thank you!' He smiled, following her in to the kitchen. 'Wow! This is a great size. Do you do much entertaining? Sorry, Claire. Stupid question. I'm not much used to small talk.'

She smiled back. 'Don't worry. Nor am I. Let's just try to be us. Why don't you sit down at the table and I'll make us a drink. Then I'll put dinner on – it won't take long. Tea or coffee? I can't offer you anything stronger – I threw all the booze out when I quit.'

'That's fine. I've got to drive back, anyway, so I wouldn't want to drink. Coffee, please.'

Well, thank God for that anyway. She put the Gaggia on. 'How long can you stay?'

'Until you throw me out, I guess. It's Sunday tomorrow, and it only takes a couple of hours to drive back, and I can sleep in tomorrow. Let's see how it goes, eh?' He smiled.

She bustled round, getting the meal ready, then served it. For a few minutes there was silence, as they concentrated on the food.

Then Philip said, 'This is good! Thank you, Claire!'

She blushed. 'Thanks. I'm not much of a cook, really. Jack did all the savoury stuff, I did the baking. But in the last year, I've had to learn how to feed myself. So long as it's one-pot stuff, I can usually manage. I can only offer you a yoghurt or ice cream for afters.'

'That's fine. I'm not sure I'd have room for anything more. This is delicious.'

Afterwards, she loaded the dishwasher, then started to wash up the rest.

Philip got up. 'Where are your tea towels? The least I can do is help to dry up.'

'In the second drawer down, over there.' She nodded in the direction, her hands in the washing-up. This was all so natural, so normal. She wasn't used to it.

Chores done, they went through to the lounge.

They spoke at the same moment.

Claire said, 'Would you like to watch something?'

Philip said, 'Where shall we go next time?'

And, catching each other's eyes, they burst out laughing.

Then Claire said, 'I don't mind. As long as there is a next time. I've had such fun today, spending the day with you.'

'My motives were entirely selfish, I assure you,' he said. 'I've been counting the days until I could see you again. When Angie died, I kind of assumed that was it, as far as love and romance were concerned. That I'd just dedicate my life to looking after Chas and hope it all worked out. When I invited you down to London for the day, I had no idea that we would hit it off so well together.'

He put his arm around her shoulders, she snuggled up against him and he kissed the top of her head.

'It may be too early to say it, but I think I'm falling in love with you, Claire. Do you mind?'

'Oh, God!' she said. 'I just don't know. Part of me wants you never to leave, but another part is still in mourning for Jack, and I'm not sure that would be very fair to you. I'm sorry. That's not the answer you were looking for. But it's the truth. It's only been a year, and I still miss him so much, every day.'

He drew her close. 'I'm sorry, sweetheart. I didn't mean to rush you. It would have been too early for me too, one year on. Let's play it by ear. I promise not to ask for more than you can give. But I wanted you to know how I feel. You're very special. Do you know that?'

Suddenly, tears welled up and Claire couldn't stop them. She didn't try. Turning her face into Philip's shoulder, she let them pour out.

Philip stroked her hair. 'There, there, my love. Everything's all right.'

It was all too much. She couldn't remember when she had last felt special, or cared for, or loved.

Wiping her eyes on her sleeve, she raised her head. 'I'm so sorry. What must you think of me? I'm just so mixed up! Being with you feels so good. Part of me feels disloyal to Jack's memory. And then, on top of it all, there's the whole not-drinking thing. It's been nearly four weeks now, and sometimes I'm desperate for a glass of wine. I'm in such a mess.'

'Claire. It's you I want. You. You, as you are. Not some ideal woman. Let's give it a try, eh?'

Resistance was pointless. She smiled at him. 'OK. As long as you know where I am. I . . . I think I might be falling in love with you, too.'

Then they were in each other's arms, kissing, clinging, holding each other, kissing and kissing again.

Her body was on fire. It had been so long. So long.

Chapter Sixteen

Although Philip stayed the night, they did not make love. Claire froze at the last minute. She pulled away from him and fled to the en suite, where she crumpled into a sobbing heap on to the cold tiles.

Moments later, she heard the door open

'Hey, hey,' he murmured, taking her into his arms. 'If you're not ready, you're not ready. I'm sorry, I didn't mean to rush you. Come back to bed and let me just hold you. Come on, Claire. Come on, sweetheart.'

Still sobbing, she let him guide her back to the bed. 'I'm so sorry. You didn't deserve that. But it's too soon.'

'It's me who should apologise. We've got all the time in the world. It's late. Let's get some sleep. Unless you want me to go?'

'No! No, I don't want you to go. I want you to stay. I need you to stay. But I can't . . .'

He gave her a gentle hug. 'It's OK. It really is. Let's get some sleep.'

'Wake up, sleepyhead! The sun's shining and it's a beautiful day. I've made you a mug of coffee and fed Baggins.'

She opened her eyes and there he was, smiling down at her. She struggled into an upright position and took the coffee. After a long drink, she smiled. 'Thank you! That's good.'

'I'll wait for you downstairs. No need to hurry.'

She was downstairs, showered and dressed, in twenty minutes. They had breakfast, then Philip said that he'd have to get off. 'Sunday's my usual housework day, and my place is a tip!' He grinned. 'Are you free next weekend?'

She managed a smile. 'That would be lovely. Where shall we go?'

'Let's have a think and I'll give you a ring in the week.'

He pulled his car keys from his leather jacket pocket and headed for the door. 'Give me a hug before I go.'

A tight hug, a quick kiss, and he was gone.

She went back into the kitchen, now so empty, and started clearing the breakfast things. Before long, tears were streaming down her face. What was wrong with her? She could use a drink. She couldn't cope with all this.

She grabbed her house keys, let herself out and was soon walking down to the Co-op to buy a bottle of red. She spent some time standing in the wine aisle, fighting with the Wine Witch. Only her Chose Life ring stopped her from taking a bottle off the shelves and heading for the checkout. She tore herself away and grabbed a big bar of chocolate instead.

Shaking, she walked out of the shop. She trudged back home, rushed upstairs and logged on to the Facebook group.

OMG that was a close one. I actually walked into the Co-op to buy myself some wine, and it took everything I'd got not to. It's been nearly four weeks now – when is this going to ease up? LL

Back came the reply, from one of the women she had made friends with over the past few weeks:

Dear LL, first of all, WELL DONE for not giving in! Every time you beat the Wine Witch, she gets weaker. The first couple of months are probably the most vulnerable – after that, not drinking becomes more of a habit. Or at least, that's what I found. But you need to know that she will raise her ugly head at ever widening intervals for a good long while yet – whenever something upsetting or wonderful happens, anything that is outside your usual routine. We've all been through it on here or are still going through it. Stay close and post as often as you need to. Hugs xx

Relieved, Claire posted:

Thank you for the reassurance. I can't believe I'm finding this so hard, and I'm so grateful for your support. LL xx

She logged off and reached for her journal.

I am in such a mess. We had a lovely day at Bourton-in-the-Water yesterday, then I invited Philip back.

What must he think of me? He must think I'm a real tease. But I'm not. I just couldn't. It's too soon. Thank God he accepted it. I think he understands. Oh, God, have I ruined everything now? He seemed to be OK about it, but I don't know how long he'll wait. And I'm not sure how long it's going to take me to be ready for a physical relationship.

But I think I'm falling in love with him. He's so kind and gentle, and he makes me laugh. I haven't felt this good in a long time. Maybe Jack would understand. It's been so long since I've felt so loved, so special. It's hard to believe that it's wrong to feel such happiness. Surely Jack wouldn't begrudge me that?

This not drinking is so bloody hard. Every time something out of the ordinary happens, happy or sad, my first instinct is to reach for a drink. I'm so proud of myself for resisting this morning, but it came that close.

I wonder if he'll ring. I'll die if he doesn't. I'm not sure I could bear to be alone again. These last couple of weeks have been so wonderful. And then I've gone and screwed it up by freezing.

No, that's not fair. I wasn't ready. And he seemed to respect that. I hope he rings.

Either Philip would ring, or he wouldn't. And she would have to deal with it. She put her journal away, went back downstairs, made another coffee, then decided to go for a walk, followed by some writing.

A brisk walk around the village cleared her head. When she got back, she made herself a scratch lunch, then returned to the study. She had spent half of the previous Friday working out a new outline for her Dani novel, so spent the afternoon working on the first chapter.

Soon she was fathoms deep in her writing and, by the end of the afternoon, she had completed a first draft of most of the first chapter.

Satisfied, she shut down the laptop, and went downstairs to make herself some dinner and watch some TV. The morning's alarms were a lifetime away.

Two days passed and no word from Philip. Claire went through the days on automatic pilot – Monday at work, Tuesday the usual round of housework, gym, and writing. And trying to sit, wait on God. Which was nearly impossible. Her heart wasn't in it. Why hadn't he got in touch?

She immersed herself in the first of the Carnegie short-list titles, which had arrived in the library on Monday. She chose to start with the latest Philip Reeve, as she'd enjoyed reading his *Mortal Engines* series. So far, it was living up to its promise.

She wondered whether she would ever write anything that good. She doubted it.

She finished her first draft of the second chapter of *Dani* on Tuesday afternoon, and the scene was now set for her heroine to set off on her first assignment. But she couldn't decide which pilgrimage to tackle first. Getting stuck this early on didn't seem to be a good omen for the novel's future.

She was four weeks AF now and the promised better night's sleep had started to kick in. Before she had quit, she had usually woken up around two with a dry and foul-tasting mouth, needing to get up, have a drink of water, and clean her teeth before getting back to sleep.

These days, she was sleeping like a baby. Falling asleep was still tricky without the alcohol to sedate her but, once asleep, that was it until the alarm woke her.

She woke up feeling refreshed and set about getting ready for work. But she was so not in the mood and was tempted to ring in sick. However, her sense of duty was too strong, and the other staff didn't deserve that of her.

So she drove to work and did what needed to be done, fiercely concentrating on the job in front of her. She was relieved when Miriam arrived at lunchtime. She almost ran to her car to get away.

Once home, she changed into her favourite pair of tatty, but very comfortable, jogging bottoms, which she only wore in the house, ate her lunch, then trailed upstairs to the study to try to recapture her lost writing mojo. She'd just logged in to her laptop, when her phone rang.

'Hello, Philip, how are you?' she asked, trying to sound casual.

'Hey, Claire! I'm fine, thanks. I'm ringing to see whether you'd like to come down to Bath this weekend? You remember we were talking about Harry Potter? Well, Emma Watson is Belle in the live-action version of *Beauty and the Beast*, and it's on at my local cinema. I thought we could go and see it, and then maybe you could come back for dinner. What do you say?'

'That sounds lovely,' she replied, the knot in her stomach unravelling. 'What time is it on? I've no idea how long it would take me to get down there . . .'

'There's more than one screening, so up to you. It took me about an hour and a half to get back last Sunday, but the traffic would be worse on a Saturday, so maybe you'd better allow at least two hours, more if you want to include a break. So if I book us in for the late afternoon showing, you could plan to get here about lunchtime, we could have a snack and then a leisurely stroll down to the cinema. Does that sound all right?'

'Yes, that sounds great.'

He laughed. 'I'm so glad you can make it this weekend, honey. It's my last free weekend for a while – next Saturday I've got to drive up to York to pick Chas up for the end of the Easter holidays. Which is a complete pain in the proverbial. It's the best part of five hours each way, so I'm going to be knackered when I get home. And then Peggy is bound to want us to go over and see her on the Sunday . . .'

'Peggy?'

'My dear not-so-beloved mother-in-law. She was great when Chas was younger, after Angie died – she used to cook us meals and such like. But lately, she's got very possessive around Chas and I think he's finding it hard. And she's never liked me very much – I was never her idea of an ideal husband for her daughter.' He paused. 'Sorry, Claire. I didn't mean to unload that on you – I'm just not looking forward to her particular brand of patronising busy-bodying.'

'Oh dear, that sounds tough. Still, we've got this weekend together, at least. I'm really looking forward to it.'

'You're right. "Sufficient unto the day" and all that. Right, I'd better ring off now – I'm supposed to be reviewing a case study for a new client, but wanted to touch base with you first. Can't wait to see you on Saturday, sweetheart. Bye for now.'

'Me too – see you then. Bye, Philip.'

Grinning, Claire turned back to *Dani*. She wrote the pilgrimage destinations on slips of paper, folded them up and then chose one at random. She could always swap the order round if it didn't work out as the plot unfolded.

Oberammergau.

Hugging herself, she searched out the souvenir book she and Jack had bought when they had seen the Passion Play all those years ago. It had been an awe-inspiring experience, which she still fondly remembered.

By the time Baggins came nagging for his tea, she had written the first part of Chapter 3 and had some good ideas for the rest of it. She closed down her laptop and followed the cat downstairs.

Two evenings later, she was back at the Red Lion with Lucy and sipping her Beck's Blue.

She leaned forward. 'I've got some news for you.'

'What kind of news? Tell, tell!' Lucy said, also leaning forward, looking for all the world like a plump little robin expecting some breadcrumbs.

'Well . . . You remember I told you about meeting Philip and Helen at the writing conference in February? And how nice it was to see them both again? I've seen Philip again since then. Twice in fact. We went down to London for the day together a couple of weeks ago and last weekend we went to Bourton-on-the Water. And . . . it seems to be turning into something more than a friendship.'

'Blimey, Claire – you're a dark horse! Why didn't you tell me before?'

'Because I wasn't sure whether it would come to anything. But now he's invited me down to Bath on Saturday.'

Lucy fell back in her chair. 'Wow! You two are dating? When did this start? Tell me all about it!'

So Claire shared the story – how they'd gone down to the *Radical Eye* exhibition together, about the bracelet he had bought her, and about their lovely day out in Bourton-on-the-Water. But nothing about Philip coming back to hers. That was private, even from Lucy.

'Well! Good for you! I've got some news of my own,' Lucy said. 'I'm dating too! I've met a gorgeous guy called Mark at the gym. We were on treadmills next to each other, and got talking. He's asked me out tomorrow.'

'That's great news. What do you know about him?' Claire said.

'Oh, not much. But he's really fit – he was going so fast on the treadmill, made me feel like a right plodder.' She laughed.

'Where are you going?' Claire asked.

'To the pictures. An action thriller. Not really my cup of tea, but I don't care. I'll be with Mark.'

'That's funny. Philip and I are going to see *Beauty and the Beast* tomorrow – the live action version,' Claire said.

'Lucky you! I'd much rather see that,' Lucy said. 'But never mind, I'm sure I'll enjoy it.'

'Well, take care of yourself,' Claire said.

'I will, don't worry,' Lucy said.

111

Chapter Seventeen

By ten next morning, Claire was driving towards the M5. It had been a while since she had done a motorway journey – not since the writing conference in fact – and the traffic, as Philip had predicted, was much heavier on a Saturday.

So she was relieved when the sign for Michaelwood Services came up. After coffee and a cake, she was soon back on the road.

An hour later, she was at Philip's door. There was an intercom system with one of the buzzers marked 'Bateman'. At least she had found the right place. She took a deep breath and pressed it.

Seconds later, Philip's voice came through the speaker, sounding metallic and tinny. 'Claire? Is that you? Come on up! I'm on the second floor.' The sound of a click, as the door was released.

She was halfway up the stairs when she heard footsteps above.

'Hey, sweetheart! You're a sight for sore eyes! How was the journey?' He gave her a big hug.

'Not too bad, thanks, but I'm gasping for a coffee.'

'Here we are - Palace Bateman. I'll put the coffee machine on straight away. It's all ready to go.'

She walked in. There was a narrow hallway, off which several doors opened. Following the sound of his voice, she came out into a light and airy high-ceilinged living room with marble-effect fireplace, a battered old leather sofa, a comfortable-looking armchair, a coffee table, which was nearly invisible under a pile of papers and a laptop, and the biggest television she had ever seen. Alcoves on either side of the fireplace were lined with bookshelves. She wandered over to learn his taste in books.

Philip re-appeared. 'Black, isn't it? I've also got some rather nice ginger stem cookies from Marks, if you fancy one. Or would you rather wait for lunch?'

She swung round. 'Yes, black, please, and I'd love a ginger stem cookie!'

'Cookies it is! Make yourself at home, I won't be a minute.'

Claire smiled. It was quite sweet, being waited on like this.

Moments later, he came in carrying a large tray, on which were balanced two large mugs of coffee and a packet of cookies. He set it down on the one free corner of the coffee table, then passed her a mug and the packet.

'Here you are – enjoy!' He sat down in the armchair and smiled. 'So, how's my girl?'

She smiled back. 'All the better for seeing you, thank you! This was a good idea of yours – I loved the original and can't wait to see what it's like as a live-action film. What time are we going?'

'There's a showing at three thirty, so I've booked seats for that. It's 2D – I hope you don't mind – I hate having to wear dark glasses in the cinema.'

'No, that's fine. Me too.' She paused. 'It's a celebration day for me today – my first soberversary. I've managed a whole month without wine! So it's lovely to be doing something special today.'

'Hey, that's great. Well done, you. How's it been?'

Bless him, he really wanted to know. Claire knew she could share her struggles with him without being judged. She told the tale of her various wobbles and how close she had come on several occasions to giving in to temptation.

Philip listened in silence, giving his full attention. When she had finished, he came over and sat with her on the sofa.

'Claire, you are so strong. I take my hat off to you.' He gave her a swift, hard hug.

She let out a big sigh and reached for his hand. He grasped it tightly. She saw a beaming, understanding face.

113

'It's so good,' she said, 'to be listened to and understood by somebody I care about. Thank you.' She leaned forward and kissed him on the cheek. 'It's been tough, but I've made the commitment, so I've got to stick with it. And,' she laughed, 'I'm sleeping like a baby these days!'

'That's good to hear,' he said, leaning over and kissing her on the forehead. 'Now,' he said, drawing back, 'we'll have lunch in a few minutes. It's only bread and cold meat and cheese, with Greek yoghurt and grapes to follow. That suit you?'

'Sounds good to me.'

The film was magical – Emma Watson was perfect as Belle, even if Claire detected an occasional touch of Hermione in her performance. She wondered how Lucy was getting on with Mark and the action thriller. No doubt she'd hear soon.

When they came out, it was still light, as the clocks had changed the previous weekend. They walked back, arm-in-arm, discussing the film. Dinner comprised an Indian takeaway – Philip had decided not to cook, because he wasn't sure how early she would want to get off. By the time they had eaten and cleared away, it was nearly 7.30.

'How long can you stay?'

'Until tomorrow, if I may. I've emailed Mum and Dad to postpone our monthly Skype conversation, and the neighbours are feeding Baggins.'

'You're so lucky to still have your parents,' Philip said. 'My mother died young, of a sudden heart attack, when she was only in her sixties, and I lost my father to Alzheimer's a good five years before his death. It used to break my heart, going along to visit him every weekend, watching him realise he knew me from somewhere, and I was his friend, but having no inkling I was his son.'

'I sometimes think,' Claire said, 'Alzheimer's is harder on the loved ones than on the sufferer. My friend Dawn, you know, from the Lion, is in that situation at the moment. Her mum still knows her but has to be told everything over and over again. At first, Dawn had her to live with them but, in the end, she needed more care than

114

Dawn could provide. They're having to move her to a home which specialises in Alzheimer's patients. Dawn feels so guilty, but her mum had started to forget how to use the oven and she was terrified she'd burn herself or leave it on all day.'

'That happened to Dad, too. But it was a stroke that got him, in the end. It's been nine years since he died. At least Chas has some memories of him, although I'm not sure he remembers him whole. My mother died before Chas was born. She knew that Angie was pregnant. She was so excited at the prospect of becoming a grandmother. She died when Angie was six months along. I'd hoped Chas would be a girl so we could use her name as a middle name. We named him after my father.'

'What a lovely thought.'

'It was the right thing to do. Chas is so like him in many ways. He shares Dad's neck-or-nothing approach to life. It frightens me sometimes. I wish he'd think for a moment before leaping into new situations. I've tried to bring him up right, but it's been so hard on my own.'

'At least he had her for twelve years. They say that the fundamental character of a child is formed by the time they reach seven. I'm looking forward to meeting him.'

'I'm very proud of him. Now. It was touch and go for a while. After Angie died. He went through a very wild phase in his mid-teens. Fell in with the wrong crowd, started drinking, skiving off school. Once, he was even suspended for fighting with another boy. He broke the other lad's nose.'

'What turned him round?'

'Being suspended gave him a fright. I persuaded him to do his A levels at the local FE college. That gave him a fresh start. He realised he actually enjoyed learning new things. He fell completely in love with history, thanks to an excellent teacher. Luckily, he was also Chas's personal tutor. If it hadn't been for him, Chas would not have gone to university.'

'You must be so proud of him.'

'Yes, I am. Well, enough of this serious stuff. Come here.'

Shortly after ten, Philip stood up. 'Time for bed!' he said.

115

Claire's doubts came flooding back. She bit her lip.

'Claire, nothing will happen unless and if you want it to – scout's honour. You could sleep in Chas's room, if you like. It's reasonably tidy, with him being away.'

She looked at him, his kind face absolutely open to her. He obviously meant it. A wave of longing swept over her.

'I don't think I'd like that. Let's just see what happens.'

'I've got hot chocolate or Horlicks,' Philip said. 'Which would you like?'

'Hot chocolate would be lovely, please.'

He grinned and went to put the milk in a saucepan to heat. Minutes later, they were on the sofa, sipping their drinks.

All too soon for Claire, it was bedtime. She felt an instant of panic. But everything would be OK. He'd promised.

He stood up and offered her his hand to pull her up. 'This way, sweetheart,' he said, leading her to the bedroom. 'I'm sorry it's not very tidy, I wasn't expecting you to stay.'

Which set her mind at rest. It was a very masculine room, with pale grey walls on which a couple of abstract prints hung, darker grey carpet, and a gun-metal grey king-size bed. The duvet cover was like a Mondrian print. An untidy pile of clothes was heaped on a chair. She smiled, remembering her own, very feminine bedroom, all flowers and soft colours.

'I can offer you a T-shirt as a nightie, and here's a towel. You know where the bathroom is. I'll go after you.'

Ablutions complete, she waited nervously for his return. She was still not sure how this was going to go – would she freeze again, or would she be able to relax? She closed her eyes and began to concentrate on her breathing to quieten her beating heart. Then she heard the door creak and opened her eyes. There he was, dressing gown wrapped round him, looking down at her.

'It's OK, sweetheart. Let's have a cuddle and see how it goes.'

He slid into bed beside her, opened his arms, and drew her into him. For a while, she lay there, listening to the beating of his heart, reassured by his warm presence.

Gently, he stroked her body, exploring her curves and folds. 'You are so beautiful,' he murmured. When he kissed her, her body took fire. As she passionately returned his kisses, she made no protest when he moved down between her legs. Within seconds, she felt a flood of emotions and feelings she had forgotten she ever knew. He was a gentle and considerate lover. She felt so loved, so held.

Afterwards, as she lay in his arms, she occasionally turned to kiss his chest, his chin, any part of him she could reach. 'Thank you,' she said softly. 'That was – special.'

'For me too, my darling. What a gift you have given me, Claire! You are so beautiful.'

They talked quietly for a while, then Claire felt a yawn coming. She tried to stifle it, but it was no good. She was so tired.

Philip laughed. 'Am I keeping you up? I'm so sorry.'

'It's been a long day and I've got to drive home tomorrow. I'd like to stay here for ever but I know I can't.'

His arms tightened around her. 'There will be other times, Claire. We're just at the beginning of all this. Goodnight, my sweet.'

He kissed the top of her head and let her go. She turned on to her side and was soon asleep.

Next morning, she was woken by Philip bumbling around the bedroom like a bee in a bottle.

'What time is it?' she said, barely awake.

'Nearly nine,' he grinned. 'You slept well?'

'Yes, thank you.' Ridiculously happy, she smiled back. 'Give me a few minutes and I'll be there.' Swinging back the duvet, she grabbed her towel and headed for the bathroom. Twenty minutes later, lured by the smell of frying bacon, she wandered into the kitchen to find Philip putting together a cooked breakfast.

'Mm, that smells good! Can I help?'

'All under control. But you can stay and talk to me, if you like. What's up, honey? No regrets, I hope?'

She shook her head and smiled at him. 'No regrets,' she said.

'How could I regret last night? I haven't felt so loved, so cared for, for years . . .'

'Me, neither. There hasn't been anyone for me since Angie, you know. I thought I was going to spend the rest of my life alone. It's hard to believe that I've found happiness again with you.'

The cooked breakfast – bacon, sausages, fried eggs, and mushrooms – was wonderful. After they had washed up, Philip led her through to the lounge where they settled on the sofa. He held her close.

Claire's eyes filled with tears. She brushed them away. 'I'm not sad, I'm happy,' she said. 'This is ridiculous. I've turned into such a watering-pot since I stopped drinking. The least little thing sets me off. And this hasn't *been* the least little thing.'

His arm tightened around her, his other hand tipped her chin up. He kissed her. Each touch of his lips aroused her, and they ended up making love again. She couldn't seem to get enough of him – it had been so long since she had made love with Jack, and her body welcomed the return of such loving attention.

Jack – she hadn't even thought of him for the last 24 hours. She stiffened in Philip's arms. What madness had possessed her? Then she shrugged and forced her body to relax again. But he had noticed.

'Claire, it's OK. You don't need to feel guilty. Nothing we have done together can sully your memories of Jack, or mine of Angie. They were them and we are us. Let's enjoy us.'

She looked at him. 'Are you telepathic or something? How did you know I was thinking about Jack?'

'A certain sadness comes into your eyes, which I recognise because I've seen it in my own. Don't beat yourself up, my sweet, let's just grow us. We've got all the time in the world.'

She nodded. He was right, of course, but a little beating-herself-up was going to happen on the journey home.

They shared a last cup of coffee, finished off the ginger stem cookies, and then it was time for her to go.

Philip walked her to her car and held her close in a final hug. 'I love you, Claire.'

118

'I love you too, Philip.'

Then she started the long journey home. The traffic was much lighter today, and she made good time. To her surprise, she was only feeling slightly guilty, remembering Philip's hands and lips on her body, luxuriating in the sense of feeling so loved.

She still missed Jack like crazy, but the raw edge of her grief was now beginning to heal. Perhaps it was time to choose to let him go, to embrace the new possibility of happiness with Philip.

When she got home, there was one final job to do. She Skyped her parents.

After the usual greetings, her father said, 'Where've you been? Why couldn't you Skype us yesterday?'

'Do you remember Philip, Dad? Jack and I shared a flat with him and Angie at university. Well, I've met him again, and . . . We're dating. I've been down in Bath, where he lives. I knew I'd be getting home too late to Skype so that's why.'

'Dating, daughter? Are you ready for that?' her mother said.

'Joan, leave her alone. She's an adult now – we can't dictate what she does with her life.'

'Don't tell me what to do, Gordon. I've a perfect right to ask her the question.'

'Mum, Dad,' Claire said, 'it's no big deal. I've mourned Jack for more than a year now. I want to move on, find some happiness again. I'm only fifty-three, after all.'

She saw her mother's mouth open, ready to protest further, but her father cut her off. 'Now leave it, Joan. Claire knows what's best for her.'

'Thanks, Dad,' she said. 'I'm not going crazy. We've only met three times in a month. I'm not going to rush into anything I can't handle.'

'Well,' he said, 'I suppose you know yourself best. Take care, my love.'

Afterwards, Claire leaned back in relief. She hadn't expected the conversation to be easy and was glad it was over. At least she'd told them some, if not all, of the truth.

Chapter Eighteen

'Something's happened, Claire?' Beryl said the following Tuesday after they came out of their customary silence.

'How did you know? I haven't told you anything yet.'

'I'm sensing that a weight has lifted from your heart. You seem to be lighter, happier. What's happened?'

'Well,' Claire said, pausing to gather her thoughts. 'Do you remember me mentioning Philip? The kind guy who was concerned about me at the writing conference?'

Beryl nodded.

'Well,' she said again, 'I was going to spend the anniversary of Jack's death alone, so I didn't make a fool of myself in public again. But then Philip messaged me on Facebook, inviting me to go with him to an exhibition down at the Tate Modern, and it seemed like manna from heaven. So I went and we had a gorgeous day together. And I've seen him twice since, once at Bourton-on-the Water, and once last weekend, when I went down to Bath to spend some time with him.'

'Manna from heaven?'

'Yes, because I was afraid of spending the day alone – I was scared the temptation to drink would be too strong and I wouldn't be able to resist. So spending the day out with someone seemed like a great alternative.'

'I'm sensing it was more than that?'

'Ye-es. I don't know how, and I don't know why, but something has clicked between us. I've known Philip for donkey's years, we

120

were all at college together, but he had Angie, and I had Jack, so we were always just good friends, almost like brother and sister. Then Angie passed six years ago, and Jack and I went to the funeral. And since then, Philip and I have kept in touch and he came up for Jack's funeral. But I'd never thought of him as anything more than a good friend. Then that day . . .'

'And that day?'

'It was so different to what I had expected! I'd expected to spend the day feeling miserable and alone and ended up having a brilliant time. He's such good company and it's been ages since I've enjoyed myself so much. Then we were browsing round Covent Garden, and he bought me this.' She held out the dainty daisy bracelet.

'Daisies! How beautiful, Claire! And . . .'

'Well, I reached up and kissed him, you know, to say thank you, and then he was kissing me, and it seemed so right! It's been so long since I've been held and loved. He caught me when I was vulnerable.' She laughed. 'And now I don't know what I should be feeling – part of me is loving every minute I spend with him and the other part is feeling disloyal to Jack's memory. I'm so mixed up!'

'Claire . . . can you sense the presence of the Spirit in this?'

'I don't know – I think so – yes! I just know that when I'm with him, part of me comes alive again – the part that knows how to have fun, to enjoy herself. I haven't felt that for so long . . .'

She paused, then continued, 'And I don't think Jack would begrudge me this chance of happiness. Philip was his friend too. I'm sure he wouldn't want me to mourn him forever, cutting myself off from light and hope.'

'Is that how you've been feeling – cut off from light and hope?'

'Oh God, yes! Some days I've felt it's hardly worth carrying on – that my life was an empty sham with no purpose and meaning. But now I can feel a tiny sprout of hope in my heart, that it might be possible to find happiness again. He's a good man, and kind.'

'Then I'm glad for you, my dear. He will never take Jack's place

121

in your heart, but in due time he may find his own. But take it slowly – let this relationship grow naturally. Don't try to hurry it. If it is meant to be, it will unfold in God's own time.'

'Thank you. That helps. I'll remember.'

That evening, the phone rang.

'Hi, Claire. It's Geoff.'

'Oh, hello, Geoff! Lovely to hear from you! How are you?'

'Good, thank you. And how are things going with you?'

'Oh, not so bad, you know. I've joined a Spirituality Book Club and I've been reading a wonderful book about Celtic Christianity. And trying to learn how to sit in silence.'

'And how's that working out?' Geoff chuckled. 'From what I know of you, sitting still is a challenge . . .'

'How right you are!' Claire said ruefully. 'It's *so* difficult. My mind's all over the place.'

'It takes a lot of practice to empty the mind, Claire,' Geoff said. 'Keep persevering, and you'll get there. And talking of perseverance, how is the not drinking going?'

'It's going!' she laughed. 'Over a month, now. I'm really proud of myself. It's been so hard, and I've nearly given in to temptation so often, but my ring has helped, and also your words.'

'*My* words?' Geoff asked.

'Yes, what you said to me on the doorstep as I was going. "After all, if you make a promise to God, you can't break it, can you?" You've no idea how much those words have helped to keep me on the straight and narrow. I'm so grateful.'

'I'm glad they've helped you,' he replied. 'You're doing really well, Claire. I'm proud of you.'

'Thank you, Geoff. That means the world to me,' she said.

'Keep it up – you know you can. Bye, now.'

'Goodbye, Geoff, and thank you for ringing.'

Friday evening, Claire was down at the Red Lion, sipping Beck's Blue, when Lucy said, 'And where were you on Saturday night? I went past the house in the evening, and your car wasn't there, and it still wasn't there on Sunday morning.'

'Well, if you must know, I stayed the night at Philip's.'

'My God, are you sleeping with him already?'

'Lu–cy!' Claire said angrily. 'It is absolutely none of your business whether I'm sleeping with him or not! You're my friend, not my mother.'

On the edge of tears, Lucy slumped back in her chair. The snug had gone quiet. They'd been overheard.

'I'm sorry, hun,' Claire said. 'I didn't mean to over-react. But some things are private. It's all a bit new at the moment and I'm feeling quite protective about it. You didn't deserve that – I'm sorry.' She reached out across the table, and after a moment Lucy took her hand.

'I'm sorry too,' she said. 'Me and my big mouth. I didn't mean to be nosy – forgive me?'

'Of course. I'll tell you more when I'm ready – I promise. How about you? How did your date with Mark go?'

'Oh, not so bad. The film wasn't my idea of fun at all, but he enjoyed it,' Lucy said.

'Oh! That doesn't sound good,' Claire said. 'Are you seeing him again?'

'I don't know!' Lucy wailed. 'I've been waiting and waiting for him to ring, but not a peep out of him all week.'

'There's still time,' Claire soothed. 'Don't give up on him yet, Lucy.'

'Oh, I suppose you're right. When am I ever going to find another decent bloke?'

'I'm sure you will. Maybe he's just not the right one,' Claire said.

Soon after Claire reached home, her phone pinged. Philip.

Heard this on the radio today, and thought of you, xx

Clicking on the link, she heard the glorious voice of Christine McVie singing Fleetwood Mac's *You Make Loving Fun*.

Her heart melted – what a lovely thing to do. She texted back:

Thank you! That is so lovely! And, me too. I'm going to really miss seeing you this weekend . . . safe travels. Love you xx

I'm going to miss you too, sweetheart. We'll have to get together over the Easter weekend . . . not the Monday, I'll be taking Chas back, but any other time. Love you too xx

Claire stared at her phone. She had completely forgotten Easter was so close. And with Easter came the end of Lent. Which meant she'd be able to drink again!

Then she heard Geoff's voice: 'After all, if you make a promise to God, you can't break it, can you?'

Damn it! She was going to have to re-commit to not drinking once Easter Sunday was past. Maybe she'd better get that sobriety book back off the shelf.

She hadn't yet answered Philip's text, so typed quickly:

That would be lovely – do you want me to come down to you, as Chas is at home? xx

That would be great – I'm going to tell him about us on the journey home. Watch this space! ☺ Off to bed now – I've got to get up at a ridiculous hour tomorrow. Goodnight, sweetheart xx

Goodnight, darling xx

Claire sighed. How close they'd grown! But with Philip not around, the Wine Witch was bound to pay a visit. Well, she wouldn't give in to her. She'd keep herself busy and put two fingers up at her. That'd show her who was in charge.

Next morning, she was up bright and early. She dressed in her gym clothes and, after a quick breakfast, hit the gym, returning home

124

feeling much better. She sat sipping a mug of coffee, while pondering on how to spend the rest of the weekend.

'Right,' she told Baggins. 'I have to do some batch cooking for next week, so that's one thing. I'm halfway through Dani's adventures in Oberammergau, so that's another. And I want to finish the Philip Reeve book so that I can start on the next one. From the blurb, it looks like quite a tear-jerker. Think I'm going to need some tissues. Then I could even go to church on Sunday morning. Why not? Which just leaves Sunday afternoon and evening to fill, which I guess will be more writing. There, sorted!'

After lunch, she washed up and got ready to cook. She had decided to do one of her mother's recipes, Texas Hash, which was lovely and warming at this time of year, and a true one-pot meal as a bonus. After half-an-hour or so of preparation, she decanted it from the frying pan into a casserole dish, put it in the oven, and set the timer for fifty minutes.

It wasn't worth going up to write for that short time, so she fixed herself a herbal tea and went through to the lounge to finish the book. It was exciting, and she was worlds away when the pinger went. She took the Texas Hash out of the oven, put it on the hob, and rushed back to her book.

Ten minutes later, she had finished. That was good. If the others are up to that standard, it would be really hard to choose.

Dividing the Texas Hash into four portions and putting foil on them was the work of a minute. She left them on the side to cool down, put the empty casserole into the sink to soak and went up to the study.

Now she'd have the rest of the day to work on *Dani*. Bliss! Moments later, she was sitting at her writing bureau, sucking the end of her pen as she tried to decide whether to make Dani a German speaker. When she and Jack had gone to the Passion Play, it had still filled them with wonder, but it would have been even better had they been able to fully understand what the actors were saying.

Looking through the beautiful souvenir book they had purchased brought back bitter sweet memories. It had been her idea to go – Jack had never been that bothered about religion – and she remembered the long hours sitting on the stone benches of the auditorium, watching the scenes unfold. The interspersion of the Old Testament tableaux had been confusing. Even Claire, who was very familiar with the New Testament, had sometimes been at a loss as to what they represented. But the final scenes – the flogging, the crown of thorns, the road to Calvary, the crucifixion itself and its aftermath – had been deeply moving. She had sobbed as Mary took her dead son in her arms, and she remembered Jack's arm coming around her – always there when she needed him. Then the renewal of hope, as Mary Magdalene met the resurrected Christ in the garden. It was one of her happiest memories.

The rest of the holiday had been spent walking in the Austrian Tyrol – which had suited Jack far more – because pilgrims were only allowed to stay for two nights in the village, so that as many people as possible could witness the Passion Play. But before they had left, they had bought a beautiful hand-carved wooden nativity set, which took pride of place on the mantelpiece each Christmas.

Remembering all this, she had plenty to write about. Putting the book aside, she started to write. A few hours later, she came to a halt, pleased with what she'd done. She'd have to revise it, of course, but at least she'd got her memories down in draft form. She looked at her watch. Five thirty. Why hadn't Baggins interrupted her?

She discovered why when she got downstairs. He had clawed open the foil on one of the Texas Hash portions, eaten most of it, and disappeared.

'Oh, Baggins! You ratbag of a cat! Now I've only got three portions for me.' She cleared away the mess, put one portion in the fridge for her dinner, and the other two into the freezer. Now she'd have to cook again mid-week. Dratted animal!

After her meal, Claire was too tired to do any more writing – and in any case, she wasn't sure where she wanted it to go. She would wait for the Inspiration Fairy to call. She spent the evening curled up on the sofa, reading the next Carnegie novel, which was as poignant as she had expected.

Baggins slunk in at about 6.30.

She shook her head. 'It's all very well for you, my lad,' she said, 'but that was my dinner!'

He jumped up on to her lap.

She didn't have the heart to scold him anymore. It had been her fault for leaving it out.

The next day, just before she left for church, Philip gave her a quick ring.

'Chas took our news somewhat silently,' he said, 'but better than I expected.'

'I hope he doesn't take against me,' she said. 'I'm not trying to take Angie's place.'

At the end of the service, Reverend Martin announced the Good Friday service would take place the following week, at eleven in the morning. She might as well attend, to mark the end of Lent.

She walked home and ate her usual Sunday lunch of bacon and egg. She wanted to talk to Philip but didn't ring him in case Chas was around.

She wasn't in the mood for Dani, nor the Carnegie shortlist.

She hadn't even thought about the next Writers' Group assignment. She got her folder out and read the instructions.

Assignment. Write a piece (either fiction or non-fiction) about your favourite hobby (not writing). The word count should be no more than 1500 words.'

Hmm. What to choose? Reading? Walking? But at least it would stop her from thinking about red wine, missing Philip or brooding about Chas.

Chapter Nineteen

The following week dragged.

In spite of her promise to herself – and God – part of her was longing to call time on not-drinking at the end of Lent. She read back her journal entries from the previous few weeks, striving to persuade herself that she had made the right choice, that her commitment to sobriety was secure. But she wasn't convinced.

She posted on the Facebook group:

> *You may have guessed from my name that I quit on Ash Wednesday. And told most of my friends that I was 'giving booze up for Lent'. Problem is, Lent's nearly over now, and I'm really struggling with the idea of continuing not to drink beyond then. Surely I've proved in nearly seven weeks that I don't have a drink problem? Perhaps I could moderate now – only drink at weekends. LL*

> *LL: this is the voice of temptation. Don't listen to it! I've followed your journey on here, and you've done brilliantly well so far, to get to nearly six weeks. But you can't give in now. The very fact that you're struggling with the idea of continuing not to drink should set off warning bells in your head. Sadly, moderation is not an option for us. Because we know that one drink will lead to another, and then another, and before we know where we are, we'll be back in the same sad mess that made us hit bottom in the first place. Don't give in now. Stay close – post as often as you need to, but DON'T DRINK!*

LL: try to play the movie to the end. I know I've said this before, but it really helps. You might start off being able to 'only drink at week-ends', but think about it – how long would that actually last? How long would it take before you'd be drinking every day again, to make the world go away? You've done so well so far – don't throw away the progress you've made. You can do this!

They were right. She had made a promise to God, and she couldn't break it. But, damn, it was so hard. She wished she could moderate but knew deep down she was fooling herself.

Her friends were right. She had to keep on keeping on, no matter how hard it was.

Thanks, everyone. You've helped me to see more clearly. Fuck off, Temptation! I'm not giving in, LL xx

Thursday evening, it was Book Group. This time, they were down to six – still enough to have a decent conversation. To Claire's surprise, two of the others were not as struck by *Waters from an Ancient Well* as she was, Pat for one.

'I really loved it,' Claire said. 'I think it was the mixture of stories, history, theology, and spiritual practices which really made it work for me.'

'Yes, me too,' Julie chimed in. 'I'm really attracted to Celtic spirituality, because it's so close to Paganism in many ways.'

'Paganism?' Pat snorted. 'Do you mean witchcraft?'

'No,' Julie replied. 'I mean Paganism – an earth-centred religion which has respect for all creation. So what McIntosh had to say about God in all creation really struck a chord with me.'

'It's not what *I* call Christianity,' Pat said.

'Pat,' Ruth said gently. 'We're here to exchange views about the book, respecting those of others. Celtic Christianity may be unfamiliar to you, but it is important to many.'

'Oh, sorry. Of course.' Pat flushed. 'I'm not used to this type of group.'

'That's OK,' Ruth said.

And the conversation continued. During the coffee break, Claire went across to Julie.

'I was really interested in what you were saying about Paganism,' she said. 'It's something I don't know anything about at all. Is it really like Celtic Christianity?'

'Yes and no, I guess,' Julie said. 'It's similar in that Pagans see the divine in creation, but very different in that they don't worship Christ. They pay homage to the God and the Goddess. And they usually do their rituals outside, in nature. There are many different branches of Paganism, and I don't know about all of them. I could lend you a book, if you like?'

'Thank you! That would be great,' Claire said.

'I'll bring it along next time.'

The next morning, Claire swithered about the Good Friday service. She had never been a regular church attender, but this book group seemed to be reconnecting her to her faith. And as she was going to be at Philip's for the weekend and she wanted to mark the end of Lent somehow, she went.

Part of the morning's Epistle from Hebrews spoke to her: 'Let us hold fast the profession of our faith without wavering; (for he is faithful that promised).'

'Oh yes,' she prayed. 'May I hold fast the profession of my faith without wavering; help me to be faithful to my promise. Help me to choose Life.'

She left the service stronger in her resolve to stay sober, and closer to God than she had for a while. She walked home with a light step and spent the afternoon writing and finishing off *The Bone Sparrow*.

She sat at the kitchen table to decide what to pack for her weekend away. She was feeling so nervous about meeting Chas. What if he didn't like her? But Philip wanted her there, so she would go.

*

Finding a parking space in Philip's street this time was much harder; she had to circle the block three times before one became free. At last, she was walking towards the flat. This was it. Butterflies or no butterflies, there was no going back. She pressed the buzzer.

'Yes, who is it?' A young, male voice.

'It's Philip's friend, Claire.'

'OK, come on up.'

The door clicked.

She was met at the door by a young man identical to Philip when she first met him all those years ago.

'Dad's in the shower,' he said. 'You'd better come in.'

'You must be Chas,' she said. 'Gosh, you're so like him!'

He grinned. 'Yeah, everyone says that. It's like being Harry Potter or something. Hang on, I'll go and bang on the door.'

She was left to take off her coat and sit down.

A few minutes later, Philip appeared, drying his hair. 'Sorry, sweetheart – I wasn't expecting you so soon.' He gave her a hug.

'Chas let me in. I thought I'd dropped through a wormhole for a minute – he looks so like you did when I first knew you!'

'Yes, there's no doubting his paternity!' Philip smiled. Then he paused. 'He's OK about it – don't look so worried.'

'Are you sure? The last thing I want to do is to cause trouble between the two of you.'

He hugged her again. 'Don't worry! It will all work out fine. Now, would you like a coffee?'

After a bread, cheese, and grapes lunch, Chas disappeared off to his room.

Philip said, 'I seem to remember you being quite a Jane Austen fan, so I thought we could visit the Jane Austen Centre. It's ages since I've been. What do you think?'

'Oh yes, I'd love to do that – thank you. What about Sunday?'

'Well . . . I'm afraid we're expected to have lunch at Peggy's. It's a family tradition on Easter Sunday. She's extended the invitation to you – wants to check you out, I expect.'

'Oh my!' Claire gasped. 'Your mother-in-law? But I haven't brought a dress with me, or anything . . .'

'It's you she's meeting, not your clothes! Don't worry, Claire. You look good enough to me.'

'Is there a Next in the city centre? I'd like to at least be wearing a pair of formal trousers – I can't turn up in jeans.'

'Yes, I think so.' His eyebrows shot up. 'Does it really matter that much?'

'Yes, it really does. Can we look it up, please?'

A moment's search showed a Next in Southgate Street so, after a wonderful visit to the Jane Austen Centre, they walked the half-mile or so through the streets and Claire bought herself a pair of unexceptional black trousers. With her black boots and her twin set, she was equipped to face Peggy.

On the way back to the car park, Philip put his arm around her. 'I'm sorry for springing Peggy on you. I didn't realise it would be such a big deal for you. But at least we've got the evening to ourselves. Chas is going out with some friends and won't be back until the early hours.'

She smiled. 'That's good – it'll be lovely to spend some time alone.'

'Don't let Chas spook you. I told you, he's OK about us – he was a bit surprised at first, but he's making his own life now, so us being together isn't going to have a huge impact on him. He's been quite curious to see what you were like, if truth be told.'

'Well, I hope I passed the test.'

'How could you not?' he chuckled, hugging her.

After a delicious moussaka, Philip and Claire settled down in the lounge, while Chas got ready for his evening out.

'I'd love,' Claire said, 'to read your novel, or at least as far as it goes.'

'Are you sure? It's not very good.'

'Yes, I am, and I'm sure it will be.'

It was a classic whodunit – a real page-turner. There were only five chapters, so far, but he had drawn his characters with a deft hand and they all seemed to have strong motives for bumping off their host.

He was plaiting his fingers, waiting anxiously for her verdict.

'I really like it,' she said. 'What made you choose detective fiction? I love reading them, especially the old-fashioned ones, by authors like Dorothy L. Sayers and Agatha Christie and Arthur Conan Doyle. But the idea of writing one . . . I'm sure I'd get as mixed up as most readers do, and leave out a vital clue, or give the solution away too early.'

'I love them too,' he said. 'Always have done. Particularly Raymond Chandler's Marlowe novels. They're so atmospheric. And I'm a big Sue Grafton fan too. As to why I'm having a go at writing one . . . I find the final resolution so satisfying – generally there is closure at the end, with all the loose ends neatly tied up and dealt with. So different to real life – most of the cases I have to deal with at work are far from neat – loose ends everywhere. And so much heartache and grief. So I guess that escapism is part of it.'

'I hadn't thought of that,' she said softly. 'I don't blame you . . . I can't wait to find out who did it. Have you decided yet?'

'No I haven't – I'm a bit stuck at the moment. It's hard to find any sustained time to write when you work full-time and irregular hours.'

'Yes, it must be. But you mustn't give up on it – promise me?'

Just then, Chas poked his head round the door. 'I'm off now – I'll be back late.'

'OK, son, remember to be quiet when you get back. We'll be asleep.'

Chas grinned at his father and nodded.

They waited until they heard the front door slam. Then, without a word, they went to the bedroom and spent the evening making love. Claire couldn't seem to get enough of their lovemaking – it had been years since she had felt so hungry for physical intimacy.

They lay back, smiling, fulfilled, exhausted. And finally, after holding each other and saying nothing – there was no need – Claire drifted off to sleep, warm, contented, loved.

At about three, they were woken by a crash.

Claire shot upright in bed, frightened.

'Don't worry,' Philip said. 'I expect Chas has dropped something. He always comes home starving.'

He got up, pulled on his dressing gown, and padded down the hallway.

'I was right,' he said when he got back, halfway between amusement and exasperation. 'It *was* Chas. He dropped the casserole dish with the remains of the moussaka in it, and we've just had to clear it up. I'd had that dish for years – it was exactly the right size. But he was very penitent . . . He usually is.'

'You're taking it all very calmly.'

'Comes with the territory,' he said. 'I was a clumsy teenager once – I try not to get angry if I can help it. Chas and I have only got each other.' He looked across at her. 'Until now, that is. Love you, sweetheart.'

'Come back to bed, darling. I'm cold.'

Chapter Twenty

They rose late and had breakfast at about ten.

Then Claire prepared for her meeting with Peggy. She wanted to look her absolute best, so spent a lot of time making her face up and checking her outfit was just so. The new trousers fitted well.

'Oh well,' she said to her reflection, 'that will have to do. She can't eat me.'

When she went back into the lounge, Philip jumped up. 'You look good enough to eat. Such a pity we have to go out!'

She threw her arms around him, and they shared a lingering kiss.

'I suppose,' he said, pulling away, 'I'd better go and wake Chas – not the easiest job in the world. Shan't be long.'

They arrived at Peggy's after an uneventful journey. Chas, pale and heavy-eyed – obviously hungover – was slumped on the back seat. Philip and Claire left him in peace.

Peggy lived in large, well-appointed house in a small village outside the city.

'Here we are,' Philip said, pulling into the drive. 'Right on time.' He kissed Claire on the cheek.

'Here we go,' Claire murmured.

'It'll be fine. No need to worry about a thing. Wake up, Chas. We're here.'

Peggy opened the door. She was slightly taller than Claire, as thin as a rake, with a beautifully permed head of white hair, sharp features, and piercing blue eyes.

She smiled in a perfunctory fashion at Philip and Claire. Then she saw Chas. Her face lit up. 'Chas, my darling! Come and give Grandma a hug!'

Chas stumbled forward and was engulfed in her bony embrace. He accepted this with good grace.

'Come on in, you're in good time.'

'Thanks, Peggy. This is Claire, an old friend of mine and Angie's – we've known each other since college days. And now a new friend of mine.'

Peggy held out her hand. 'Hello, Claire. Come in.'

And she was given a cold, limp handshake. This lunch was going to be very awkward.

They followed Peggy in.

Outside of *House Beautiful* magazine, Claire had never seen a house like it. The hall and lounge were immaculately decorated – not a spot of dust to be seen – and exquisite items of furniture were arranged at geometrically precise angles. There weren't many pictures, but they were obviously originals.

Claire shivered. This was more a show-house than a home.

A pure white Persian cat was sitting on the sofa, fastidiously grooming himself. Claire walked over to say hello but was rewarded by the swipe of a paw and a hiss. She jumped back, narrowly missing a small table on which a Tiffany table lamp was precariously balanced.

'Be careful!' Peggy exclaimed. 'And leave Alonzo alone! He doesn't like strangers, do you, precious?'

'I'm sorry – I was only trying to be friendly . . .'

'No harm done,' Philip said. 'It was only an accident, Peggy, and you need to teach that cat of yours some manners. Has he hurt you, Claire?'

'No, I'm fine.'

Peggy went over to the sideboard. 'Sherry before lunch, I think. Philip, you prefer dry, don't you? Chas, what about you? And Claire, which would you prefer, sweet or dry?'

'I'm sorry, I don't drink,' Claire said, fiddling with her Chose Life ring.

136

'Why on earth not?'

'It doesn't agree with me. May I have a soft drink, please?'

'I suppose so. Never heard of anyone not liking a sherry before lunch. Whatever next?'

And with that, she left the room.

'Oh God, Philip, I'm so sorry.'

'Don't worry, sweetheart – this is pretty mild for her. Peggy has very fixed views about the rights and wrongs of everything. I find it easier to go along with her most times, but this was definitely not one of them. I'm so proud of you!'

'Yeah,' Chas said. 'Grandma's soft as butter underneath. Don't let her get to you.'

Peggy returned with a bottle of tonic water. 'I keep this in for when I have a G and T. It's been open for a while, but it shouldn't be too flat. I'll get you a glass.'

And before Claire could protest, Peggy had poured her a large tumbler full of suspiciously bubble-free tonic water and handed it over.

'Well, sit down, sit down,' Peggy said.

Claire sat as far from Alonzo as possible and sipped the stale tonic water. Philip joined her on the sofa and Chas sprawled on a nearby chair.

Peggy sat bolt upright in an armchair. 'So, Chas, are you working hard at university?'

'Yes, Grandma, we've got two new modules this term.'

'And? What are they about?'

'They're both what the Department call survey modules. One of them goes right from Roman times to the Renaissance, and the second one's called "Citizens, Comrades and Consumers" and covers from 1650 to modern times. It's to give us a broad overview.'

'Doesn't sound like history to me – what about the kings and queens?'

'Oh, Grandma! They don't teach history like that these days. It's much broader – about whole societies, not just the upper classes.'

'It sounds much more interesting to me,' Philip chimed in.

'Yes, I'd far rather learn about the history of ordinary people and of society than just kings and queens,' Claire agreed.

Peggy glared at them. 'And how would you know? Neither of you read history, did you?'

'Leave it, Peggy,' Philip said. 'It doesn't matter.'

The interrogation continued. 'Do you have a girlfriend yet?'

Chas blushed. 'Yes, Grandma, I'm going out with a girl called Jessica.'

'Jessica. Where is she from? Is she a student?'

'She's from Derbyshire and she's a first year like me. She's reading Astrophysics.'

'Astrophysics? How's that going to lead to a good job?'

'You'd be surprised, Grandma. Good astronomers are hard to find.'

'And when am I going to meet her?'

'Have a heart, Grandma. We've only been together a few months.'

'Well, I expect you to invite her home soon, Chas, so that I can meet her.'

They went into the dining room for lunch. The table was laid as if for a banquet. A rich cream linen tablecloth, crystal glasses, and silver cutlery.

They started with soup, which Claire ate carefully, praying that she wouldn't spill on the immaculate tablecloth. Then came roast lamb.

Peggy turned to Claire. 'We always have lamb for Easter – it seems the most appropriate. How long have you known Philip, Claire?'

'About thirty-five years. We met in college. Angie, Philip, Jack, and I were all in the same year.'

'Jack? Who's Jack?'

'My husband. He died just over a year ago.' Claire swallowed, fighting back tears.

'Yes,' Philip said, looking at her, smiling. 'Claire and I have known each other for a long time. And we both love writing. We met up at a writing conference a couple of months ago and just clicked.'

138

'Yes,' Claire said, rushing in. 'Philip's got the makings of a really good writer. Of course, neither of us are good enough to give up the day job, but it's a lot of fun.'

'Seems like a waste of time to me,' Peggy remarked.

Claire sat back, crushed. For the rest of the meal, she kept her attention on her food, saying as little as possible, speaking only when she was spoken to. Peggy hated her.

Finally, the meal was over, and they moved back into the lounge. How long were they going to have to stay?

But Peggy chatted away to Chas and Philip, as if Claire wasn't there.

After an eternity – but what was really only forty minutes – Philip stood up.

'We have to go now,' he said. 'Claire's got to drive back to Brandleton this evening and it's a long drive at this time of year.'

'Well, if you must,' Peggy said, pursing her lips. 'But I do think I should be allowed to have some more time with Chas.'

'I'm sorry. We really do have to go. I'm sure you'll see Chas again soon.'

In the hall, Peggy hugged Philip and then Chas. 'My darling,' she said, not wanting to let her grandson go. She looked at Claire and nodded. 'Nice to have met you, I'm sure.'

The journey home was done in silence. Chas retreated into his headphones. Claire stared out the window. Philip tried to start a conversation a couple of times but soon gave up.

Once back at the flat, Claire marched to the bedroom, intending to pick her case up and go straight home. But Philip followed her in and wrapped his arms around her.

'Claire, I'm so very sorry for what happened. Can you ever forgive me?'

She turned on him, twisting in his arms. 'How could you let it happen? I was completely humiliated! She obviously hates the very sight of me. Making me drink that filthy tonic water. And her horrible cat – I was only trying to be friendly.' Tears were leaking down her face. 'And poor Chas, grilling him like that. She could give lessons to the Spanish Inquisition! I never want to see her again!'

His arms tightened around her. 'I'm so sorry. I really am. I'd hoped she would at least try to welcome you.'

'Well, you were wrong. That domineering, interfering bat of a cow wouldn't welcome anyone who wasn't her precious Angie!' She stopped, her hand going up to her mouth. 'I'm sorry, you didn't deserve that. It's not about Angie, it's about me. She was so hostile. I was terrified of spilling soup on her precious tablecloth, and then to be ignored after the meal like that . . . It was unspeakably humiliating.' She collapsed against him, sobbing into his shoulder.

Gently, he stroked her hair. 'I know. I should have stood up for you, and Chas too. But in all honesty, I'm too afraid of offending her – Chas and I need to keep on the right side of her.'

Her head came up. 'Need to keep on the right side of her? Why?'

Philip paused. 'You must have wondered why we're living in this flat. Well, after Angie died, we didn't have enough money to keep the house – our home – going. Angie had been self-employed, didn't have a decent pension, and the bills were too much on my salary alone. But I knew we had to stay in Bath, so Chas didn't have to change schools – his friends were important to him just then, they were the only part of his life which hadn't betrayed him by going away. But the house was heavily mortgaged and, even with the proceeds from the sale, it was difficult to find anywhere affordable to live. So I appealed to Peggy and she lent me the rest of the money to buy the flat. I think she's regretted it ever since and has made it clear I won't get another penny out of her. I'm paying it back bit by bit. I suppose I should be grateful she's not charging interest! But she adores Chas – I think he's the main beneficiary in her will. So you see, it's hard to stand up to her, with all that in the background.'

'Oh God. I'm so sorry. That must be a hard row to hoe. But all the same, I never want to see her again, I really don't.'

'I know, I understand. I'll try to avoid it. If possible. But please don't go now. You've not got work tomorrow, have you? It's a Bank

Holiday. Why not stay the night? Then when Chas and I set off for York, you can head for home. Please?'

'OK, that would be lovely.'

Fiercely she clung to him, muttering, 'She's not going to get between us, she's not!'

'Amen to that, sweetheart. I do love you, Claire, and I was so proud of you today.'

'Proud of me? Why on earth?'

'For not drinking, of course! I could tell how much you were longing for that sherry. But you didn't give in, even when it cost you a row with Peggy. You're doing so well with this. Today's the end of Lent, isn't it? I'm guessing you're going to carry on with it?'

'I've been dithering about that all week. But I guess, after today, yes, I am going to carry on. There are times when I'd give anything for a glass of red wine – not least today – but the one good thing that this –' she groped for the word, 'fiasco has shown me, is that I can manage not to cave under pressure. And most of the time, it is getting easier – it's been nearly seven weeks now and I'm not thinking about it all the time anymore – except when it catches me unawares.'

'Good for you! I know you can do this. Now, I don't know about you, but for me, the only remedy for that lunch is a doner kebab – d'you fancy one?'

'You mean,' she grinned, 'a large kebab stuffed with meat and eaten straight of the polystyrene carton?'

He nodded several times.

'The perfect antidote. Brilliant! Let's do it.'

Three large and greasy doner kebabs later, Philip, Claire, and Chas sat in the lounge, too full to move.

'Thanks, Dad, that was good!' Chas said, wiping his mouth. 'By the way, I've arranged to meet Adam and Ben tonight.'

'Don't be back too late – we've got an early start tomorrow. Have you packed yet?'

'I'll do it now. I'll be back by midnight.' He got up. 'It's been good to be home.' He turned to Claire. 'And nice to meet you too, Claire. You're good for Dad. I can tell.'

She smiled up at him. 'And good to meet you too.'

Then he ran upstairs and, ten minutes later, popped his head around the door. 'See you oldies later!' The front door slammed shut.

'Wow!' Claire said. 'I wasn't expecting that.'

'He's got good taste – like me!' Philip grinned. 'And now we have the evening to ourselves.'

His lips came down on hers, and the familiar feelings swept through her body. She relaxed against him, secure in his love, and looking forward so much to another evening of making love. Each time, it seemed to get better, as they learned each other's bodies, and found new ways to arouse the passion between them. It would be a good ending to a bad day.

Chapter Twenty One

Monday evening, Philip rang.

'On the way back,' he said, 'Chas asked me, "How long has this been going on?" – for all the world as if he was the dad, and I was the son! I told him we'd met up at the writing conference, and then about the day in London. He was silent for a while, then he said, "Well, I don't suppose I mind too much. After all, I've got Jessica, so I don't see why you shouldn't have someone. And Claire's all right." So you have the Chas Bateman seal of approval!'

'That's a relief!' she sighed. 'I'm not sure what I would have done if he'd taken against me too.'

'Yes, I get that. But he's fine about it, Claire. Which is great.' He yawned.

'Darling, you sound beat.'

'You're not wrong there. It's been one heck of a lot of driving. I'm not sure I can even be bothered to eat. See you next weekend. Love you.'

'I'm sorry, Philip – I can't do next weekend. It's World Book Night, and there's an event on at the library.'

'Oh!' he said. 'That means we won't be able to see each other for three weeks.'

'Why?' she said. 'What's going on in a fortnight?'

'They're sending me on a weekend conference,' Philip said.

'Oh, what awful timing! I wish the conference had been a week earlier. I'm going to miss you so much!'

'Me too, sweetheart. But work is paying for this one and I have to go. I'll be thinking of you every minute and wishing I was with you.'

She couldn't wait for the end of the month, when he would be coming up to Broughton to spend the whole weekend with her.

She had finished ploughing her way through the Carnegie shortlist, and had chosen her favourite and voted for it. She'd have to wait now, to see whether it won.

More importantly, one of them had given her an idea for her own book. She could interweave Dani's back story with the pilgrimages.

She tried to talk about the books she'd been reading with Lucy, that Friday evening down the Lion. But her friend's taste in reading ran to women's magazines and chick lit once a year by the pool.

'I'm sorry, Claire, I know you love these things, but I'm so tired by the time I get home, I just want to blob in front of the telly with a nice glass of wine.'

'Fair enough. I just found it such a wonderful book, that I wanted to share it with you. Never mind. Are you going to the play this year?'

'Yes, I'm going on Saturday. It sounds good. Are you?'

'Yes, Philip and I will be there. So you'll finally get to meet him.'

Lucy's eyes lit up. 'Whoo! That's exciting. I can't wait to see this mysterious man of yours.'

'He's not mysterious – he's just Philip!'

'Are you seeing him this weekend?'

'No, we've got the World Book Night event at the library on Saturday evening. And next weekend, he's got a work conference. So I'm not seeing him for ages. But I've got heaps of writing to do – I'm having another go at that novel I started when Jack was ill.'

'Working on Saturday evening? Rather you than me! Dawn and I are going into Worcester clubbing on Saturday night. I was going to invite you to come.'

'I'm sorry, Lucy, not this time,' she said. 'And in any case, I don't think I'm quite ready for sober clubbing just yet.'

'But I thought that Lent was over now? Are you still not drinking?'

'Yes, I've decided to stick with it. I'm sleeping so much better, and that pain in my lower back has gone away completely.'

'Oh well, if you must, you must. But you're going to miss out on a fab evening!'

'What's happened with Mark? I thought you'd be spending time with him?'

'Oh, I've given up on him. He was Daniel Cleaver in the flesh – completely commitment-phobic,' Lucy grimaced.

'I'm sorry it didn't work out, Lucy. Maybe you'll meet someone on Saturday.'

'I can hope!' Lucy smiled.

The Saturday evening, it was World Book Night. It had taken months of planning, but Claire and Miriam were both looking forward to it. They had managed to book a local poet and storyteller, Joss Worth, and sent invitations out to all the neighbouring primary schools. Both Celia and Gillian were coming in to help.

They were expecting thirty or so children but, including parents, more than twice that number arrived. The final hours before the event were spent setting out more chairs, and then *more* chairs, and then cushions on the floor, and serving soft drinks and biscuits. Half an hour before the start, Claire's mobile rang.

'Hello, is that Claire Abbott? It's Joss Worth. I'm stuck in traffic the other side of Evesham, but I'm hoping to be there on time.'

Oh my God! What are we going to do if he doesn't get here? 'Hello, Mr Worth. Yes, it's Claire. Any idea when you might get here?'

'The traffic's moving, but slowly. My sat nav says I should be there by six twenty-seven. Got to go, we're moving again.'

The phone went dead.

Claire went in search of Miriam.

'I've just had a phone call from Joss Worth,' she said. 'He's stuck in traffic and his sat nav reckons he's only going to get here three minutes before we're due to start. What are we going to do?'

'Cross our fingers and hope, I guess,' her friend replied. 'If he's not here on time, we'll just have to do a reading from something else, and keep them happy until he does turn up.'

Six-thirty came and went. No Joss Worth. Claire stepped up to the microphone and clapped her hands.

'Hello, everyone. Mr Worth is on his way, but he's been delayed by a traffic jam. Until he arrives, we're going to read you some poems from *The Rattle Bag*.'

There were a few groans of disappointment, but then the audience settled down. Claire and Miriam took it in turns to read poems and Miriam was in the middle of reading when the door banged open and Joss Worth strode in, his dark mop of hair streaming wildly behind him. Claire nodded to Gillian, who hurried over to welcome him. When the poem was over, she announced,

'Mr Worth has now arrived. We'll take a short break, to give him time to catch his breath. Then the fun will begin!'

The event proper finally started at seven. The storyteller had the audience spellbound – he had a deep, expressive voice, which he used to great effect. The adults enjoyed it as much as the children and the book-signing took another hour after he had finished.

Then, when storyteller and audience had left, the tired library staff had to clear everything away and put all the chairs and cushions back in their right places, before locking up and heading for their beds. It had been a great success, but so exhausting.

Claire rose late on Sunday, but was determined to get some writing done. The idea of interweaving Dani's back story into the pilgrimage episodes had fired her imagination but, to her dismay, she realised she didn't truly know who Dani was – what motivated her, what her character flaws were, where she was vulnerable, what had happened to her as a child – anything, really.

So she downloaded a character questionnaire and set to work. It was amazing how answering the simple questions helped to flesh out Dani's character. As a result, she had to give her a convincing and interesting past that would affect how she reacted to current events.

After much thought, she gave her a strict convent education, which would explain the interest in pilgrimages, coupled with a strong teenage rebellion – perhaps an unhappy love affair, or a friend's betrayal, or a drug habit. Or even a combination of all three. This was starting to sound interesting!

At which point, she then realised this was going to involve a major re-write of what she had done so far. If Dani was to be a real character, Claire would have to go deep, rather than skating along on the surface of the plot.

Damn the woman! This is going to be hard work.

She spent the evening curled up with Baggins, watching nature documentaries on BBC iPlayer. They were quite soothing. But she was on her own. She wished Philip's conference had been this weekend, not next.

'I wish we lived nearer to each other,' she told Baggins. 'I hate only being able to see him at weekends.'

Baggins took no notice. He carried on dozing and purring – as he always did.

'You've no idea what I'm talking about, have you?' she said, tickling his ears. 'All you care about is where your next meal's coming from, don't you?'

She stared at the TV for another twenty minutes. She had no idea what she was watching.

'Well, Baggins,' she said eventually, 'this is no good. It's work tomorrow so I need to get to bed. Come on, you.' She scooped him up, carried him into the kitchen and put him away for the night.

If only Philip were here.

The following Wednesday was Writers' Group. Claire had found this month's writing assignment – to write something about her favourite hobby – tricky, and she'd chosen walking. When it came to her turn to read, the members said it was good on description, but that they hadn't felt the passion. Oh well, maybe she'd do better next time.

She gasped when Duncan gave out the following month's

assignment. The genre was the paranormal. She was sure she could produce something good. It was much more up her street.

The week dragged and Claire spent most of the weekend drafting some of Dani's back story. But by ten o'clock on Monday, Dani was being so uncooperative Claire gave up. At this rate, she was never going to make something decent out of this.

She looked out of the window. It was a beautiful day. She'd go for a walk. And not just around the village. She gazed at the photo of herself and Jack on top of her writing bureau. It had been taken by a friendly passer-by while on a glorious walk on the Malvern Hills. Maybe she was ready to go there again, lay some ghosts.

She made up a packed lunch, loaded her backpack, and set off. The roads were busy – after all, it was a Bank Holiday – but in a little over three-quarters of an hour, she was parking her car at British Camp.

It was a warm and sunny spring day, ideal for walking. Shouldering her pack, she looked around. People were milling about, obviously with the same idea – but once she got on to the spine of the Hills, it would be less crowded.

It was good to be walking again. It had been so long since she had done a proper hill walk. She and Jack had loved it and had always chosen their holidays with walking in mind. Wales, the Peak District, the Lake District – they had walked them all.

She was going to do a route they had loved – from British Camp, along the ridge-top path to the hill fort, on to Swinyard Hill, then back past the Giant's Cave and the reservoir to the car park. It would take her a couple of hours, longer if she stopped for lunch.

A steep climb took her up to the Herefordshire Beacon, where she paused to catch her breath. The view was glorious – Herefordshire stretched out before her on one side, with the Welsh hills in the distance, and the gentler landscape of Worcestershire on the other.

She could hear other walkers, talking and laughing, and the ever-present bleating of the sheep. The smell of the sun-warmed bracken was intoxicating. She breathed deeply and stood for a while, drinking in the beauties before and around her. She felt so close to God up here.

Then she carried on, along the ridge top path, descending to the Silurian Pass. Once there, she had to think for a moment to remember which of the four paths to take – she thought it was the one straight ahead. If she remembered rightly, it would take her gently downhill, followed by a steep climb up Swinyard Hill.

And so it proved. As she climbed up the wide grassy track she felt at peace. Once she reached the summit, the view was spectacular in every direction. She stopped to eat her lunch and take it all in. The sun was warm on her face and, somewhere in the blueness above her, was the song of a skylark.

Munching on her cheese roll, she saw how much had changed since she and Jack had last walked this path. Before the cancer had taken him from her. Before the huge grief of his passing.

Before her new life with Philip.

Silently, she wept, glad there was no one nearby who would try to comfort her.

'I loved you so much, Jack,' she whispered, 'but even the best of my love couldn't save you. I've missed you so much. But I'm beginning to heal. I'll never stop loving you, never stop missing you. You know that. But being with Philip is helping me to move past the worst of the pain. You wouldn't begrudge me that, would you?'

In her heart, she knew Jack would be happy for her, that he would want her to move on, would not want her to remain trapped in her grief.

She packed her things away, stood up, got herself together and, taking one last look around, set off back to British Camp. The route back was less strenuous, skirting the sides of the hills, rather than up and over.

An hour later, she was back at the car park. After a restorative coffee in the little café, she climbed into her car.

Back in her study, she gazed again at the picture of herself and Jack. Picking it up, she kissed him gently, then set it back in its place.

It was time to move on, to choose life, to stop allowing her grief to define her.

★

After dinner, she decided to give Dani one more try. Before long she was lost in her writing, weaving Dani's vulnerabilities into the witnessing of Mary's pain at the foot of the cross. Hours later, she came to a natural break and sat back, satisfied. At last she was beginning to see her way clear. It was only the first draft anyway, there would be plenty of opportunities for changing her mind during the editing and polishing process, later on.

Before going to bed, she reckoned she deserved to spend a while mooching around on her iPad. She checked in to the sobriety group, remembering belatedly that this was her two-month soberversary. She posted:

Yay! It's my two-month soberversary today. I celebrated by going for a lovely walk on the Malvern Hills, then doing some writing. I really think I can do this!

Congratulations, LL! Two months is a solid achievement. But stay alert—temptation can rear its ugly head at any time.. Take it day by day.

Well done, LL! That's awesome news. The worst of it is over now— sobriety should be becoming a solid habit for you. But what SK said is right — you aren't out of the woods yet. Stay sAFe! Xx

Thank you for the warnings. I'm feeling pretty solid right now, but know I've got a long way to go, LL xx

Then she texted Philip:

How did the conference go? I've really missed you this weekend. Went for a walk on the Malverns this morning — it was gorgeous. Can't wait to see you on Friday, love you xxxx

I'm back home now, my lovely, and absolutely whacked. It was a great conference, and I've got loads to take back to implement at work, but I missed you too. Only four days to go. Love you too xxxx

Chapter Twenty Two

Friday came at last.

Claire rose early to get the food shopping and her gym session out of the way as soon as possible. Then she started on the house. She tidied, dusted, polished, scrubbed, mopped, and hoovered until every room was spotless and immaculately tidy. Her final act was to get clean sheets and a duvet set out of the airing cupboard and change the bedding. Although Philip probably didn't care about all this, she did. She loved the look and smell of a clean and tidy house and wanted everything to be just right for his first official visit.

By this time, she was hot and sweaty. She made herself a quick lunch, had a shower, then took quite some time choosing what to wear – clean, pressed jeans, and a soft pink top. She laid them out ready on the bed, then climbed back into her tatty jogging bottoms and an old T-shirt so her fresh clothes wouldn't smell from the cooking.

Humming, she laid out the ingredients. She had chosen to make a lasagne, which could easily be re-heated if he was late for any reason. She enjoyed the process of cooking and assembling it. She put it in the fridge, ready to pop into the oven at the right time. Then she prepared a colourful salad.

He was coming straight from work, so she was expecting him around 7.30. At half past six, her phone rang.

'Hey, Claire. There's been an accident.'

'Oh my God! Are you all right? You're not hurt?'

'Whoa, it's OK, it's OK. I'm not *in* the accident. What I was going to say was, there's been an accident up ahead, and I'm stuck in a long tailback, somewhere south of Tewkesbury. I was just ringing to let you know to expect me when you see me. I didn't mean to frighten you. Sorry, sweetheart.'

'Oh, thank God for that! I was imagining all kinds of things!'

'Well, don't! I'm fine, just stuck. Can't wait to see you. Oops, better ring off, we're moving again. Love you.'

And the phone went dead. Thoughts of a glass of wine crossed her mind, but she fought them off. Tea, that was the thing. Hot, sweet tea. She had heard it was good for shock.

Moments later, she was at the kitchen table, sipping her mug of tea, well laced with sugar. She wondered whether to put the lasagne on now or to wait until he arrived. She'd cook it, anyway. If he was late, he would be starving, and it would be the work of minutes to re-heat it. Soon, delicious smells were wafting round the kitchen, and she went upstairs to get changed. Then she came down and laid the table.

After which there was nothing to do but wait. The oven timer pinged, and she put on an apron to get the lasagne out. It smelled and looked fabulous, all golden brown and bubbling and her mouth began to water. She was starving but wanted to wait to eat with Philip. She thought she'd better stay in the kitchen to guard it, after Baggins' recent adventure with the Texas Hash, so she fetched her iPad and started to do the daily jigsaw.

Time passed, no Philip. By eight o'clock, she was starting to worry but knew he would ring if he could. Finally, at twenty past eight, she heard his car pull up on the drive. Dumping her iPad on the side, she raced down the hall to the front door and flung it wide.

There he was, case in hand, very weary. But as soon as he saw her, his face lit up. He dropped the case and took her in his arms.

'Thank God you're all right,' she said. 'I was so scared.'

'I'm fine, sweetheart, just tired. Let's go in.'

'Of course — I'm so sorry. Come on in. The meal's ready — just needs heating up. Leave your case in the hall.'

She let him eat in peace. He needed some time to restore himself. By the time the lasagne was eaten, he was more like his usual self.

He smiled at her. 'Well, that was a journey I don't want to repeat in a hurry. The rate we were moving, I thought I'd be on the road till midnight! It was so good to get here. I've missed you.'

'I'm so sorry. But you scared me when you rang. I was imagining all kinds of things!'

'The writer's curse,' he said lightly. 'I'm fine, just tired. I hope you haven't got any plans to go out this evening?'

'No, that's tomorrow. I want to snuggle up with you and catch up on your news.'

He told her all about the conference, which had been on the topic of child abuse, and she listened with sympathetic interest.

'I really admire what you do,' she said. 'It must be great to make a difference in people's lives. But I'm not sure I could cope with all the pain and grief of other people. Library work is much easier – the worst I have to deal with is someone's disappointment if the book they want is out of stock!'

'Horses for courses. I love my job. But it's not for everyone. You serve too, in your way. Now, enough about me – what've you been up to?'

The answer to this involved a full re-telling of her struggles with Dani, and her attempts to inter-weave her back story into the narrative.

Philip said, 'That sounds really good, Claire. I'd love to see what you've done so far.'

'Fair enough. I've read yours, after all. But I haven't got it printed out. It's all on my laptop. I could go up and fetch it, if you like? Or would you rather wait until tomorrow?'

'You're right, as usual. I'm not sure I could do it justice tonight. Let's go to bed. I've got enough energy for that!'

Afterwards, lying in dreamy, blissed-out contentment, Claire smiled over how far she had come in the past few weeks. The last time they had been here, in her bed, she had fled, afraid of her

153

feelings, unable to escape her grief. This time was so different. How little time had passed.

She was just about to tell Philip when she heard a soft snore. Easing herself out of his arms, she turned on to her side and fell asleep.

They rose late and, after a leisurely breakfast, she said, 'Do you really want to see what I've written so far?'

'Yes, absolutely. Lead the way.'

They topped up their coffee mugs before going up to her study.

'What a lovely space!,' Philip said. 'You're so lucky to have this – I have to do my writing with my laptop balanced on my knee. There simply isn't space in the flat for a writing corner.'

'It used to be Jack's office, but I've changed it into my creative centre. All my writing and art books are here.' She pointed to the bookcase. 'And I keep my art supplies in here.' She pulled open the cupboard of the writing bureau. 'It's lovely being able to leave stuff out if I'm halfway through a project.'

'Like I said, you're very lucky. It's a beautiful, peaceful space – I envy you.'

Claire hugged him, then powered up the laptop and clicked on the Dani folder.

'D'you want me to print it out or are you happy to read it on here?'

'On here's fine.' He sat down at the desk and started to read.

She hooked a book down from the shelf, curled up in the armchair and pretended to read, all the while watching him out of the corner of her eye, trying to work out what he was thinking.

Forty minutes later, Philip turned to her. 'This is good stuff, Claire! I love the way you've started to put bits in about Dani's back story among the events of the present. How did you find out so much about Oberammergau?'

'Oh, that was the easy bit. Jack and I went to the Passion Play in 2000 so I was writing from memory. The hard bit has been relating it to Dani – she's so different to me. Do you really like it?'

'Yes, I really do. Where's it going next?'

154

'I'm planning to send her on a series of journeys to pilgrimage destinations like Santiago de Compostela, Canterbury, Iona, Lindisfarne, Glastonbury, Jerusalem, and Bethlehem . . . it's going to take a lot of research, because apart from Canterbury and Glastonbury, and of course, Oberammergau, I've never been to any of them. And I'm not sure what's going to happen to her yet . . . I haven't worked out how her past is going to be impacted by what she sees. But I've done this great character questionnaire, I found it on the internet, which has helped.' She fished it out of its folder.

His eyes lit up. 'This looks really useful. Where did you find it? I could do with filling out one of these for each of my characters.'

'I googled character questionnaires, and it came right up'. She laughed. 'It's been great – it's given me so many insights into her character, which I just didn't have before.'

'Yes, I can see that.' He furrowed his brow. 'You know, it's funny your mentioning the Camino – it's something I've always wanted to do, but never got round to. Hey, I've just had a brain waggle! Why don't we do it this summer?'

'Wow! That's an amazing idea! I hadn't thought about any holiday this year. Do you think there's a website?'

He closed down the Dani folder, then went on to Google. Claire stood behind him and, before many minutes had passed, they were planning their first holiday together.

They agreed they definitely weren't up to walking the full 780 kilometres, even if they had the time, but thought that the final hundred kilometres from Sarria to Santiago de Compostela should be do-able, if they did some training first. There were specialist firms who would organise the whole itinerary for pilgrims. It was just a matter of deciding when and then booking some annual leave.

'I'm so excited!' Claire said. 'I never imagined actually doing this – it's a wonderful idea.' She kissed the top of his head.

He stood up and hugged her. 'It's going to be hard work, but great fun.' He looked at her. 'At least you're reasonably fit – it's been years since I've done any proper exercise. This is going to take a fair amount of conditioning, and some new hiking boots!'

'I'm OK at the gym, but I haven't done any serious walking for years – not since Jack became ill. Maybe we should try to get in a walk most weekends – we'll soon build up some stamina.'

The rest of the day was spent planning the walks and simply enjoying each other's company. Then Claire suggested they had better eat before walking down to the village hall.

'What would you like? I could do us some baked potatoes with cheese and a salad?'

'Sounds good to me.'

They set off just after seven. Curtain up wasn't until 7.45, but the Saturday night performance was usually a sell-out and getting there early was important, if you wanted a good seat. She told him to wear layers. 'It gets really hot in there, but it'll be cold by the time we walk back.'

They had just sat down when Lucy walked in. She made a bee-line for them. She plumped herself down on the seat next to Claire. 'Hi, Claire! We missed you down the Lion last night. You must be Philip? I'm Lucy.' She held out her hand.

'Hello, Lucy, Claire's told me a lot about you.'

'All good, I hope?' she said, tilting her head to one side.

'Yes, all good,' Claire said. 'Who are you sitting with?'

'Well, you two, of course, unless you don't want me.'

'Of course, you're welcome,' Claire lied.

The time until curtain-up was spent with Lucy telling them about her night out on the town with Dawn the previous weekend. 'You should have come with us, Claire, it was brilliant.' At long last, the drama group's front man welcomed the audience and made the usual health and safety announcements.

This year, the play was Agatha Christie's *The Hollow* and was full of the usual plot twists. It didn't take long for everyone to suspend their disbelief as they settled down to enjoy it.

'Are you coming down to the Lion for a drink?' Lucy said, as they put their jackets on to leave.

'Not tonight,' Claire said. 'I'll see you on Friday – usual time?'

'Yeah, OK. Nice to meet you, Philip.' And with that, she was gone.

'I hope you don't mind,' Claire said to Philip as they left the hall. 'I just want to go home and spend as much time with you as possible. If we go down the Lion, we'll be stuck there for ages.'

'Fine by me, my sweet,' he said, putting his arm around her. 'Let's go home and be us.'

'Bloody hell!' Philip said, looking at the website. 'This is going to be quite a challenge!'

They had Claire's laptop in the bedroom, the power cable and extension lead snaking over the duvet to the distant socket.

'My first thought,' he continued, 'was sixty-two miles in seven days – that's about nine miles a day – should be a cinch. But now I'm realising it's nine miles a day with a full pack – quite a different proposition.'

Claire looked at him. 'You haven't changed your mind, have you? You still want to do it?'

'Ye-es, but God!' he said, blowing out his cheeks. 'I'm so unfit. I think we'd better plan this for September rather than the summer, to give me more time to toughen up. Nine miles a day with a full pack is going to take some doing.'

'The heat shouldn't be as bad then, either. Let's have a look and see if we can find some training programmes for long-distance walks.'

But first she clicked on to a tour company's website they'd come across during their search, which offered packages for people wanting to walk different sections of the Camino. Moments later, she let out a whoop of delight. 'Philip, look! They do baggage transfers – we'll only have to walk with day packs!'

'Oh, that's epic! That makes life a lot easier. Well spotted.'

She downloaded the website's *Camino Guide*, which they read together. It seemed to be very well-organised – they could start each day with a continental breakfast, then walk with a day pack to the next hostel. The company offered 24/7 phone support, as well as the baggage transfer option, which cost more, but would be worth every penny.

'Now all we've got to do is to decide when to go!' Claire said. 'How much annual leave have you got left?'

'Well, like you, I'm guessing, my leave year starts on the sixth of April, so the short answer is most of it. I'll talk to my line manager on Monday. September shouldn't be much of a problem.'

'That's great. I'll do the same. But let's check our diaries. Hang on, I'll fetch my Filofax from the study.'

'You Luddite, Claire! I've got all my appointments and everything on my phone.'

'I tried that, but it's such a hassle. I kept forgetting to check it, or to put new stuff in. I'd far rather have a hard copy, which I can flick through instantly. My Filofax is my Bible – it's got everything in it. I'd be lost without it. Be right back.'

After some discussion, they decided on the third week in September, and agreed to try to book it off with their respective employers.

'I'm so excited about this! I never imagined in a million years that I'd actually be able to walk the Camino,' she said, hugging him. 'It was a wonderful idea of yours.'

'Aw, shucks!' he said. Then he grinned. 'Yes, it really was. I can't wait either.'

'I suppose we'd better get up and have some lunch. What time do you have to leave?'

'Not until early evening. Plenty of time yet. But, yes, let's have some food to stoke our energy levels.'

'Philip Bateman! You've got only one thing on your mind!'

'Are you complaining?'

She smiled back. 'Who? Me?'

After lunch, they went back to bed. They were lying entwined, talking softly, when the bedroom door opened, and Baggins leapt on to the bed.

'All right, you tyrant, I get it – it's teatime.' Claire threw back the duvet, reached for her dressing gown and went downstairs.

A few minutes later, Philip followed her.

'Oh,' she said.

'What?'

'You've dressed.'

'Yes – well –'

'I thought we might . . . No, you're right. It's high time I got dinner.'

After she had dressed, she said, 'I've got us pork chops for dinner – I've found a lovely recipe in my *Fast, Healthy Food* book – in a barbeque sauce, with a pine nut and raisin pilaf. That OK by you?'

'Mmm, sounds delicious. Is there anything I can do to help?'

'No, just sit yourself down and talk to me, please.'

He watched as she gathered together the ingredients.

'Gosh, you're methodical,' he said. 'I'm usually halfway through cooking when I realise I've forgotten something crucial.'

'My mother calls it setting your stall out properly. I find it easier this way. Everything gets weighed and measured out first, then I follow the recipe. Help yourself to a coffee if you like – you know how it works.'

'Thanks. Do you want one, too?'

'Not now, I'd only spill it or something. I'll wait until it's all cooking.'

Before long, appetising smells were filling the kitchen. Claire prepared the pilaf, then said, 'Right, that's it. It should be ready in about fifteen minutes. I'll have that coffee now.'

They sat at the table, while the meal finished cooking. When the timer pinged, she got up to dish.

'Mmm, mmm, this is good!' Philip said around a mouthful of chop. 'Can you give me the recipe, please?'

Claire blushed. 'I'm so glad you like it! I'll type it out this evening and email it to you.'

After washing up, they watched the news, then Philip stood up.

'Sorry, sweetheart, but I really need to make a move – I won't be home until gone nine as it is.'

'I know. I'm going to miss you. What are we doing next weekend?'

'Well, we've got about four months before the Camino, so I don't suppose we need to start training yet.' His eyes twinkled. 'Do you think the neighbours would look after Baggins again? Or shall I come up here?'

'Would you mind? I don't feel I can ask them more than about once a month.'

'Sweetheart, I'm all yours. I hope the journey up isn't as bad next time. I think I'll come up early on the Saturday morning. I hope you can come down to Bath at the end of the month. It's Chas's birthday on the Bank Holiday Monday.'

'I'll ask them. I'm sure they won't mind, if they're around. But if it is the Bank Holiday weekend, they may not be.' She paused. 'If push comes to shove, I could put him in a cattery, but he'd hate it.'

One final embrace and he was out of the door and in his car. Before he backed off the drive, he blew her a kiss, which she returned, and then he was gone.

Without him, the house was so empty, so quiet.

Claire gave herself a little shake. She'd had a whole weekend with him, and she'd be seeing him next weekend. She just had to deal with it. It wasn't as if she wasn't used to being on her own.

She trailed upstairs to type out that recipe.

It had been a fabulous weekend. But, now, it was over, and the silence would begin again.

A glass of California Red would put that right. It would keep her company.

No, a *large* glass. Even better company.

She clutched her Chose Life ring, then typed out the recipe. Back to reality.

Chapter Twenty Three

But getting back to reality proved to be tougher than she had thought. In the days that followed, Claire swithered between missing Philip – it had been so good to have him sharing her life for that short time, and phone calls, however loving, just weren't the same – and feeling guilty about betraying Jack. She almost phoned Beryl a couple of times but stopped herself. This was something she needed to work through on her own.

On the Wednesday, the conflict in her heart came to a head. She spent the afternoon in the study, researching Iona as a pilgrimage destination, when she glanced up and saw the photo of Jack and herself on the top of the bureau. All at once, she was seized with a huge sense of guilt – what was she doing, sleeping with another man, even if that man *was* Philip, when Jack, her precious Jack, was only a year gone? Philip's words, that nothing they were doing could sully Jack's or Angie's memories, suddenly rang hollow.

God, this was too difficult. How she needed a drink! If she could only stop going round and round like a squirrel in a cage and come down on one side or the other.

When she was with Philip, she was so happy. But when he wasn't here, she was surrounded by the life she had made with Jack. And then the reality of Philip wasn't so real.

Maybe she should move. With the proceeds from the house, and from Philip's flat, they could buy somewhere together and make a fresh start.

What was she thinking? She'd been with this guy for only a

couple of months. She had no right to ask Philip to sell up just like that because of the way she felt.

Hang on a minute! Slow down!

Her whole life was here. Her job, Beryl, Lucy, the gym, everything. Did she really want to give all that up?

She didn't have to. He could find a job here and they could move somewhere local.

But wasn't that jumping the gun? Sure, she was having a good time with him – and the sex was amazing – but was she ready to make a deeper, more permanent commitment? Wasn't she on the rebound, grabbing the first chance of happiness that had happened to come along?

'Oh, I don't know!' she wailed, throwing her head into her arms and bursting into tears. 'I don't know!'

Straight away, there was temptation. At her shoulder. Whispering in her ear. 'Have a drink . . . Just one little drink. You know it'll help you calm down. After all, you know you're not addicted anymore.'

She fought it, longing to give in, longing for a glass or two of wine – anything to make this pain go away.

Geoff's line echoed in her head. 'After all, if you make a promise to God, you can't break it, can you?'

She wiped her eyes, blew her nose, and reached for her laptop. Her sobriety group friends would help.

Hello, I'm in bits. I've just had a wonderful weekend with my new boyfriend, and now I'm feeling like total shit, because of thinking I'm being disloyal to my late DH's memory. And now temptation has come to call, and I'm that close to listening to it. LL

That sounds like a tough one ((LL)). Remember HALT – I'm guessing you're feeling pretty lonely at the moment, and that's one of the triggers for temptation to show up. Can you call a friend? Talk it through? If not, just try to be gentle with yourself. Eat something you really enjoy, have a nice hot bubble bath, read a good escapist book. But Don't Drink! Stay sAFe, xx

Thanks. Just talking to you helps. I know I can't give in to it, but dammit, it's sooo hard sometimes! LL x

Then another, from the friend who had been so sympathetic about Jack, having been through the same thing herself:

Dear LL, I know it's hard, but like I've said to you before, you will get through this, and your DH wouldn't want you to be this unhappy. You're doing brilliantly well so far – more than two months, isn't it? Does your new man understand the situation? If so, why not give him a ring? If not, stick with the usual remedies – treat yourself to something you enjoy, but stay sAFe. It's just not worth it. Hugs, xx

She rang Philip.

'Hey, Claire, how are you, sweetheart?' It was so good to hear his soft Welsh voice.

'Feeling lonely tonight, so I thought I'd ring. You're not busy with something, are you?'

'No, sitting amid the remains of a takeaway curry, watching the box. Hang on, I need to mute it. Now, what's up with my girl?'

'I'm such a mess,' she sobbed. 'We had such a wonderful time at the weekend, and I'm loving being with you, but . . . it's Jack. I love you but I still love him too.'

'Oh sweetie, of course you do!' he soothed. 'I can never take Jack's place with you. And I don't want to. I'll never forget Angie either and the years we had together. Am I putting too much pressure on you? I know it's not been that long since Jack passed; it's different for me. Finding you has been so wonderful, after the loneliness of these past years. Please tell me you don't want to end it?'

'No, of course I don't! I love you, Philip. And I'm happy when I'm with you. It's just so hard, being here, surrounded by all the things Jack and I chose together. And you not being here to help me forget. I'm sorry, that sounds so self-centred. I'm so worn out with this to-ing and fro-ing in my heart.'

'Mmm, that's rough. In a way, I was lucky, having to move after

Angie died. At least the flat isn't full of reminders. But what do you want to do? What do you want *me* to do?'

'I wish we could be together more often. The weekends are so wonderful, but the weeks are so hard.'

'What are you suggesting? I think it's too early for us to move in together, as much as I'd love to. And then there's my job. If I moved up to Brandleton, I've no idea whether there would be a job for me.'

'I know.' She sighed. 'I'm being silly. But I feel so lonely tonight. I've been fighting temptation. I could murder a glass of wine, to make all this go away.'

'Claire, sweetheart,' he said, 'don't give in. Drinking won't make this go away. It will add self-loathing to the rest of the mix. Don't give in now. You've been doing so well. I am so proud of you! Consider yourself hugged. I'll set off really early on Saturday so we can have as long as possible together. I love you, sweet Claire.'

'I love you too, Philip. Thank you for understanding. Think I'll have a long, hot bath now, then an early night. Bye, darling.'

'Bye for now, love you too.'

Fortunately, it was Book Group the following evening. Claire was enjoying exploring books which she would never have read on her own account, and was gaining new insights about herself and the world. This month's book was *The Return of the Prodigal Son: A Story of Homecoming* by Henri Nouwen, and the conversation had been fascinating. When she got home, she needed to get her thoughts down on paper.

So much of what he writes resonates with me. He examines the painting, and the parable from the Gospel of Luke, from every conceivable angle.

His exploration of the painting and the parable takes place in the context of his own life, his own spiritual journey. At first he strongly identifies with the younger son, the prodigal son, who is lost, adrift, but heading home, hoping to be reconciled with his father, forgiven and accepted once more as his son. The phrase Nouwen repeats, over and

164

over, is 'You are my Beloved, on you my favour rests.' Such a wonder-
fully reassuring promise!

This longing to be at home, to be loved by God, to be accepted 'just
the way I am', is very strong in me. Nouwen explains that we are like
the prodigal son every time we look for unconditional love in the wrong
places. I could recognise myself in that.

He cannot understand that love, whether divine or human, is infin-
itely elastic in its nature. This has helped me so much with Jack and
Philip – my having loved Jack to pieces doesn't mean that I can't love
Philip too. There is more than enough room in my heart for both of
them. Here I can get a glimpse of the father's unlimited compassion and
love for both his sons; and of the Father's unbounded compassion and
love for all of humankind.

She sighed and put her journal away. What a writer! If only she
could move people like Nouwen did. Time for bed.

Chapter Twenty Four

When Claire walked into the Red Lion on Friday evening, Lucy was already there, nursing her usual large glass of red wine. Claire ordered a Beck's Blue and joined her.

'Hello, Lucy, how are things?'

'Not too bad, I s'pose. I lost another two pounds at Slimming World this week and,' she took a sip of wine, 'I've got a date for tomorrow night!'

'Oh, wow, that's great! Tell me all about it.'

Lucy grinned. 'You remember Dawn and I went clubbing a couple of weeks ago? Well, I met this guy there, and we exchanged phone numbers, and then he didn't ring, and I thought that was it. But then yesterday he texted me and we're going for a drink in Worcester tomorrow!'

'What's he like? Tell me everything!'

'Well, his name's Sam, and he works in IT in Birmingham and commutes every day. He's about our age, I think, and he's gorgeous! Tall, slim, fabulous bum, gorgeous smile. I'm feeling so nervous — don't know what to wear. I want to make the right impression.'

'How about your lovely gypsy top? You always look fab in that. Then skinny jeans and ankle boots. Where are you meeting him?'

'Ooh, that's a good idea. We're meeting in the Dolphin and then he's taking me for a meal. Hang the calories for once. I'm going to enjoy this!'

'And what's he like, apart from to look at?'

'We didn't talk for very long. But we like the same sort of

music – soul and Motown. He's a really good dancer. And I think he may be divorced too, but it didn't really come up. I expect I'll find out more tomorrow.'

'I'm glad you're meeting him somewhere public. After all, you don't know him. Make sure you don't go anywhere alone with him.'

'Claire, you're such a worry-wart! I'm a big girl. I can look after myself.'

'I know you can, Lu, but be careful. I'm rather fond of you! It was different for me. I've known Philip for more than thirty years, so I knew I could trust him straight away.'

'I'll be fine. I'll give you a ring on Sunday evening and let you know how it went.'

'You deserve some happiness after all this time.'

'Are you seeing Philip again this weekend?'

'He's coming up tomorrow morning. He had a dreadful journey here last Friday night – there'd been an accident on the M5 – so he's leaving really early tomorrow.'

'He seems such a nice guy, Claire. You're lucky.'

'I know it. But then, I've known Philip was a nice guy for over thirty years! In our final year at uni, Jack and I shared a flat with him and Angie.'

'How long have you two been together now?'

'Just over two months. I wish he lived closer though. It's so lonely not seeing him Monday to Friday.'

'Yes,' Lucy said. 'I can understand that one. It must be hard on you.'

'Yes,' Claire said, taking a deep breath, 'and I'm also finding it hard not to feel guilty.'

'Guilty? Why on earth should you feel guilty?'

'Because it's only been just over a year since Jack died and I'm feeling disloyal finding another man so soon.'

'Mmm. But I'm sure Jack would want to see you happy again. He wouldn't want you to mourn him for the rest of your life. Not the Jack I knew, anyway!'

'Do you really think so? I'm beating myself up something fierce about it.'

167

'Yes, I am sure. Didn't you say Jack and Philip were old friends? Then I'm sure he'd be happy that you were in good hands now he isn't here for you. Crikey, Claire, if I'd found such a nice guy, I wouldn't be hesitating!'

'Yeah, you're right. Thanks. You've no idea how bad I've been feeling about it. It's so difficult not to feel guilty.'

Lucy leaned over and touched her hand. 'Don't do this, Claire. We're put in this world to be happy, not to beat ourselves up. Jack wouldn't want you to be miserable, would he?'

'Thank you, Lucy. You're a good friend. Oh, let's talk about something else. What did you think of the play?'

Sunday evening, after Philip had gone, Lucy rang, bubbling over with the story of her date.

'Hi, Claire. How are things? Did you have a good weekend with Philip?'

'Yes, thank you – it was lovely. How about you? How did your date with Sam go?'

Her friend sighed. 'Oh, Claire, it was wonderful. He is so nice. We had a couple of drinks in the Dolphin, then he took me to an Italian restaurant in Crowngate and we had a gorgeous meal. He's so easy to talk to!'

'So, tell me more. What's he like? Is he divorced?'

'Yes, and with two kids, who he only sees every other weekend. Both teenagers. The older girl's in her first year at university and the younger is doing GCSEs this year.'

'Mmm, how do you feel about that?'

'Well, you know I've never been much on kids, but after all, I needn't see them very often, if he only sees them every other weekend.'

'All the same, that adds a whole other dimension to things. He's not a heart-free singleton, is he?'

'Don't rain on my parade! Mark was one of those, and that was a disaster! I'm sure it's going to be fine. Anyway, I'm meeting him again on Tuesday evening. We're going to the pictures.

'Ooh, that sounds fun. I hope you have a wonderful time.'

Putting down the phone, Claire smiled. Lucy was so impulsive! But she hoped that this Sam was the decent bloke she thought he was. Lucy had been deeply hurt by her divorce and Claire didn't want her to be hurt again. She wondered how long it would be before he appeared down the Red Lion. Knowing Lucy, it wouldn't be that long.

Claire spent most of her spare time the next week working on her Writers' Group assignment. She had swithered over what to write about – a ghost story, superpowers, or something to do with magic.

After a few false starts – she thought about setting it in a call centre, fielding calls about malfunctioning magic, or a classic ghost story. In the end, she went with the idea of parapsychic powers, such as predicting the future, telepathy, or healing, being scientifically recognised as a normal part of life. She made her heroine a triage nurse who discovers she has healing powers. Reading back over it, she was pleased with the result. The story came together on its own. She couldn't wait to share it with the Writers' Group the following Wednesday.

As she printed out copies ready for the meeting, she wished she were telepathic. It would be fabulous to talk to Philip, mind-to-mind, any time she liked. Their planned weekend together hadn't come off. He had phoned her the previous evening.

'I'm really sorry, sweetheart, but I won't be able to make it this weekend. I've got another bad case. Can't tell you the details, but I need to be get-at-able in case it goes critical. I'm so sorry. I'm going to miss you loads.'

Her heart sank. This was the second time in two months this had happened. For a fleeting instant, she wished he was an accountant or worked in insurance – or something. Anything 9 to 5, Monday to Friday. But this was irrational. If he hadn't followed his dream, he wouldn't be the man she fell in love with

'Oh Philip. I'm sorry too. I'm going to really miss seeing you. Don't worry about me. I'll spend the weekend with Dani.'

'You're a gem, sweetheart! Thank you for not stressing out about it. It's the last thing I want, believe me. But I don't have a choice. We'll make up for it the Bank Holiday weekend. Three whole days together!'

'Ring me when you can, won't you? Love you.'

'Love you too, my sweet. I'll ring when I can.'

So that was that.

After lunch, she started work on Dani's trip to Iona. She would book in for one of the Gathering Space weeks and would be changed by her experience of living in a Christian community, sharing worship and work, all away from the distractions of the modern world.

She vaguely remembered someone at St Mary's talking about their time on Iona. Now who had it been? It would be great to have a first-hand report. After all, even the best website could only give a flavour of the experience. She'd go to church on Sunday and see if she could find out.

In the meantime, she put herself in Dani's head, and worked out how she would react to being under authority. With Dani's convent background, she would either relax into it. Or resent it fiercely.

By the end of the afternoon, she had got as far as she could without a first-hand account. She spent the evening reading the next Book Group book, *I and Thou* by Martin Buber, Baggins curled up on her lap. She found it very heavy going.

The next morning, she set off for St Mary's. Not having been since the Good Friday service a month before, she felt a bit guilty. But at least she was going to the Book Group.

She needn't have worried. When she walked in, Reverend Martin's face lit up. 'Claire! How lovely to see you!' Smiling back at him, she took her usual seat at the back.

It was a lovely and uplifting service. As the Church year was moving towards the Feast of Pentecost, the readings were testimonies of the work of the Holy Spirit. She particularly enjoyed Psalm 100, which exhorted everyone to 'Make a joyful noise to the Lord'. After this, Claire, along with everyone else, belted out the hymns with extra fervour.

170

Afterwards, during coffee hour, she sought out Ruth. 'Can you remember who gave that talk about Iona?' she said. 'I'd really like to talk to them.'

Ruth smiled. 'That's easy. It was me! How can I help?'

'Oh, gosh! I'm sorry – I should have remembered. As to how you can help . . . I'm writing a novel and I need some information about a typical day in the Iona Community.'

'Goodness!' she said, taking a deep breath. 'Where do I begin?'

'Mind if I take notes?' Claire said, getting out her notebook and pen.

'What? Oh, not at all. Well, for a start, the accommodation's pretty basic. Everyone shares a room. And there aren't that many facilities. No TV. No Wi-Fi. No phone signal. So you're really cut off from the outside world. Which is marvellous. Everyone mucks in with meal preparation, cleaning and washing up. There are morning and evening services at the Abbey.'

'Every day?'

Ruth nodded. 'Yep. Every day.'

'Did you have to go to every one?'

'Up to you,' Ruth said. 'It all depends on why you're there . . . Anyway, formal sessions of the programme are in the Chapter House. We relaxed in the Common Room. Oh yes, and the Library's fabulous. All wood panelling, and wonderful books. Which should appeal to you.'

Ruth took a sip of coffee while Claire caught up with her notes. Claire looked up from her notebook and said, 'What are the formal sessions like?'

'Formal's a bit strong, really. Usually, there's a theme for the week.'

'Theme?'

'Yes, you know – peace, justice, living in community, that sort of thing. So the sessions are a mixture of learning and sharing on the theme.'

'I see,' Claire said, still scribbling.

'Let's see,' Ruth carried on. 'What else can I tell you? They're strong on making music, singing, and learning crafts. And, oh, yes, they hold a lovely welcoming service on the Saturday evening and then a Blessing service on the Friday morning. Mondays, there's a ceilidh in the village hall, which is wonderful – lots of singing and Scottish dancing.'

She paused while Claire caught up.

'And then, of course, there's the island itself. It's so beautiful.'

'And what did you get out it? Personally, I mean.'

'Me?' Ruth said. 'Oh, it's life-changing. Was for me, at any rate. It's like being translated into a different time and space. Like magic. I don't mind saying, the ferry journey back to the mainland was like waking up from a dream.'

'It sounds fabulous.'

'Oh, it was! If you get the chance to go, do!'

'Yes,' Claire said. 'Maybe next year. Thanks, Ruth.'

It would be so wonderful to go to Iona next year. Would Philip be up for it? Maybe not . . . though it wouldn't hurt to ask. But they had to get the Camino done first.

Chapter Twenty Five

The Friday before the Bank Holiday, the journey down to Bath took her nearly four hours, twice as long as usual, because the traffic was nose-to-tail. So, when she finally got to Philip's at half past six, she was ready for some coffee.

'Ahh,' she sighed. 'I needed that.'

'And now we've got three whole days together,' he said. 'I thought, if the weather was nice tomorrow, we could have a go at the Bath Skyline walk. You brought your trainers, I hope?'

'What's the Bath Skyline walk?'

'It's a six-mile walk along the hills and valleys around Bath. I haven't done it for years, but from what I remember, it's steepish in places, but not too difficult, and should be beautiful at this time of year.'

'Sounds great. Six miles is going to be pushing it for me though. I haven't done a walk that long for some time. But we can rest on Sunday. I'm in!'

'Chas is going out with friends on Sunday, so we'll have the flat to ourselves.'

'Sounds good to me!' she laughed. 'Where's Chas?'

'He's gone to get himself some Jack Daniels. He's meeting some friends later. He should be back soon. I've never known him to miss a meal!'

'I've got him an Amazon gift voucher for his birthday. D'you think that will be OK?'

'Ah, that was sweet of you. You needn't have done. I'm sure that will be more than acceptable.'

'Oh, good. I didn't know what to get him. I don't really know him at all . . .'

'Not still worried? I told you, he likes you! Now, what've you been up to? How did Writers' Group go?'

'Really well!' She laughed. 'Duncan said it was the best story I'd ever written! And everyone else said nice things about it. I was so chuffed!'

'I bet! But I'm not in the least surprised. You're a good writer, Claire.'

'Aww, thank you. And I saw Ruth at church on Sunday, and she's been to Iona, so I asked her loads of questions.'

'Iona? Oh, of course, Dani. That's great. So much better to give an authentic account.'

'Yes, and it sounds absolutely marvellous. If we weren't doing the Camino . . . talking of which, we'd better book it, hadn't we? Have you heard from HR yet? I've got that week booked as annual leave.'

'Yes, finally. On Thursday. It's on!'

'Oh that's wonderful. Let's book it tonight!'

Philip hugged her, laughing 'Yes, we'll book it tonight!'

When they woke up on Saturday, the sun was shining through the bedroom curtains and, when Philip drew them back, the sky was a deep blue. After a quick breakfast, they packed a few necessaries into a backpack, left Chas a note, and set off.

They drove out to Bathwick Hill, the starting point for the walk. It was wonderful. They visited what remained of Sham Castle, then walked through Bathwick Wood, stopping often to admire the views. Then through a kissing gate, pausing to kiss, happy to be with each other. The sun was glimmering through the new green of the leaves and birds were twittering all around them. The very air smelled of spring.

'This is wonderful, Philip. Wonder-full, in the best sense of the word.'

'You're right, it's beautiful. I'd forgotten how beautiful.'

'What are these rows of stones?'

'Hang on,' he said, pulling out the leaflet. 'Oh my, it says here that they're "the remnants of a tramway built in the 1700s to transport stone from the quarries in these woods to the canal, for distribution to Bath and beyond." Well, I never knew that!'

They emerged from the wood into an open, grassy meadow, profuse with wildflowers.

'This is like *The Sound of Music*!' Claire exclaimed. 'Can we stop here for a while and have a break?'

Philip dropped the pack on to the ground, and they sat for a while, munching protein bars and drinking from their water bottles. High above them a skylark filled the air with its heart-lifting song.

Then he stood up again – too soon for her liking.

'Come on! We mustn't sit for too long or we'll stiffen up.'

'Oof, you're right,' she gasped. 'I'm getting old!'

'You don't look it to me. Come on, sweetheart, we've got a long way to go yet.'

'So,' she said. 'Tell me about your case – that is, if you're allowed to.'

'Well,' he said, 'I can't tell you much. The mother is an alcoholic and has three children by three different fathers, none of whom are on the scene right now. The oldest was placed in foster care a while ago, and seems to be settling down. But her carers can't take the younger two. So we're trying to find a placement for them together. But the middle one is so damaged that I'm not sure we'll find anyone to take him. It breaks my heart, how the children are always the ones that suffer for the sins of their elders.'

'Isn't there any other family who could take them?' Claire said.

'Unfortunately not. The grandparents are nearly as bad – the grandfather has a police record as long as your arm, and the grandmother also drinks.'

'Ah, that's sad. It must be hard work to let it go at the end of the week,' Claire said.

'You're right there,' Philip said. 'They haunt my dreams sometimes . . .' He shook his head. 'Let's change the subject. I don't want to spoil the rest of the weekend worrying about them.'

She hugged him and they walked on. After a few minutes, the worry

175

lines began to smooth out of his face as he came back to the present. They continued over Claverton Down to Prior Park, at the head of Lyncombe Vale. There was a wonderful folly there, peacefully set amid trees and grass. Claire spotted a green woodpecker. Then they wandered through Smallcombe Woods, thickly carpeted with bluebells, which smelled so sweet. The final leg threaded through fields and an orchard, then they were back at Bathwick Hill, tired, but with a great sense of achievement.

By the time they got back to the flat, Claire's legs were aching, and by the weary slump of his shoulders, Philip had obviously felt the distance too.

Chas popped his head out of his room. 'Hi Dad, Claire! How did the Skyline – oh, God, you two look knackered.'

'Well, we did it,' Philip said, rubbing the back of his legs. 'Six solid miles.'

'Wow! Well done, you.'

'Yes,' Claire said. 'And we'll be doing a lot more like it in the next few months. Has your dad told you about the Camino?'

'Oh yeah,' he said. 'You're doing some pilgrim walk in Spain, right? Rather you than me. Spain's for sitting on a beach, my arm around a girl, or checking out the nightlife.'

'Well,' Philip said. 'Horses for courses, I suppose. When I was your age, that would have been my idea of a good time too.'

After Philip and Claire had showered, the three of them had a supper of sausage, egg, and chips. As Chas then disappeared until Sunday evening, they settled down for the evening. They snuggled together for a while on the sofa, watching a film. Soon, though, they were dozing, so went to bed.

And slept.

Sunday, they didn't leave the flat, making love, cooking and eating meals.

When Chas finally rolled in, looking shattered, Claire was replete and content.

'Hello, Chas,' she said. 'Good time?'

'Yeah, cool, thanks. Just going for a shower.'

'I don't expect he's been to bed,' Philip remarked, after he'd gone. 'Oh, for the stamina of youth!'

'I was so stiff this morning,' she said. 'We're going to have to put a lot of practice in this summer – we'll be walking half as far again every day for more than a week.'

'But we've made a good start. Yesterday was gorgeous. By the way, you may want to give Chas your present this evening. I don't expect he'll have surfaced by the time you leave tomorrow.'

So, after the evening meal, she fetched it from the bedroom.

'This is for you, Chas. Happy Birthday for tomorrow.'

'Wow, sweet!' Chas said, ripping open the envelope. 'Cheers, Claire!' He came over and gave her a peck on the cheek.

Claire blushed. He really was accepting her. 'You're welcome.'

'God,' Philip said when he rang on Tuesday evening, 'I'm so sick and fed up of Peggy! She's been on the phone, giving me a hard time, because I didn't take Chas to see her this weekend. Bloody woman. She doesn't own us!'

'Oh love, I'm so sorry. What did you say?'

'I told her you'd been down for the weekend and there hadn't been time. So, of course – *of course* – I got the whole "You care more about your new girlfriend than you do about me" routine. She makes me sick to my stomach!'

'Ow!' Claire said. 'I'm so sorry that I've caused this.'

'Oh, it's not you, it's her. She simply can't understand we don't want to spend all our spare time with her. I wish she didn't have this hold over us.'

'Oh, you mean the loan? When are you due to pay it off?'

'Not for years. And she's never let me forget it, either. Not for a moment. She's used it to browbeat me into doing whatever she wants for far too long. Well, I've had enough. She's not going to dictate who I see.'

'She doesn't have the right,' Claire snapped. 'She's going to have to get used to me.'

'Too right, my sweet. Now I've found you, I'm not letting you go.'

'What matters is I love you, not what she thinks. Let it go, darling. Don't give her that power over you.'

He sighed. 'I know that, sweetheart, but you've no idea how hard she makes it for me.'

'I'm so sorry,' she said again. She didn't know what else she could say.

'Ah, don't worry about it. I've weathered Peggy's rants before, and I'll weather them again. I can't wait to see you this weekend. What are we doing?'

'I thought we'd go for a walk on the Malvern Hills. They're beautiful this time of year. Should give us some good practice. Lots of ups and downs!'

'Not *more* ups and downs,' he said. 'I have enough of them with Peggy.'

Claire laughed.

'Looking forward to it, sweetheart,' he chuckled. 'Love you.'

'Love you too.'

The following week, Claire shared her feelings with Beryl.

'Honestly, Beryl, Peggy is a pain. She doesn't seem to appreciate Philip is moving on – that he's found some new happiness with me. I wish he could move up here and get shot of her.'

'Move up here?'

'Yes, I don't see why not,' she rushed on. 'He could get a job up here and move in with me. I've got plenty of room. Or we could sell my house and pool the proceeds from that and the flat and find somewhere new together.'

'Do you think you're ready for that, Claire? Think for a moment before you answer.'

'Oh, I don't know. We've been together for nearly three months, which seems like no time at all. On the other hand, I'm like two people at the moment. Happy and fulfilled when I'm with him, lonely and depressed when I'm not. And I have known him for over thirty years, after all. Do you think I'm being too hasty?'

'I wonder whether you've really thought this through. It isn't so very long since you were in such grief about Jack.'

'I know! And I still have spasms of missing him like mad. But being with Philip has made a difference. I think that the healing process has started. It helps that he's been through the same loss. So he understands that part of me will always love Jack, like he loves Angie still. I honestly think the two of us could make a fresh start together.'

'Have you mentioned this to Philip yet?'

'No, I've only just thought of it now, talking to you. I don't know. Maybe it's a bad idea. But it seems so right!'

'Then I suggest you take it to God in prayer and work through the pros and cons before you leap into such a fundamental change in your life. And how's the not drinking going?'

'It's getting easier as time passes. I had my three-month soberversary on Thursday. But whenever I get stressed out or sad, I still want to numb my feelings with wine. Do you think there will ever be a time when my go-to solution isn't alcohol?'

'You're doing really well. And yes, that time will come, but it may take longer than you expect. But I am concerned that bringing such an upheaval into your life may test your resolution to the limit.'

'I guess you're right. But I still think it could work. I've mourned Jack's passing for so long, and I want to move on.'

'Like I said, take it to God in prayer and try to discern what is the next right step. I will be holding you in my thoughts and prayers.'

Over the next few days, Claire prayed about the idea. But no matter how hard she tried to think of the possible pitfalls, the prospect of having Philip with her all the time was becoming more and more attractive.

At the weekend, she said, 'You know you had that run-in with Peggy after the Bank Holiday?'

'Don't remind me, I'm still having nightmares about it.'

'Well, I was wondering . . . What if you weren't dependent on her anymore?'

'That's just not going to happen.'

'Well, it could . . . If you found a job up here.'

Philip stared at her for a moment, then broke out into an enormous grin. 'You mean move in with you? I'd love to!' Then he frowned. 'But are you ready for that? I don't want to rush you.'

She smiled. 'I know, it's quite soon to be thinking about it. But honestly, Philip, I'm so happy when you're here and so lonely and fed up when you're not. Then I got to thinking – maybe that would be the solution.

'After all,' she said, 'it's not like we've just met. I've known you for most of my life and, since I've been with you, my grief for Jack has started to heal. I genuinely believe I'm ready to find new happiness. And I want to find it with you.'

Philip nodded. 'Me, too.'

'So, I thought, you could move up here first, then sell the flat. Then we'd put this house on the market, find somewhere new together, and pay Peggy what you owe her. It wouldn't be right for us to live here. It has so many memories of my life with Jack.' She stopped for a moment, looked away, gathered herself. 'And it wouldn't be fair on you.'

Philip's mind appeared to be elsewhere. 'Claire,' he said softly, 'if you really think you're ready, I'd love to.' He smiled. 'But finding a job isn't going to be easy. I'd have to go on to the BASW website . . .'

'What's that?'

'Oh . . . British Association of Social Workers. Anyway, I'd have to do that to look for vacancies up here. It may take a while to find something and I can't contemplate moving without a job. Then there's Chas. It would mean leaving all his friends in Bath.'

'He shouldn't mind too much,' Claire said. 'After all, he's pretty much left home now, hasn't he? And he and Jessica seem to be getting quite serious.'

'He could always stop at Peggy's if he wanted to see his old friends.'

180

'Or sleep on someone's floor . . .'

'Or sleep on someone floor. I'll talk to him next weekend. He's coming home for Father's Day.'

'So let's leave it there for now. But I would like to try . . .'

They hugged tightly.

'God, Claire, I hadn't dared to hope you'd feel ready for this so soon. I love you so much.'

Chapter Twenty Six

Because of Baggins, Claire spent only Saturday in Bath. So they agreed Philip would wait until Sunday to talk to Chas. He phoned her after dropping Chas at the station.

'So, what did he say?'

'His first response was, "Leave Bath? But all my friends are here." I pointed out he was away at uni for most of the year and that he could always stay with them if he needed to. He went silent for a while, then he said, "But you've only been with Claire for a few months. Are you really sure about this, Dad?" I had to laugh. Talk about role reversal!'

'What did you say?'

'I told him that, although we had only been dating for three months, we've known each other for more than thirty years, so it's not as if we're jumping into this blind. I told him how much I've missed Angie and I never thought I'd find happiness like that again but that I've found it with you. So, I said, I really want to do this, but I needed his blessing. He thought for a while, then said, "I never thought about you needing that sort of thing. My bad. I suppose if you must have someone else after Mum, I'm glad it's her."'

'I hope you stressed that I in no way want to replace Angie with him?'

'I didn't say that, but I think he understands. So now, *all* I've got to do is sell the flat and find a job! That is going to take months. But maybe that's not a bad thing. If you get cold feet, there'll be plenty of time for you to change your mind.'

'I don't think I will. Wow! That's quite a bundle of news. Have you started looking for jobs yet?'

'Have a heart! I've only just got back from dropping Chas off at the station. But when I get off the phone, I'll have a look at the BASW website. It's got a good section on vacancies.'

'Oh my, this is sounding so real, all of a sudden.'

'Not having second thoughts, are you? Because we can't do this unless you're truly ready.'

'No, no second thoughts. But part of me is still catching up with the idea. We only talked about it last weekend, and now it's starting to come true.'

'Let's take it day by day, eh? There may not be any jobs, although I'm going to cast my net wide. After all, I could commute to Birmingham, so it's not like I'm limited to Worcestershire. And then I'll have to go through the recruitment process *and* get the job! So it'll be months before I can move. Which means Chas will have at least one more summer holiday in Bath.'

'That's true. Fingers crossed. I love you, Philip.'

'Love you too, sweetheart. Bye now.'

Ten days later, he phoned again. 'Claire, you'll never guess,' he said. 'I've found a job I'm going to apply for. It's with the National Fostering Agency in Birmingham and Warwickshire. I think I tick all the boxes, so I've applied. It will be quite similar to the work I'm doing at the moment and at a comparable pay grade, but with a lot more driving. But I don't mind that. And they pay a car allowance as well.'

'When's the closing date?'

'This coming Friday. So I've only just got it in in time. They're interviewing the second week in July. Send up some prayers for me, sweetheart.'

'Wow, of course I will. That's amazing. I never expected you to find something so quickly. If you get it, how much notice will you have to give?'

'Three months, but that's fairly standard, and the new people will expect that. But if all goes well, I could be moving up by the end of October, which would be a lovely birthday present!'

'Let's not count our chickens. I'll be keeping every finger and toe firmly crossed. And praying hard, too.'

The next few weeks were hard. Claire had to fight the temptation to drink on more than one occasion while she waited to hear whether Philip had got the job. One particularly bad evening, she rang Geoff.

'Hello, Geoff, Claire here,' she said. 'I'm really struggling tonight.'

'What's up, Claire?' he asked.

'I'm waiting to hear whether my boyfriend has got a new job up here,' she said. 'If he gets it, he'll be able to move in with me. If he doesn't, I don't know what I will do. And I could murder a drink.'

'That's just temptation messing with your head, Claire,' Geoff said. 'It would be fatal to listen. You're over the worst now – more than four months, isn't it? You just need to remember what I told you – it's a total commitment and you can't break a promise to God once you've made it.'

'I guess you're right,' she sighed. 'But it's so damned hard sometimes.'

'I know,' he said. 'But you can do it, Claire. Chin up!'

'Thank you, Geoff. I needed to hear that.'

Philip was called for interview in the second week of July but wouldn't hear for least a fortnight or so while they took up references.

It was difficult for them to think about anything else. They met at weekends, sometimes in Bath, sometimes Brandleton, and got in a few good long walks. They were getting fitter, which was a good thing, as the Camino was only a couple of months away.

She didn't tell anyone yet – in case it all came to nothing. She did her best to carry on as normal going to the Writers' Group, reading the latest book for Book Group, working at the library or on her Dani novel, seeing Lucy and Dawn every Friday and, most difficult of all, not telling Beryl and her parents.

So it was quite a relief, in among it all, to go out for a meal to celebrate Lucy's birthday during the second week in July. Fortunately, for Claire, Lucy was so full of her new relationship with Sam, she did most of the talking.

'He's really lovely! He treats me like I'm someone special. And I've met his girls. I'm not sure what they thought of me, but I quite liked them, which was a surprise.'

'I'm so glad it's going well for you. You deserve some happiness, after all this time.'

'Thanks, hun. And I'm losing weight too. I don't need to comfort eat so much anymore. Another few weeks and I should hit target.'

'That's great. Well done, you! I thought you were looking rather svelte when you walked in.'

'You noticed? Aw, that's great. Thanks, Claire.'

Claire smiled at her friend, even fonder of her than usual. She was so pretty in a new wrap dress which accentuated her curves. But the real difference was subliminal. She had lost the hungry look in her eyes and was emanating contentment. Claire hoped Sam was the one.

The following Thursday was Book Group. After the customary check-in, it was time to share their views about that month's book, *God has a dream: A vision of hope for our time* by Desmond Tutu.

'I loved it,' Claire said. 'My favourite thing was the way he opens each chapter with the words "Dear Child of God". I'd never really thought of myself as a child of God before, but he made me realise that *everyone* is a child of God, from the most saintly to the most wicked. And that there's hope for us all – anyone can become their best selves. Which would make the world a better and happier place.'

'I don't know,' Pat said. 'Isn't it a bit idealistic? I mean, you couldn't include people like Hitler and Stalin in God's family, surely?'

'I think we have to,' Ruth said slowly. 'After all, he and Nelson Mandela were in the thick of the battle against apartheid in South Africa, and must have seen so many atrocities. But they somehow managed to overcome their desire for retribution and set up the Truth and Reconciliation Commission.'

'I really loved the concept of *ubuntu*,' Julie said. 'That every human being is in inter-relationship with every other human being. The idea of belonging to a greater whole. That really spoke to me.'

'The part that made me sit up and take notice was that bit about the difference between loving and liking your enemies,' Claire said. 'That it's impossible to like everyone, especially people who've hurt you, but you *can* try to love everyone, or at least, to act lovingly towards them. What a message!'

'Yes, I think that's what Jesus meant too,' Ruth said. 'Such a challenge, such a call to action. Which is why Tutu can still talk of hope, I guess, after all he has seen and suffered. His faith is in a loving God, and in the capacity for humankind to be loving and good and compassionate and caring.'

There was a murmur of agreement from the others.

The Reading Agency's Summer Reading Scheme started at the library at the beginning of the school holidays. The theme for the year was Animal Agents, and the launch had been at The Hive, Worcestershire's Central Library, on the first of July. The idea behind it was to keep primary school children in the reading habit over the summer holidays, by challenging them to borrow and read at least six books. Claire enjoyed organising the events, which this year included a visit by a representative of Guide Dogs for the Blind, together with a beautiful chocolate Labrador named Coco. She and Miriam took it in turns to host the daily story time, and had great fun sourcing suitable animal stories. It was her favourite time of the year, at work.

The last weekend in July, it was Claire's turn to go to Bath.

Philip was waiting for her with a big grin on his face.

'I've got it!' he said. 'I've got the job! I didn't want to tell you until I was sure, but they sent me an email today.'

She flung herself into his arms. 'Oh Philip, that's brilliant news! When will you be starting?'

'Well, I've got to hand in my notice on Monday, so it will be the end of October or beginning of November. But I've got a few days' leave owing so I'll make my last day the twenty-fourth of October. That'll give me a few days to move up. Which means I'll be able to spend my birthday with you!'

'Oh, that's fabulous! Have you told Chas yet?'

'No, he's spending a couple of days up in Derbyshire with Jessica. I'll tell him when he comes home. I'd rather do it face to face. But now, my sweet, we celebrate! I've got us a bottle of fizz.'

She couldn't believe her ears. Surely he wasn't expecting her to have a drink? True, she was longing to do just that. Break open a bottle and celebrate. Surely this once wouldn't hurt? After all, it *was* a special occasion.

Then, through the roaring in her ears, she heard him say, 'Don't worry, sweetheart, it's alcohol-free. I nipped out and bought it as soon as I got the email.'

The combination of relief and regret was so intense, it almost brought her to her knees.

Seeing her face, Philip took her in his arms. 'You surely didn't think I'd forget, did you? We can celebrate just as well without the booze. In fact, if I move in with you, I might take the pledge myself. I don't drink very often, and I won't miss it.'

'Yes, let's celebrate. I'm so happy for you. For both of us. I can't quite believe it's happening.'

'Well, it is.'

And they kissed before he headed to the fridge for the bottle.

Their joyful celebrations continued for the whole weekend. They spent some time looking at estate agents' websites, found one they liked the look of, and emailed them to arrange a valuation.

Claire was so happy when she got home on Sunday evening. But lying in bed that night, suddenly it all hit her. Was it happening too fast? Was she really ready to have him move in? *What had she done?* Was it too late to back out now? He's got the job. He's selling his flat. Was she up for this?

Maybe writing it all out would help, get some clarity. She fetched her journal and plumped up her pillows.

Such an exciting weekend! I got down to Bath to be greeted by the news that Philip has got the job and can move up at the end of October. Most of me is thrilled, but part of me is getting serious cold feet about the whole thing. I wasn't expecting it to happen so quickly. But now Philip's committed. He's got the new job and will be resigning his old one tomorrow.

This is ridiculous. For weeks and weeks, you've been wishing you could spend more time with him and now it's happening and you're having doubts. What's wrong with you?

I guess I'm just feeling a bit of out of control. Always a red flag for me. I love Philip. I truly do. But it's going to be so weird having him here, in this house, where Jack and I have been so happy, and so sad. I think it would be best if we moved to a new place together, straight away. Somewhere that will be ours, not mine and Jack's with Philip living there.

Or would that be one change too many? I don't know. I guess it wouldn't do any harm to look for a four-bedroomed house locally, so that we'll have both a spare room and a study, and to check out how much this place is worth. But I'll have to wait until Philip knows how much he's getting for the flat, and how much he can bring to the new place.

So calm down. You can't do anything about it now. You'll just have to possess your soul in patience and wait and see how it goes. It's late. You've got work in the morning. Time to sleep.

The following Tuesday, she saw Beryl.

'Well, the die is cast. Philip's found a job up here and resigned from his old one yesterday. All being well, he'll be moving up here at the end of October. I'm so excited! But a bit scared too.'

'Scared?'

'It's all come together so quickly. I'm not a hundred per cent sure I'm ready for this. But it's too late to back out now. I love Philip and

I do want to spend the rest of my life with him, but it's going to be so weird, him living in the house. It's so full of memories of Jack.'

'So, what is your heart telling you?'

'I was thinking that, when Philip knows how much profit he's going to make from the flat sale and after he's paid off Peggy, we could look for somewhere bigger. Because there will have to be a bedroom for Chas, one for us, a study, and a spare room. I think it would be better to move to a new place, where we could make a fresh start together. It all depends on how much money we've got to play with. Because I don't have a mortgage, so anything we make on my house could be put towards a new one.'

Beryl nodded. 'I think that's a wise decision. It would be hard for you to have Philip in your house, where you and Jack were so happy. Are you *sure* you're doing the right thing, Claire?'

'I think so. No, I know so. Since I've been with Philip, I've felt my grief about losing Jack begin to heal. I know Jack would approve – he was very fond of Philip. And when I'm with him, I'm so happy. He really is a good man, you know. It feels like I'm choosing Life.'

'Then I'm happy for you and I hope it all works out as you think it will. Take your worries to God. He is always listening.'

That evening, she shared the news with her parents.

'But you've not known him for more than a few months, daughter,' Joan said. 'What's the big hurry?'

'I've known him for more than thirty years, Mum. And I'm like two people at the moment – happy and fulfilled when Philip is around, grey and lonely when he isn't. I want to be heart-whole again.'

'But can he really give you happiness?' her father said.

'Yes, Dad. I'm beginning to get over the worst of my grief about Jack – it's been well over a year now – and Philip lost his own wife six years ago, so he understands what I've been going through.'

'Well, it's your life, my dear. I just hope he can make you happy.'

★

A couple of days later, Philip rang. 'Hello, sweetheart. You're never going to guess what they've valued the flat at. I'm flabbergasted.'

'Well, go on – tell me!'

'They reckon I'll get £365,000 for it – £350,000 if I want a quick sale. I paid two hundred and fifty-five for it, of which a hundred came from Peggy. So even after I've paid her off, and paid the mortgage off, I should be able to clear nearly seventy grand! I just don't believe it.'

'That's great news. So if we sell my house, and add your seventy grand, we ought to be able to find a four-bedroomed house somewhere local.'

'Hang on. You want to move?'

'I did tell you. This house has so many memories of Jack, and it wouldn't be fair on you. And hard for me too.'

After a brief silence, Philip said, 'I'm sorry, sweetheart. I hadn't thought. Stupid of me. Of course, you're right, but we'll have to wait until my sale's finalised. You do still want to do this, don't you? You're not getting cold feet? Because I've rather burned my boats down here. I resigned on Monday.'

'Of course not. It's just that it's all happening so quickly and I'm struggling to keep up. But no, of course not. I can't wait for us to be together.'

'Are you sure? Because it's not too late. I could go into work tomorrow and withdraw my resignation. But you'll have to decide now. I'm having to make decisions here.'

'Oh, Philip! Of course I don't want you to do that. It's just my old, stupid need to be in control thing. Ignore me. I'm so excited for you, for us! I'm counting the days.'

'Well, if you're sure?'

'Yes, I am sure. I love you, darling. When you come up this weekend, we could see what house prices here are like. I've lived here so long I've absolutely no idea what this place is worth. About the same as yours, I expect. Broughton isn't half as trendy as Bath!'

He laughed. 'God, you scared me just then! I thought it was all going to go belly up.'

'It's not. I can't wait. I miss you so much when you're not here. It's going to be fantastic having you around all the time.'

'That goes double for me, sweetheart. I love you, Claire.'

'Love you too. Goodbye, my darling.'

'Bye, sweetheart.' And he was gone.

Claire sat back, exhausted by the mix of emotions.

Chapter Twenty Seven

August was always a difficult month. For the past 22 years, the Bank Holiday weekend had been permanently overshadowed by memories of her daughter's brief life.

Laura was born on a sultry evening, one 24 August, spent all of her short life in the neo-natal intensive care suite in Worcester Royal Infirmary. She slipped away six days later.

The labour had been long and arduous, and Claire and Jack were relieved and happy when Laura finally appeared. But it wasn't long before those joyful firsts she had anticipated – holding her baby to her breast, cuddling her close, listening to her breathing – came to nothing. The delivery room became a scene of fear and despair.

Laura was taken away from her. Nurses, midwives, and doctors talked together in low tones. But she and Jack caught the words 'cord around the neck' and 'brain damage' and were filled with dread.

What was wrong with their Laura, their precious little daughter? Tears leaked down her face, past her ears and on to the bed.

'Jack! What are they saying?'

That was the start of it.

Laura was rushed to the neo-natal intensive care unit. The diagnosis was brain damage due to lack of oxygen during labour.

Claire spent as much time as she was allowed in the neo-natal ICU sitting in a wheelchair, Jack at her side, watching their daughter struggle for life. So many wires attached to the little body and to the softly pulsing skull.

'Come on, little one,' she whispered again and again. 'Come on, Laura. You can do this.'

The doctors operated to try to relieve the pressure on the brain. The long hours of waiting, unable to rest, weeping, unable to sleep, weeping, praying her daughter would live through this, would get well, would come home.

But when Jack walked into the little side room of the post-natal ward, she knew the worst had happened.

His face was grey, twisted in grief. He fell to his knees beside the bed and burst into tears. 'We've lost her.'

'Oh, my baby, my baby!'

Three weeks later, the tiny white coffin was laid to rest in the graveyard at St Mary's. After that, Claire and Jack tried to rebuild their lives. Although the doctors were emphatic that it was just one of those accidents, Claire never stopped blaming herself. Deep in her soul, she believed her failure to conceive again was a punishment.

For the rest of their married lives, they never celebrated that particular holiday.

And then, this old grief was joined by a new one last year. Jack's birthday was on 8 August, so that day was filled with memories of their years together. Their whirlwind, fun-filled courtship at university, the happy early years of their marriage building a satisfying life together. Then the grief of losing Laura, which had brought them even closer together. And now, the shocking diagnosis of the cancer, the difficult years of his illness, and then his death.

All through that, she had soused her grief in red wine, listening to music they had shared, crying herself into a stupor.

And if that wasn't enough, this year, she fought a full-scale pitched battle with the temptation to drink.

Come on, you deserve a drink. Just for today.

I haven't had a drink for more than five months now.

You need the support.

Surely it won't hurt to drink today?

That's right. It will make the pain go away.

193

I'll go back to being sober tomorrow.

Geoff's words: 'If you make a promise to God, you can't break it.'
Why can't I break it?

Because then you'll be throwing away all the progress you've
made so far.

Go on to the sobriety group page and ask them.

She flounced upstairs, logged on, and posted:

*It would have been my DH's birthday today and I'm desperate for a
drink, to make the pain go away. Surely it wouldn't do any harm to
drink today? I can go back to being sober tomorrow, LL*

*I'm so sorry to hear about that. Anniversaries are always hard. But
you mustn't give in. You've done so well up to now. More than five
months, isn't it? Try playing the tape to the end. You might feel better
for a drink at first, because it will numb the pain, but imagine how shit
you'll feel tomorrow, knowing that you've given in.*

*Oh my dear! I'm so sorry for your loss. But don't give in. I'm guessing
you're feeling pretty lonely at the moment. Is there anyone you can
reach out to, talk to? You know the old saying, a problem shared is a
problem halved. Whereas, if you have a drink, it will be a problem
doubled. Phone a friend and then treat yourself to something gooey and
fattening to eat and have a hot bubble bath. Hugs.*

OK, I'll try. Thank you x

Damn. She knew they were right. But God! She thought she'd be
over the worst of it by now. She couldn't phone Philip now. He was
at work. She'd go to the Co-op and treat herself to one of their
gooey cakes, or even two. She'd have them with a nice cup of tea.
Sighing, she grabbed her purse.

An hour later, she was in the lounge, licking the last of the cream
off her fingers, when Baggins jumped on to her lap.

'Hello, you,' she said. 'Come for a fuss, have you?'

It was soothing to sit there, the cat purring contentedly. She shuddered at how close she'd come to drinking. Again. She still missed Jack so much. Would there ever come a time when the memory of him didn't bring grief?

Early evening, she rang Philip.

'Hello, Claire. How are you?'

'Oh, Philip! It's been such an awful day! It would have been Jack's fifty-fourth birthday today and I've had to fight temptation to the mat again. I'm so sick of this. It's been more than five months now and my go-to solution for anything is *still* a drink.'

'Oh, love, I'm so sorry,' he said. 'That's a tough one. But you didn't give in, did you?'

'No, but it came *that* close. It was only thanks to my sobriety group friends that I beat her.'

'Why didn't you ring me?'

'I didn't like to disturb you at work.'

'I wouldn't have minded. Not for that. Don't you know I love you, sweet Claire?'

Her eyes filled again. 'Oh, Philip. Whatever would I do without you?'

This month's Book Group book was peculiarly appropriate: Harold Kushner's *When bad things happen to good people*. Reading it helped to heal some sore places in her soul. She journaled:

Such a healing book! I'm so glad we've had to read it this month, of all months. Kushner lost his son after fourteen years – even harder than our loss of Laura,, because he had been in Kushner's life for so much longer. But I've always blamed myself for her death, and he's helped me to understand that it wasn't my fault, that bad stuff just happens, and that the question I need to ask myself is not 'why did this happen to me' but 'now that this has happened, what shall I do about it?' It's helped me to come to terms with her death, and even, a bit, with Jack's. At least I know not to blame God any more. Kushner's made me understand that what God does is to inspire people to help others,

who are grieving and lost. As I have been. And I've had Beryl, and
Philip, to help me through this. I think it's actually helped restore my
faith in Him. Which is pretty amazing.

Philip was struggling too. After an initial flurry of interest in the flat, he was starting to wonder whether it would ever be sold. One buyer had looked promising but couldn't get a mortgage large enough.

He was also becoming increasingly frustrated by the time-wasters – people who had no intention of buying the flat but just wanted to fill a spare afternoon.

'Honestly, Claire, it's driving me mad,' he said one evening. 'I really thought that woman would be the one, and then to get the email yesterday, saying her mortgage arrangements had fallen through . . . So it's back to square one. At this rate, I won't have sold by the time I have to move up.'

'I'm sure someone will come along soon. It's a nice flat in a good location. What's not to like?'

'Perhaps I ought to lower the selling price.'

'What does the agent say?'

'I'm beginning to hate the very sound of his voice. He's so damned upbeat all the time. "I'm sure we'll find a buyer very soon, Mr Bateman." Well, I'm not.'

'Philip, you mustn't think like that. Someone will come along. Just hang on in there, sweetheart. And get some writing done. That will take your mind off it.'

'You're right, I suppose. Ah, don't take any notice of me. It's just getting me down. What are we doing this weekend?'

'I thought we could clear out the garage so there's plenty of room for your stuff, while we decide what's going to go where. Then go for a long walk on Sunday. What do you think?'

'Sounds like a plan.'

'The other thing I was going to mention was, do you think Chas and Jessica would like to come to Brandleton for the Bank Holiday weekend? We could have a barbeque in the garden.'

'That's a great idea! It'll be good for Chas to see where he's going to be living after October and, if Jessica's with him, he'll be on his best behaviour. I'll ask him this evening.'

'So,' Claire said in the lounge of the Red Lion the next evening, 'how's Sam?'

'Oh, so-so,' Lucy said. 'He's on holiday with the girls at the moment, so I won't be seeing him until after the Bank Holiday. I'm so fed up about it.'

'Poor old you! That's hard. But I guess he can only see them for any extended period during the school holidays.'

'Oh, I know that. But when he talked about going on holiday, I was kind of hoping he meant with me. Then he started talking about father-daughter time with the girls and I realised I was the last thing on his mind. Why can't I find a decent bloke without school-age kids?'

'Poor Lu! I'm so sorry. That really sucks. Maybe you'll be able to get away with him later in the year. A long weekend, perhaps?'

'Claire, you're a genius! I'll suggest that to him when he gets back. With any luck, he'll be fed up of the kids and will jump at the idea of a civilised adult weekend away.'

'Let's hope so. But I wouldn't put it like that!'

Lucy grinned. 'Don't worry – I *can* be tactful, even if it's not very often!'

Just then, Dawn arrived. 'Dawn!' Claire said, 'I haven't seen you for ages.'

'I know, I haven't been down here for a while,' Dawn said. 'Jake and I have been away for a couple of weeks. I splashed out and booked us an all-inclusive holiday in Tenerife – it's the first time we've been away for more than a couple of days since Mum . . .' she paused, 'since Mum became ill. And he's got his exam results due soon, so I thought it would be a good opportunity to show him how much I've appreciated him.'

'Aw, that's lovely. Did you have a good time?'

'It was wonderful,' she said. 'Not that I saw much of Jake, except

197

at mealtimes. He made friends with a group of lads his own age, and spent most of the days in the water. So I had the chance to have a proper rest, do some reading, and work on my tan.'

'You're certainly looking rested,' Lucy said. 'Maybe I should go away on my own – fat chance of a holiday with Sam.'

The following day was hot and dirty work. When Claire unlocked the garage door – with some difficulty, she hadn't been in there for ages – Philip let out a whistle.

'Blimey, Claire! It's lucky you don't have a car which needs putting away at night.'

'I know. We've been using this space for storage ever since we moved in, and that's over twenty years ago. I did warn you it was going to be a big job.'

'So, how d'you want to tackle it?'

'Well,' she said, looking up into a clear blue sky, 'I checked the weather forecast this morning and it's supposed to be staying fine all day. So let's get everything out on to the lawn and drive and then divide it into four categories – stuff I want to keep, things I can give away on Freegle or recycle, things I can sell, and the rest to the dump. I bought some industrial strength bin bags during the week but, looking at this lot, I'm not sure it's going to be enough. Could you move your car off the drive, please?'

Philip's eyebrows shot up. 'I like a woman who knows her own mind. You're the boss.'

By the time the garage was completely empty, Claire was beginning to wonder whether she'd been crazy to imagine that they get it all done in one day. Every inch of the drive and lawn was covered with storage boxes, cardboard boxes with faded labels, garden tools, and household tools. Not to mention pieces of furniture and other odds and ends.

'Right, that's stage one finished,' she said, pushing back some stray hair which had come loose from its ponytail. 'I don't know about you, but I need a break. Let's go inside and have a cold drink and some biscuits.'

'Excellent. This is going to be a long haul.'

'You don't mind helping, do you? I thought you said you were up for this?'

He hugged her. 'Of course I am. Don't be daft. It's to make room for my stuff, after all.'

They tackled the big stuff first – the furniture and the tools, most of which she decided to put on Freegle. The only thing she wanted to keep was a footstool, which was badly in need of a clean.

'This was Jack's mother's,' she said, softly. 'I couldn't part with this. Once I've cleaned it up, it can go in the lounge.'

Then she put her hands on Jack's old toolbox. 'You'd better look through this. Jack built up quite a good collection over the years, and if there's anything here that you haven't got, we'll need to keep it.'

'This must be hard for you. You're not just clearing out a garage, are you? You're also clearing out your old life.'

She burst into tears. Philip caught her and held her

'It's all right,' he said, stroking her hair. 'Everything's all right.'

'I'm sorry,' she said after a few minutes. 'Don't take any notice of me.' She dried her eyes. 'It's so hard, parting with stuff we bought together, or were given. It's like giving away memories.'

'I remember having to go through Angie's stuff after she died, and it was a wrench to pack it all up and send it to Oxfam.'

After a quick lunch, they started again. As Claire had anticipated, going through the storage boxes was the most difficult part. She kept coming across old belongings of Jack's, and things like concert programmes, which brought back so many memories of their time together, that she spent much of the afternoon on the edge of tears.

By teatime, with Philip's gentle encouragement, they were finally done. The keep and sell stuff was put neatly back on the shelves at the back of the garage, the Freegle stuff near the front for easy access, and the rest heaved into both their cars for trips to the local recycling centre. It took three trips in all, even with the back seats down, because neither of them had big cars, and by the time they were finished, they were shattered.

199

Hot and sticky, they showered, then went out for an Indian take-away. An hour later, they were in the lounge, dog-tired.

'You certainly know how to give a man a good time,' Philip said.

'Philip! That's not fair!' Then she saw the twinkle in his eye and relaxed back against him. 'Oh, you rotter! I thought you were serious for a minute!'

'We've done a good day's work there, sweetheart. But I have to say, I'm hoping that our walk tomorrow isn't too strenuous – I'm knackered.'

'You have a point – I feel pretty shattered myself. I'd planned for us to do a circular walk around Bredon Hill, which starts and ends at Great Comberton. I've had a look on the website, and it's about eight miles. D'you think we're up to it?'

'I suppose we ought to. After all, the Camino's less than a month away now.'

'In which case, we'd better get an early night.'

She smiled up at him, saw his disappointment. He'd obviously had other ideas. She was so full of love for this man, sometimes she could hardly bear it.

The next morning was warm, promising to get hotter, so they took plenty of water. The website had mentioned moderate climbs and they weren't convinced that the writer meant the same thing as they did by the word 'moderate'. By the time they were halfway around, they were running with sweat.

'Why did I think that a long walk in this heat would be a good idea?' Claire wheezed. 'It's beautiful, but, blimey, I'm boiled!'

'Have another drink of water. According to my Fitbit, we're more than halfway.'

'Well, thank goodness for that!'

They shouldered their packs and walked on through open fields, some already harvested, and others awaiting it. The highlight of the walk was Parson's Folly, an eighteenth-century tower next to Kemerton Camp. Although its appearance was spoilt by large mobile phone aerials, the view was spectacular, and they agreed it was worth the climb.

After that, they were on the home stretch, and got back to the car more than three hours after they had left, feeling very pleased with their efforts.

'Let's hope it's not this hot in Spain next month!' Philip said on the drive back.

'I looked on the website the other day and it's supposed to be several degrees cooler, at least when we'll be there.'

'Thank God for that!'

The rest of the day was spent overhauling the long unused barbeque, which had been sitting in the garden shed for the past few years. They were surprised it still worked.

'Looks like next weekend's on!' Claire said with a smile. 'I was beginning to think I'd have to buy a new one. Well done, you!'

'All part of the service,' he said, with a bow. 'Now, we'd better have something to eat, then I must make tracks.'

That evening, he phoned to let her know that Chas and Jessica would be coming with him the following weekend.

'He seemed to be quite excited at the prospect. Jessica was going to spend the weekend with us, anyway, so it's just a change of venue. I'm looking forward to you meeting her. She's very good for him.'

'Me too. She sounds like a lovely girl. See you on Friday, darling.'

Chapter Twenty Eight

Mid-week, Claire texted Philip in a panic.

I just thought. Do either Jessica or Chas have any food dislikes? Because I'm shopping on Friday and I'll need to get stuff I know they'll eat. Also, could you bring the booze for the weekend with you? I can handle other people drinking here, but I don't think I'm up to actually buying it yet. And please could it not include red wine. Not sure I could deal with that! Finally will they want to share a room? I'll need to put the air mattress up in the study if they're not.

Don't panic! Chas eats anything and everything – except fish – and I don't *think* Jessica has any food gremlins. But I'll ask him this evening and let you know. I'll get the booze. Are you sure you're up for that? I won't drink, if you'd rather I didn't. I'll get something for the kids. Probably Jack Daniels & Coke. And yes, they'll definitely want to share a room

Thanks, darling. Thought I'd better run it past you. I want this all to go right!

Don't worry. It will all be fine. See you on Friday xx

Looking forward to it very much xx

Claire put her phone down and sighed. Sometimes she wished Philip wasn't so easy-going – she loved him for it, and it was good for her, but he didn't understand her need to have everything just so. She wouldn't change him, but it was hard to get used to.

But he was as good as his word and phoned her later that evening. Jessica was vegetarian, but otherwise not picky. He had picked up the drink on the way home. So everything was all right.

She went to the gym early on Friday, then did the food shop. As there were only going to be the four of them, she kept it simple – meat and Quorn burgers, vegetarian and ordinary sausages, burger buns and hot dog rolls, packets of crisps and nuts, fresh salad, and some fruit to make fruit kebabs. Plus a few bottles of AF fizz for herself and Philip.

As an afterthought, she added a couple of tubs of Carte d'Or ice cream. She'd buy the bread fresh from the Co-op on the Saturday. The rest of the day was spent cleaning the house from top to bottom. She wanted it to look its best.

They rolled up just after half past seven. She had a vegetarian moussaka waiting for them. Afterwards they went into the lounge, where Claire was able to have her first proper look at Jessica.

How beautiful the girl was. Long legs in skin-tight jeans, slim figure, an oval face, very dark eyes and long, straight, black hair.

'It's kind of you to ask me here, Claire,' Jessica said. 'I've been dying to meet you ever since Chas told me about you.'

'I've been wanting to meet you too. You're at uni with Chas, aren't you?'

'Yes, we're both going into our second years. We shared halls last year and started dating after Christmas. I'm studying Physics with Astrophysics,' she beamed. 'It's really hard work, but I'm loving it!'

'That sounds hard. I've always been a humanities person myself. I flunked science at school and got put off it.' She blushed.

'Oh, that's a shame! I love it. Especially the astrophysics part. I've got the chance to spend a year abroad working in an observatory in third year, and I can't wait.'

'Yeah,' Chas said. 'It's going to make my year out seem dead ordinary by comparison.'

'You're so lucky to have these chances, aren't they, Philip?

Sandwich years weren't available to Psychology or Librarianship students when we were at uni, or at least, not at ours. I really envy you.'

'Yes,' Philip said. 'But we didn't have student loans to contend with. So we were lucky too.'

'That's true. I think it's so unfair to saddle you with that much debt, before you even start your working lives.'

'Would you mind,' Chas said, 'if me and Jess went down the pub, Claire?'

'Of course not. Turn left at the end of the road, and it's about half a mile on your right. Hang on, I'll give you the spare key.'

When they had gone, she turned to Philip with a look of dismay. 'God, I feel so stupid. I've no idea how to talk to students. I made a complete fool of myself.'

He hugged her. 'No, you didn't. Don't worry so much, Claire. Just relax and be your normal friendly self. I expect Jessica was more scared of you than you were of her!'

'Well, I wouldn't have known it. I envy her easy self-assurance. At her age I was gauche in the extreme!'

'They've grown up in a different world, sweetheart. It was ages before I stopped calling Peggy "Mrs Hartman", but these kids are on a first-name basis straight away.'

'I was the same with Jack's mother. I was terrified of her. But she was lovely.'

'Lucky you!'

'Is Peggy being difficult?'

'Nothing out of the ordinary. She's made it very clear she disapproves of the move, of me, of you. But she's not changing my mind.' His arm tightened around her.

'I should think not! You'll be well shot of her, Philip.'

'You're so right about that. Now, what are our plans for the weekend?'

'I thought we could take Chas and Jessica into Worcester on Saturday, let them – and you – have a look around, then we could have a meal out together in the evening. There's rather a nice Thai

204

restaurant in Evesham. But I'll have to book it now. They get quite busy on a Saturday.'

'That sounds great! Then the barbie on Sunday. This is going to be fun!'

'I hope so.'

'I do wish you wouldn't worry so! It's all going to be fine.'

He was right. They had a lovely time wandering round Worcester. Chas and Jessica went off by themselves, while Claire and Philip visited the cathedral.

Philip was impressed by its Gothic beauty and by the magnificent Victorian stained glass. Then they went for a walk by the river, admiring the swans.

'Some years,' Claire said, 'the Severn bursts its banks and the whole area gets flooded. I've seen photos of the swans floating serenely through the streets.'

'That must be quite a sight.'

'Yes,' she said. 'But I'm glad I don't live here. It must be so hard, knowing that there's an annual danger of being flooded out. It must be impossible to get insurance.'

They met Chas and Jessica, spent a couple of hours at home, then drove into Evesham for the Thai meal. The food was delicious and, to Claire's relief, the conversation flowed more easily than the evening before.

Sunday dawned bright and warm. While Philip showered, she went downstairs, only to find that half the loaf she had bought for the barbeque was gone. It looked as if Chas and Jessica had helped themselves when they got home from the pub. They had, at least, washed up their plates and the breadboard, for which she supposed she ought to be grateful. But how dare they take her food without asking?

She rushed back upstairs. 'They've eaten half the loaf I bought for the barbeque!'

'Oh dear. Well never mind, they'll have to eat less later.'

Claire considered this response to be rather less than adequate. She folded her arms.

'I'm not sure I can do this. Are students like this all the time?'

'I'm afraid they are. Or at least Chas is. Take it as a compliment. If they'd thought you would mind, they wouldn't have done it.'

'I suppose so. I'm just not used to this.'

He looked at her curiously. 'It's really bothering you, isn't it?'

'Well, yes, it is, a bit. Like I said, I've never had to deal with students before.'

Her anger was beginning to subside in the face of his phlegmatic attitude. He came out of the shower and gave her a damp hug.

'Try to go with the flow, sweetheart. It will save you a lot of angst. I know it's easy for me to say, and hard for you to do, but try to accept them as they are. You're not going to change them.'

'I suppose not. I just want everything to go right, and here I am already,' she laughed, 'stressing out over some missing bread.'

His arms tightened around her, and he tipped up her chin to kiss her. 'Don't worry, sweetheart, it's going to be fine. I'll go down to the Co-op and replace it, if you like. But I'll need to get dressed first.'

'No, let's leave it,' she said. 'Like you say, they'll have less to eat later. Let's have breakfast and get on with the preparation.'

'That's my girl!' he said. 'Let's do that.'

Most of the work was done by the time Chas and Jessica wandered into the kitchen, yawning.

'Hello, you two!' Claire said. 'Good night?'

'Yeah, they're nice people, your neighbours. We stayed until gone midnight.'

'Yes, closing time's fairly flexible at the Lion. Do you want anything to eat?'

'Yes please, Claire,' said Jessica. 'But I can make us something if you like. We don't want to put you to any trouble.'

'That's all right. I was just going to put lunch together for us. We're having bacon and egg, but I know you don't eat meat. Would a mushroom omelette be OK?'

206

'That would be lovely, thank you!'

A few minutes later, they were all sitting round the table eating brunch. Chas was quite pale, his eyes cast down.

'Chas,' Claire said, 'I've got an old box of Recovery sachets in the back of my medicine cupboard, if you'd like one? I think they're still in date.'

He blushed. 'How did you know?'

'Been there, done that.'

'Yeah, OK, thanks.'

After the Chas and Jessica had left to shower and dress, Philip smiled at her. 'That was kind.'

She shrugged. 'I could tell he was feeling awful. The colour of his face, and the way his eyes were squeezed almost shut. I know what it's like.'

Later on, the conversation continued. 'How much longer have you both got left at York?' Claire said.

'Two years of study,' Jessica said, 'plus a sandwich year in the middle.'

'Have you got any ideas for that yet?' Claire said.

'I'd love to spend the year on La Palma, in the Canary Islands. It's got a fabulous range of telescopes, including the Gran Telescopio Canarias, which is one of the biggest in the world, and also special telescopes for studying gamma rays and other energies and a couple of solar telescopes. I went for a visit in the spring and it looks fabulous!'

'How do the placements work?' Philip said. 'Does York have arrangements with particular observatories, or do you have to set up your own?'

'Oh, we're responsible for finding our own placements but the university helps. Like I said, I've already visited the observatory and managed to speak to the personnel department. And the island itself is so beautiful! I'm really hoping it all works out. It would be a dream come true for me.'

'It sounds wonderful. I hope it works out for you,' Claire smiled. 'How about you, Chas?'

'Oh, mine won't be as exciting as that,' Chas said, flashing Jessica a grin. 'If I want to spend a year abroad, I have to apply in the autumn to transfer to the four-year course. I've been having a look, and I think I'd like to go to the University of Utrecht. The modules sound brilliant and, more important for me, they're taught in English! I *should* be able to get in under the Erasmus scheme, if my grades are good enough and if Brexit doesn't screw it all up.'

'Oh, blimey, Chas! I hadn't thought of that angle. When will the new arrangements come into force?' Claire said.

'I've been keeping an eye on it and it looks as though I might squeeze in under the present arrangements. Fingers crossed,' Chas said.

'What about you, Claire?' Jessica asked. 'What are your dreams for the future?'

'I haven't really thought about it,' she said. 'If you'd asked me this time last year, I would have said my main aim was simply to survive. But now,' and she glanced at Philip, 'I seem to have the possibility of a new life. Which will be a dream come true for me, too.'

'More than a possibility,' he replied. 'I should be here for good by the end of October. And that's my dream too,' he added, looking at Jessica and Chas.

But in spite of the happy atmosphere, part of Claire was feeling edgy. It was still hard, this not drinking when other people were.

Then Jessica said, 'D'you have any wine around, Claire? I'm getting a bit fed up of Jack Daniels. It's more Chas's drink than mine.'

'I'm sorry, Jessica, I don't have any wine in the house. I can offer you Beck's Blue or lemonade.'

'No wine? That's unusual.'

'I gave up drinking at the beginning of March,' Claire said. 'So I don't like having wine in the house. I hope it's not too much of a problem for you.'

'Oh, God, I'm sorry,' Jessica said, blushing. 'I didn't know.'

'No reason why you should. It's no big deal but, there it is,' Claire said, not altogether truthfully. 'Philip, I think the Co-op should still be open. D'you want to pop down and fetch a bottle of white? I assume it's white you prefer?'

'Yes, that would be lovely. If you're sure you don't mind?'

'No, that's fine.' Thank God for small mercies. At least she didn't want red wine.

Philip stood up. 'What sort of white do you prefer?'

'Chardonnay, please. But I don't mind paying . . .'

'Don't be daft! One bottle of Chardonnay coming right up. I'll be back before you know it.'

True to his word, he was back in fifteen minutes.

'Here you are,' he said. 'One bottle of Chardonnay.'

'I'll get you a glass,' Claire said, heading indoors.

'Now,' said Philip, once they were all back together. 'Let's decide what we're going to do tomorrow. Claire and I really ought to go for a walk. The Camino's only three weeks away now. Are you two up for a long walk?

Jessica grinned at him and held up a shapely leg. 'I'm not sure these shoes are suitable!'

Claire looked at the flimsy ballet-style pump the girl was wearing and said, 'I see what you mean! What size are your feet?'

'I usually take a five and a half or a six.'

'Then you can borrow a pair of my trainers. They ought to fit you.'

'Thanks, Claire. That sounds great.'

By the time it got to ten o'clock, Claire was tired. She stood up. 'I don't know about you lot,' she said, 'but if we've got to get up early tomorrow for the walk, I think we'd better start clearing up now.'

'You're right,' Philip said. 'Come on, you two. Many hands make light work.'

He, Chas, and Jessica brought the remaining food into the kitchen and put it on the table. Claire transferred anything worth keeping into plastic containers, binned the rest, then loaded the dishwasher and turned it on.

'Good night, you two,' she said.

'Night, Claire,' they chorused, then burst out laughing.

Later, in bed, Philip said, 'You did well there.'

'How?'

209

'When Jessica asked for wine. I'm proud of you!'

'It was touch and go,' she admitted. 'She completely blind-sided me. I wasn't expecting it at all.'

'But you coped. You coped brilliantly. I was so surprised when you sent me out for a bottle of wine.'

'I surprised myself!' Claire said. 'I couldn't have done it a few months ago. I'd have fallen apart. But it's been nearly six months now and I'm used to seeing Lucy drinking wine when we're down at the Lion. But it wasn't easy.'

'I know. As I've said many times before, you're a strong woman, Claire Abbott.'

'Not sure I could have done it without you,' she said, snuggling up to him.

The next day, they went for a walk along the top of the Malverns with Chas and Jessica gaining a healthy respect for Claire and Philip's fitness and stamina.

'Not bad for a pair of oldies!' Chas laughed.

'If you're as fit as we are, by the time you get to our age, you'll be very lucky!'

'Only kidding, Dad. Respect!'

Chapter Twenty Nine

The three weeks leading up to the Camino walk were not easy for Claire. She wrote and re-wrote her packing list, frequently consulting the helpful 'What to pack' advice. She already had most of the items, a legacy of walking holidays with Jack, but this was different, as they would be walking such distances every day.

After all, it wasn't as if they were going to the back of beyond. Even if they forgot something, there'd be shops.

At the same time, Philip had his own anxieties.

'Honestly, Claire,' he said one evening, 'I'm getting seriously worried about this. If it doesn't sell soon, I don't know what I'm going to do.'

'Do you need to move *all* your stuff up here? You'd still own the flat, after all. You could leave a bare minimum of stuff there – so that it looks like something out of *House Beautiful* – and I bet it would sell in no time.'

'That's a great idea! And the agents already have a set of keys, so I wouldn't have to be down there for viewings.'

'I'm sure it's going to sell soon, Philip. There are lots of people looking for nice flats these days.'

'You're right. And if it comes down to the wire, I'll do what you suggest. I suppose I'll have to go back down every couple of weeks and make sure it doesn't look too dusty. But God! I hope I've sold it by then!'

'How is the packing for the Camino going?' she said. 'I've been through the list so many times I'm feeling dizzy. I keep worrying about forgetting some essential item. After all, it is less than a week away.'

'I'm sorry, sweetheart,' he said. 'I know it is. But I've always been a bit of a last-minute merchant as far as packing is concerned. I expect I'll sort it out the day before.'

'The day before?' Her voice went up an octave. 'You can't leave it that late! What if you haven't got some vital article – like Compeed or something?'

He laughed. 'Well, if I haven't, I'm sure you will. I'm sorry, honey, I can't get worried about stuff like that, not at the moment. I've got to help Chas get organised for uni, because he'll be leaving the week after we get back, and most of the rest of my brain is filled up with the flat and work.'

'Sorry, Philip. I didn't mean to nag. Of course, you're right. And it's not as though Spain doesn't have shops, after all.' She forced a light laugh.

'Whoops, there goes the door; Chas must be home. I'll see you on Friday.'

She shook herself. This was going to take a bit of getting used to. Jack had been as much of a perfectionist as she was. Philip was obviously a lot more easy-going. She sighed and headed upstairs to work on her latest writing assignment. She had to get it done before they left. Writers' Group was the Wednesday after they returned.

Write a short story set in a specific place – setting is everything. Word count: should be no more than 1,500 words.

This was going to be easy. She could re-jig the Oberammergau chapter from Dani. She'd have to edit it a bit, but she was sure she could turn it into something good.

A couple of hours later, it was done and dusted. She wandered downstairs to shut Baggins up for the night. She was quite pleased with herself. She'd managed not to rant at Philip and got her latest story finished in good time.

*

212

Friday afternoon, Claire was packed and ready to go, apart from a few last-minute things like toiletries, which she'd have to use next morning. She hoped Philip would have a reasonable journey up the M5. She remembered only too well the delays he'd suffered the last time he'd driven up on a Friday evening. And they had to leave at six next morning.

'I know,' she told Baggins, 'I'll go for a walk round the village, then come back and start on dinner. That should keep me nicely occupied until he comes.'

It was a lovely mid-September day. As the weather had cooled down from the heat of August, she enjoyed her stroll. The first leaves were beginning to turn yellow and she was looking forward to autumn, one of her favourite times of the year. She had always enjoyed the in-between seasons the most – summer was too hot, and winter was too cold, but spring and autumn were perfect.

In the spring, she loved watching everything unfurl and turn green, and in the autumn, she felt a pleasant melancholy as the trees and plants died back, to rest in dormancy before the next growing season.

And for some reason – she guessed because of spending so much time in or connected to the educational system – September always felt like a New Year. Whereas 1 January was just a man-made mark on the calendar, at least for her.

Back home again, she got out her faithful *Fast, Healthy Food* cookery book and turned to one of her favourite recipes, Moroccan chicken with couscous. As she hadn't cooked it for a while, she read the instructions carefully. It really was fast. Most of it needed doing immediately before it was served. So she prepared the ingredients that it needed, then read for a while. There would be no point cooking it all in advance. Philip would probably like to rest for a while before eating.

She was deep in *Pride and Prejudice* when she heard his car draw up. Seven thirty.

'Philip! You've made such good time!' she said, opening the door and giving him a big hug.

'Hey, sweetheart! I'm so glad that's over. I left work early to avoid the rush and it's still taken me four hours to get here.'

'Oh no! Dinner will be a little while. Can I get you a drink?'

He followed her into the kitchen. 'That would be lovely. Thanks, sweetie.'

'I could just sit here with you for ever,' she said, snuggling up to him on the sofa after they'd eaten and washed up.

'Me too, my lovely. But we'd better have a fairly early night, if we're starting out at six. Have you got the tickets and everything?'

'Of course I have. I've only checked everything about three-and-a-half million times this week. Oh, I'm looking forward to it so much! I hope it lives up to my dreams.'

'I'm sure it will. But even if it doesn't, it will still be our first holiday together, and that makes it special in my book.'

Smiling up at him, Claire gave him a kiss on the cheek. 'You're so right.'

After a long and tiring journey – by car, minibus, plane, then two more buses – they finally reached Sarria.

'I feel as though I've been travelling for ever,' Claire said.

'Me too! Let's hope we can find the hostel quickly. I could do with a shower and something to eat. I'm starving!'

'You're not the only one. I could eat an elephant, if there was one handy!'

'Goodness! Such greed! But if truth be told, I could too.'

After they'd settled into their rooms – single-sex dormitories, with bunk beds, the standard accommodation along the Camino – they went down to eat. When the food was served, it came with big carafes of red wine.

She turned to him in dismay. 'Oh no! Surely they've got something else we can drink. God, it smells so good!'

'Don't worry, sweetheart,' he said. 'I'll ask.'

Fortunately, the server spoke English, so they were provided with fresh orange juice instead. But Claire could smell the wine the rest of the pilgrims were drinking. As soon as decently possible, she walked out.

Philip found her in the courtyard, leaning against a wall, breathing deeply.

'That was so hard. It smelled so wonderful. It was all I could do not to pour myself a glass, and just glug it back.' She shuddered.

'But you didn't. You're doing so well, Claire. Over six months now. Stay strong.'

'Oh, God! I hope I can. I wasn't expecting that. I hope it's not going to be like that every night.'

'I'm afraid it may be. But you'll get through it somehow. You always do. I trust your strength of mind and I'll be there to support you.'

'Damn it! Why didn't I realise? Is there ever going to be a time when I can watch other people drinking red wine and not care? For two pennies, I'd go back in there and pour myself a large one.'

'Don't think about it, sweetheart. We can do this!'

They went for a wander round Sarria.

It was a beautiful place with many old stone buildings as well as more modern hotels and hostels. Claire guessed that it had expanded greatly in the last half-century as the Camino became more popular for walkers, not just pilgrims.

Two buildings in particular caught their eyes. The ruins of the old castle, with its round tower and its walls with greenery growing from them, and the thirteenth-century Convento de la Magdalena, originally a hospice for pilgrims.

'What a lovely place to start our pilgrimage. I'm so glad you're here with me, Philip.'

'Yes, it's going to be quite an adventure. But I think we'd better get back to the hostel now. We've got a long old day tomorrow – nearly fourteen miles.'

'Oh my! I hope we can do this. *Why* didn't we register they were splitting the mileage up over five days rather than seven? It's going to be quite a challenge.'

*

They woke up to a bright sunny morning with a light breeze. They picked up their pilgrims' passports and scallop shells and set off.

The walking was very pleasant. The roads and pathways were lined with trees, which gave some welcome shade. Before very long they reached the stone pillar marking the beginning of the final hundred kilometres to Santiago.

Two lads in their early twenties, who introduced themselves as Matt and Steve, asked Philip whether he'd mind taking a photo of them in front of it.

'Sure. Will you do the same for me and Claire?'

'Of course,' said Matt. 'Have you just started? We've been on the road for more than four weeks now. Right from the beginning.'

'Oh, you lucky things!' said Claire. 'We could only get a week off work, so we're just doing the final stretch. It must be wonderful to walk the whole Camino. Are you students?'

'Yeah, we're members of the uni rambling club, so we decided to do this over the Summer. It's been quite tough. The heat a couple of weeks ago was knackering.'

'I'm so glad it's cooler now. I'm not sure we could manage this in the heat. And you guys have got full packs, too.'

'Yeah, I was wondering about that. How come you two have only got day packs?'

'We're doing this with a regular walking tour company, so we pay extra to have our baggage transferred from place to place.' She shrugged. 'So we did.'

The boys looked at each other.

'Oh well,' said Steve. 'Better crack on. Nice to meet you, Claire, Philip.'

When they had got out of earshot, Claire said, 'Well, that put us in our place! They obviously thought we were bumbling amateurs, and shirkers to boot.' She laughed. 'But you know what? I don't care! We're doing this our way.'

'Too right, sweetheart. Let's do it!'

The path started to climb steadily among quiet fields still dotted with wildflowers until they reached the high point of Pena dos

Corvos. The views over the Galician countryside were spectacular. They were thrilled to pass the 90km marker before they reached Portomarín, where they were spending the night.

To their dismay, the Camino route into the town was up a steep flight of stairs and through a stone arch. They had to force their aching knees to bend and straighten, bend and straighten.

'Gosh, my legs are tired!' Claire said, as they plodded up the cobbled main street. 'Why are there always cobbles at the end of a long day?'

'Always cobbles?'

'Yes, I was thinking about the time I did the London Marathon. There's a cobbled stretch at about mile twenty-two and it nearly killed me.'

'Well, we're here now' he said. 'Let's find our hostel, freshen up, and then go and find something to eat. I'm ravenous!'

The next day started badly. They were very stiff, Claire in her knees and Philip in one hip; he also had a large blister on one heel. So out came the Deep Heat and Compeed, and they treated themselves before setting out rather more slowly than the previous day.

But, as they walked, they loosened up and their aches and pains subsided. After a while, the path flattened out and soon they were wandering through fields, farmland and little hamlets. After stopping at Castromaior for coffee, they visited the tiny Romanesque Church of Santa Maria.

'These little churches,' Claire said, 'are so different to ours, aren't they? All curves and no pointed arches.'

'I see what you mean,' Philip said. 'But I like the gothic grandeur of our cathedrals – you know, the way everything points up towards heaven.'

Smiling, she turned to him. 'That's exactly how I feel! Lifted out of myself. At one with the Divine.'

'Well,' he said, 'I wouldn't go quite that far. But I have to admit those medieval architects certainly knew what they were doing when they designed those buildings. Even an agnostic like me can feel uplifted by visiting them.'

'I'm glad,' she said, clutching his hand. 'My faith has helped me so much in the last year or so. It's good to know you're not against it.'

'Of course I'm not,' he said. 'But I'll never share your faith, Claire. You know that.'

They walked on. This part of the Camino was busy, even at this time of year, and they passed, or were passed by, several groups of walkers, some chatting busily, others spending the time more reflectively in silence. They themselves were talking less than usual. There was a certain discipline imposed by the task of walking, which seemed to invite contemplation. Claire was centring down, becoming one with the landscape, one with the experience of being on pilgrimage.

They were delighted to pass the 70km way marker before arriving at the large village of Palas de Rei. A lovely little park beckoned. So, before they found their hostel, they walked across the grass and settled down under the inviting shade of a tree.

'Well, we've done it!' Claire said. 'That's the second day over. It's been so special for me – as though we'd left the ordinary world behind. I guess that's how the old pilgrims must have felt. Let's see how far we've got to do tomorrow.'

Philip got the guidebook out and turned to the relevant page.

'Blimey, Claire. It's even further tomorrow. Twenty-nine point five kilometres. That's more than eighteen miles! We should've organised this independently. At least we could have spread the walking out over more days.'

'I know,' Claire said. 'Still, by the end of tomorrow we'll be nearly three-quarters of the way there. Look! The last two days are shorter. Eighteen kilometres and twenty-two point five. We should be able to do those in our sleep after tomorrow. And I don't want it to end – it's so peaceful here, doing this with you.'

'Hmm, I guess you're right. It's certainly a change from my usual holiday! Hup you come! We'd better find our hostel and then replenish our energy levels with a good meal.'

Chapter Thirty

Reading a post on her phone the next morning, Claire was less than impressed to find the Spanish referred to today's walk as 'the leg-breaker', because of its length. But she was also grateful it was otherwise a comparatively easy day, with few ascents and descents. Perhaps her knees would have a chance to recover.

They made an early start. The Camino path wended its way through a series of small villages and towns, so they could fill their water bottles regularly. As it was the hottest day so far, this was a real blessing.

When they took a break at the village of Lobreiro, Claire opened the guidebook.

'Listen,' she said. 'You see the building over there?' She pointed. 'It says here it used to be a pilgrims' hospital. Look, there's the coat of arms of the Ullo family, who founded it. Imagine what it must have been like to walk along here eight hundred years ago and see this!'

'Yes, it gives you a real sense of history, doesn't it?'

'More than that. It gives me goosebumps to be walking the same path pilgrims have walked for all those centuries. Wouldn't it be marvellous to be able to go back in time and talk to them?'

'Maybe you could use that as a reflection for Dani.'

At lunchtime, they reached Melide, an important staging post for pilgrims down the centuries as it marked where the Camino Primitivo joined with the Camino Frances. Later, they were delighted to be walking through a forest of oak and eucalyptus trees. The smell was wonderful, a combination of verdant growth and Vick's Vapour Rub – green and minty, with a hint of honey. And so was the shade.

They reached Arzua at five o'clock. They had done it! The longest leg of the walk was behind them.

They booked in to their hostel and shed their packs.

'I'm going to have a shower before I do anything else,' Claire said. 'And then I think we deserve to have a celebratory coffee and a wander.'

'Sounds good to me! See you in half an hour.'

The next day was far easier, although there were more ups and downs to contend with. They walked past sturdy oak trees and lush meadows. When they reached Santa Irene, they washed their hands and faces in the Fountain of Eternal Youth. According to legend, it meant they would never get old.

'Well, we can hope!' Philip grinned.

'I'm not sure I want to never get old,' Claire said, thoughtfully. 'I've enjoyed my life so far. My thirties were better than my twenties and my forties were better than my thirties. Jury's out on my fifties. I have been more miserable and more happy in the last few years than I could ever have imagined.'

'You're right, of course. I want to grow old with you, my sweet.'

'Aww, thank you, Philip. That's really lovely.' She gave him a kiss. 'Well, we'd better get going.'

A couple of miles down the road, they caught up with a younger woman in her thirties.

The woman, Kate, told them, 'I'm here in memory of my best friend, Jane. We'd always said we'd do this walk together but I lost her to motor neurone disease last year. So I decided to walk it anyway to try to reclaim some meaning in my life.'

'I'm so very sorry,' Claire said. 'That's a wonderful thing to do. How are you coping? Has it helped?'

'The first few days were hard. I spent a lot of the time raging at God for taking her from me. But as the miles have gone on, and I've faced the pain of doing them alone, the edge of the grief has seemed to soften somehow. And the countryside is so beautiful. I've felt its serenity seeping into my soul.'

'You're so brave. I lost my husband eighteen months ago to cancer, so I know how hard it is to move on and build a new life.' She stopped. 'Would a hug be welcome?'

Kate's eyes filled. 'Oh yes!'

They hugged tightly, cheek to cheek, eyes closed, tears welling up. 'I hope you find happiness again,' Claire whispered. Then, blushing, wiping her eyes, she stepped back and grasped Philip's hand. 'I have.'

When they stopped for a coffee, Kate left them. 'I'm hoping to make it to Santiago today,' she said. 'I hope I see you there.'

A final hug, and she walked on, her back straight, her stride determined.

'She is so brave,' Claire said, watching Kate go. 'I'm not sure I could have done a long walk like this in memory of Jack. It would have been too hard. But it seems to have worked for her.'

'Come on, let's get going,' Philip said. 'Not far now. It's our last day of walking tomorrow. It's gone so quickly! When we started off, it seemed like it would take for ever and now we're nearly there!'

'I know. I can't wait to get to Santiago. I'm so glad we decided to book an extra day, so that we can go to the Pilgrim's Mass on Friday and explore Santiago properly. I've got so much material for Dani. Goodness knows how I'm going to condense it into anything readable.' She smiled at Philip. 'I'm so glad we've done this together. It's made it so special for me. I hope Kate finds someone special to love her.'

On the final morning, the sky was overcast and cloudy. They walked through Lavacolla and came to a river.

'Hey, listen to this,' Philip said, reading from the guidebook. 'It's a quote from the *Codex Calixtinus*. Apparently, that's –'

'I know,' Claire interrupted. 'The twelfth-century guidebook to the Camino –'

'By Aymeric Picaud,' Philip finished. 'How do you know that?'

Claire smiled. 'Carry on.'

He went back to the book. '"And,"' he read, '"there is a river called Lavamentula, because in a leafy spot along its course, two miles from Santiago, French pilgrims on their way to Santiago take off their clothes and, for the love of the Apostle, wash not only their private parts, but the dirt from their entire bodies."'

'How lovely! A ritual cleansing, preparing themselves for coming into the city of the saint.'

Another four miles on, they came to Monte del Gozo, the Mount of Joy.

Claire grabbed Philip's arm. 'Look! Those are the spires of the cathedral at Santiago. We're nearly there!'

'Yes, we're nearly there. Thank goodness. Let's stop for a while and think about what we've accomplished. I'll just take a few photos of the monument and then let's find a café.'

'Good idea. I'd like to do some writing in my journal too.'

I can't believe our pilgrimage is nearly over . . . it seems to have gone so quickly! When we got here, four days ago, the prospect of walking for a hundred kilometres seemed daunting, but here we are, just a hop, skip, and jump away from Santiago.

It's made me appreciate why people went on pilgrimage in the olden days – the pilgrimage routes and destinations are such thin places – so full of God's presence. I have felt nearer to God walking here, in spite of all the aches and pains, than I have done for years. I'm really look-ing forward to getting to Santiago.

And it's been wonderful to share it with Philip. I know he doesn't believe in God like I do, but it's been so special, to share this journey with him.

Leaving Monte del Gozo, they came across a pile of shoes and train-ers among the bushes.

'Pilgrims,' Philip said, 'doing the final kilometres barefoot, I expect.'

Claire stared at the footwear for a moment. 'Shall we do that?'

'You *are* joking, aren't you?'

She shrugged. 'I'm not sure.'

'Well, I am,' he said. 'And I'm not.'

They walked on.

As they reached Santiago de Compostela, they passed the spectacular monument at the Praza da Concordia, wended their way along the final stretch of the Camino and entered the old town.

Claire noticed a bronze waymark in the familiar shape of a scallop shell set into the pavement. Ahead was another. They followed the trail past many churches and grand buildings of brick and old stone into the great square in front of the cathedral, crowded with pilgrims and tourists.

Claire turned to Philip. 'I can't believe we've actually made it! Isn't it magnificent?'

'It surely is. But let's take our time. We've got the rest of the day and all tomorrow to explore. Let's find the Pilgrim Office and get our certificates. Then I'd like to dump our packs and have a shower before anything else.'

It was an exciting experience to receive their certificates, which proved they had walked at least the last 100 kilometres of the Camino. They were asked their motives for doing the Camino. Claire chose 'religious and other'; Philip chose 'other'. So the certificates they received were different. Claire's read:

The CHAPTER of this holy apostolic and metropolitan Church of Compostela, guardian of the seal of the Altar of the blessed Apostle James, in order that it may provide authentic certificates of visitation to all the faithful and to pilgrims from all over the earth who come with devout affection or for the sake of a vow to the shrine of our Apostle St James, the patron and protector of Spain, hereby makes known to each and all who shall inspect this present document that Claire Abbott has visited this most sacred temple for the sake of pious devotion. As a faithful witness of these things I confer upon her the present document, authenticated by the seal of the same Holy Church.

Deputy Canon for Pilgrims

Whereas Philip's was a simpler document, which read, *The Holy Apostolic Metropolitan Cathedral of Santiago de Compostela expresses its warm welcome to the Tomb of the Apostle St James the Greater; and wishes that the holy Apostle may grant you, in abundance, the graces of the Pilgrimage.*

When they came out of the Pilgrim Office into the September sunshine, they were no longer pilgrims, but tourists. So now all they had to do was find their final accommodation – not a hostel but a hotel. Which, after consulting the map, was easy.

It was the first time they had shared a room since starting the Camino and Claire was thoughtful as she sat in front of the mirror, brushing her hair. Then she got out her journal and began to write.

> *It's so weird, the way I've got accustomed to being Philip's other half. It seems so natural to be here, settling in to our room, as though we'd been doing it all our lives. I feel so comfortable in his company and it all seems so right.*

She could hear Philip showering and singing in the little bathroom.

> *Well, that's one thing that's different! I don't think I ever heard Jack sing in the shower. He's got quite a good voice too. Who knew? I guess there are a good many things I don't know about Philip yet. But it's fun finding out!*

He came out, drying his hair with a towel. 'Ah, but it's good to be back in civilisation! I've really missed having a decent shower and space to move around in at night.'

Claire smiled at him. 'You're right there. But being in the hostels was part of the experience somehow. I don't think it would have been quite the same if we'd been in hotels every night. I felt more like a proper pilgrim in my little bunk bed.'

'True enough. Are you ready to go out now?'

'Give me a few minutes to freshen up, and I'll be ready.'

*

As they explored the Old Town, a UNESCO World Heritage Site, for an hour or so, Claire consulted their Camino guidebook.

'Look, Philip. What luck we started the walk when we did! It says here that the great censer is operated every Friday at the seven-thirty p.m. Pilgrim's Mass. Do you remember watching that bit in the Simon Reeve programme, when it was swinging high over all the pilgrims? Let's go to the evening Pilgrim's Mass instead of the lunchtime one. I wouldn't miss that for anything!'

'It looked highly dangerous to me. But if that's what you want, then we'll do it.'

Next day, they spent a luxurious morning in bed, then visited the cathedral before returning for the Pilgrim's Mass in the evening.

It was a magnificent building, imposing in its granite splendour and more than eight hundred years old. It was one of the largest Romanesque cathedrals in Europe. They were awed by the intricate facades – each one different, but all splendid – although their view was blocked at some points by some very modern scaffolding.

When they walked inside, through the Portico da Gloria, Claire halted in her tracks. Ahead of them was the impressive barrel-vaulted nave, with its many decorated pillars, designed to lead the eye to the ornate, golden high altar.

'Wow! Can you imagine arriving here at the end of your pilgrimage and being faced with this?'

'It's certainly impressive,' Philip said. 'No wonder it's been such a popular pilgrimage destination for all these years.'

Following the example of other pilgrims they touched the left foot of the statue of St James to signify they'd reached their destination. They noticed a groove had been worn in the stone by the countless hands down the centuries.

Claire said, 'It makes me feel so small and insignificant – to realise that I am only one among so many thousands of pilgrims who have come to this place. But also connected with all of them.'

'Yes, it has a great historical feel to it. This is quite a place.'

In the evening, they attended the Pilgrim's Mass. The square in front of the Cathedral was crowded with pilgrims, all on the same mission.

As they filed in through the Portico da Gloria, Claire whispered to Philip, 'This morning, we were tourists, now we're worshippers.'

'There's such an expectant feel in the air,' he whispered back.

The music started and the ornately clad priests began to process into the sanctuary. When one priest read out the nationalities and numbers of the pilgrims who had received their certificates in the last twenty-four hours, Claire squeezed Philip's hand and beamed at him.

The high point of the service came with the lighting of the huge incense burner and eight red-clad officials starting its swing, filling the with smoke and perfume of frankincense.

Claire bowed her head and gave thanks to God for the time of pilgrimage and the grace of arrival.

They had done it. They had walked the Camino.

Chapter Thirty One

The journey back to Brandleton was long and tiring, and they were relieved to finally get there. After unpacking the car, they ordered a takeaway, which they were almost too tired to eat.

'Why,' Claire said, 'are journeys home so much more exhausting than journeys away?'

'I guess it's because you've got the adventure to look forward to on the way out.'

'I suppose you're right. And, golly, wasn't it an adventure! I don't know how I'm going to make it meaningful for Dani.'

'I'm sorry, my pet,' Philip yawned, 'can we talk about it in the morning?'

'Of course!' Claire laughed. 'Let's go to sleep.'

The next morning, Philip drove home to Bath, because he had to take Chas to York on the Monday. Claire set about unpacking, sorting out all the washing and then reading through the notes she had made during the week.

It was good to be home. After a week of sharing accommodation with strangers, however pleasant, it was good to walk from room to room in peace and quiet. But she missed the peace of walking the Camino, communing with God.

She sat in her armchair in the study, appreciating the space. So peaceful, so quiet.

The next thing she knew, Baggins had jumped into her lap. Startled, she woke up.

'My goodness! I must have been tired,' she said to him. 'I *never*

227

sleep during the day normally. Oh well, I must have needed it. All right, all right. I get it. It's teatime.'

Cat fed, she thought maybe she should get herself something. If she remembered correctly, there were a couple of ready meals in the freezer. One of them would do for this evening. But she'd have to do a mini-shop after work tomorrow.

Just then the phone rang. 'Hi, Claire!' Lucy said. 'I saw you were back. Did you have a good time?'

'Lucy! How lovely to hear you! Yes, thank you, it was marvellous, but I'm so tired. We walked over sixty miles in five days.'

'Wow! Respect. I'm not surprised you're knackered. I'd be dead by now. Well, I won't keep you. I was just ringing to see whether you'd be down the Lion on Friday?'

'Yes, I'll be there. I'm looking forward to catching up with you.'

'See you later then.'

By Wednesday evening, Claire was back to normal. It was the Writers' Group and, as she had hoped, her Oberammergau story went down well. Encouraged, she spent Friday working on the Camino chapters for Dani.

They came together more easily than she expected. The events of the week were so fresh in her mind, the words simply flowed out of her. There was no substitute for first-hand experience if you wanted to write vividly. They'd need revising, but at least she'd got her impressions down.

Satisfied with the day's work, she walked down to the Lion with a light heart, looking forward to sharing her adventures with Lucy.

'Bloody men!' Lucy cried, even before Claire had sat down. 'You can't trust them!'

'Why, Lucy! What's wrong? Is it Sam?'

'Yes, it damn well is. That toad of a git.'

'What on earth's happened? I thought things were going OK between you.'

'Well, they're not. You know you suggested hinting about a city break in October? Well, I did, and he turned the idea down flat. Said

228

he hadn't got enough leave left, because he's got to have the girls with him for half term. I could just spit!'

'Oh, Lu, I'm so sorry. That's tough. I know how much you were looking forward to going away with him.' She hugged her friend, then sat back. 'But if his leave year ends in December, he *might* just be telling the truth. Did you ask?'

'I did not! We had a blazing row and I swept out. And since then, I've been eating for England. God, I'm so miserable.'

'When did all this happen? Has he been in touch since?'

'Tuesday night. I've been waiting by the phone, hoping he'd ring, but he hasn't. And it was Slimming World today and not only have I not lost any weight, but I've even put on a pound!'

'Oh Lucy, I'm so sorry,' Claire said again, taking her friend's hand. 'How much do you want to be with him? Or is it over for you?'

Lucy burst into tears. 'I really miss him. But after what I said, I don't deserve him.'

'Of course you do.' Claire sipped her drink, then said, 'I think the only thing to do is to bury your pride and ring him. There's no room for pride in a relationship. I know that from me and Jack. We once had a dreadful row – I can't even remember what it was about now, except that I was probably in the wrong – and I spent a really miserable few days, enjoying being the victim. But it was no good. It didn't work. In the end I apologised. And he was sorry too.'

'I'd give anything,' Lucy moped, 'to unsay what I said.'

'What was so dreadful?'

'Oh, that he cared about his girls more than he did about me and I wasn't going to play second fiddle to anyone. The usual jealous stuff.'

'Oh dear. Not good. What are you going to do?'

'Ring him and apologise, of course.'

'You could go into the garden,' Claire said. 'There's no one there.'

Fifteen minutes later, Lucy returned, her face still tear-streaked, but smiling. 'He apologised too! He was going to ring me tomorrow. We're going out tomorrow evening.'

'That's great. I'm really happy for you.'

★

The next day, Claire drove to Bath.

'Hey, my sweetheart,' Philip said, hugging her. 'I've missed you so much this week!'

'Me, too. Did Chas make it back up to uni all right?'

'Yes, but I was shattered by the end of the day. Claire, I've got some bad news.'

'What? What is it?'

'It's Peggy's birthday a week on Monday, and she's issued a royal invitation for us to have lunch with her on the Sunday. I've explained that Chas won't be there, but she still wants to see us. I dread to think what she's got in mind.'

'Well, thank God for that! I was imagining all kinds of things. What can she do to us? Eat us?'

'I thought you'd refuse to come. Hopefully, it will be the last time I need to see her before Christmas.'

'We'll get through it somehow. I even feel a bit sorry for her. She won't see Chas nearly so often once you're both up with me.'

The next day, a young couple came round to view the flat and seemed to like what they saw.

When they had gone, he said, 'They sounded really keen, didn't they? Oh God, I hope they'll make an offer. I'm getting so stressed out about this. It's going to be so much harder to sell once it gets nearer to Christmas. Nobody buys a house in the lead-up to Christmas. It's even affecting my writing. I'm completely blocked at the moment. Not a thought in my head.'

'Maybe they'll be the ones. Philip, it *will* sell, I'm sure of it.'

When she got home, she Skyped her parents and told them all about their wonderful Camino experience.

'The walking was tougher than we'd imagined. I've only just stopped feeling stiff!'

'It sounds wonderful, Claire,' her father said. 'You'll have to send us some photos.'

The following Tuesday Claire got an excited phone call.

'They've offered the asking price! And they're first-time buyers, so there isn't a chain. They've just got the mortgage to sort out but seem to think it will be OK. Oh, Claire, I hope it will go right this time.'

'Yay! That's great news. I'm sure it will all be fine now.'

The next day was her spiritual direction session with Beryl. She told her about the Camino walk, how it had changed her, and her excitement about Philip finally coming up to Brandleton.

'But,' she added, 'I'm not looking forward to next Sunday at all. Philip's mother-in-law, Peggy, has invited the two of us round for lunch. It's her birthday. The last time I was there, she was really foul to me. Made it perfectly clear I was no substitute for her beloved daughter and humiliated me about not drinking. I've said I'll go. But now I wish I hadn't.'

'Yes, I remember you telling me about her. I wonder whether you've looked at things from her point of view?'

'What do you mean?' Claire said defensively.

Silence.

Claire hated it when Beryl did this. It was a sure sign she had seen something that she, Claire, had not.

'I suppose you think she's justified?' she said. 'That's not fair! I went there, tried to be friendly and she was horrible to me.'

'Does she have other family?'

'Not really. Her husband died about ten years ago, I think, and her son lives in the States . . . Oh. And now I've come along, and she thinks I'm taking the last two members of her family away from her . . . But I'm not . . . Damn it . . . I am, aren't I?'

'I'm guessing that's how it looks to her, Claire. Try to put yourself in her shoes for a moment. She has helped Philip and Chas out financially all these years and seen her grandson regularly. Now, you've come along and they're moving away to be with you. How would you feel?'

'Fairly hostile, I suppose. Oh, Beryl, does that mean I've got to be nice to her?'

Silence.

'I suppose you're right. But honestly, she was really horrible to me. I've never felt so humiliated in all my life.'

More silence.

Claire sighed. 'I guess I need to talk it over with Philip, and see how we can include her. I wonder if she's got Skype?'

'I knew you'd see it, if you gave yourself the time to listen to the Spirit.'

'I suppose so. But oh, I sometimes wish I didn't have a conscience. It makes me do things I really dislike.'

'You can only do your best. I have great faith in you.'

The next evening, Claire said to Philip, 'I can see Beryl's point. It must look to Peggy as though everything that gives her life meaning is moving away.'

'Yes, I hadn't thought of it like that. I'd like to meet your Beryl some time. She seems a really special person.'

'Oh, she is. I don't know what I would have done without her these past few years. She kept me sane throughout Jack's illness and was a true anchor in the aftermath of his death. But what can we do about Peggy?'

'Well, I can think of one thing, but I'm not sure whether you'd like it. Chas has a reading week in early November and usually comes home for it. Perhaps we could ask Peggy to come up to Brandleton for the weekend? Or we could go down there?'

'I think I'd rather invite her up here. At least then I could hide in the study if she's too obnoxious. And she might be on her best behaviour if she's away from home.'

'Let's ask her on Sunday.'

Sunday came too soon for Claire's liking. But at least she was prepared this time. Determined to follow Beryl's advice and be as pleasant as she could, she bought Peggy a Yankee Candle as a birthday present. She packed a bottle of Shloer, so that she'd have something palatable to drink, and a posh frock.

When they drew up on Peggy's drive, she said, 'I'm feeling so nervous. What if she's as bad as she was last time?'

'Then we'll leave. I'm not having her treating you like that.'

She took a deep breath. 'Come on, let's get it over with. She can't eat me, after all.'

As before, Philip was given a stiff hug, and Claire a limp handshake.

'I'm sorry Chas couldn't make it this time, Peggy,' Philip smiled. 'But he only went back to uni a week ago.'

'I suppose,' Peggy said, her lips pursed, 'I'll hardly be seeing him at all in the future.'

'Not at all,' Claire said. 'In fact, we'd like to invite you up to Brandleton the first weekend in November, when Chas will be home for his reading week.'

Peggy's finely manicured eyebrows shot up. 'To Brandleton? You mean, to your house?'

'Yes, to my – I mean, to our – home. I know it will be hard for you, Peggy, not having Chas so close at hand, but we'd like to keep in regular touch with you.'

'I suppose I ought to be grateful,' she said.

'Actually, Peggy, I think you ought,' Philip said. 'We've owed you a lot, Chas and I, down the years, and we've been grateful for all the help you've given us. You're Chas's grandmother and my mother-in-law and we don't want to lose touch with you. But you could at least give Claire a chance. She's doing her best to be friendly and you're not meeting her halfway. How about it?'

'How dare you speak to me like that, in my own home?'

'Because it's time you faced the truth,' Philip carried on. 'Claire and I are together and are going to continue to be together. I will never forget Angie, as Claire will never forget Jack, but we've found new happiness together, and I don't intend to let you come between us. It's up to you. You can either accept the situation, in which case you will be welcome to visit us, and we'll do our best to keep in touch in between times, or you can hold on to your pride, and that will be it. Your choice.'

Peggy's face crumpled. A tear trickled down. She swiped it away.

'I really don't know how you can speak to me like that, Philip. After all I've done for you and Chas.' She paused. 'But I can see that your mind is made up, so I will bow to the inevitable. I don't wish to say any more about it.'

233

'Thank you, Peggy,' Claire said. 'That means a lot to us. Here's your birthday present.'

'And here's one from me and Chas,' said Philip.

'Thank you. I'll open them tomorrow. Now, may I offer you a drink before lunch?'

'I've brought a bottle of Shloer,' Claire said. 'I didn't want to put you to any trouble.'

'As it happens, I had remembered your idiosyncrasy and bought one myself.'

'Thank you, Peggy. That was very considerate. I'm very much looking forward to lunch.'

'It will be served at one o'clock. How is my grandson, Philip?'

When they left, as soon as was decent after lunch, Claire said, 'Do you think she'll accept that we are us?'

'She'd better,' he growled. 'Thank God we're moving away.'

'I actually felt sorry for her. She must be so miserable. She's a lonely old woman, Philip. I think we need to do our best to keep in touch. After all, she won't be around for many years longer.'

'I guess you're right,' he sighed. 'Ah well, that's the last time for a while.'

Chapter Thirty Two

Claire drove down to Philip's the next two weekends to help him to pack for the move. She enjoyed going to Book Group, sharing her experience of the Camino with the others. And she came back early from Bath the next weekend to attend the Harvest Festival at St Mary's. She had so much to be thankful for just now that the traditional hymn 'Come, ye thankful people, come!' resonated strongly.

A few days before Moving Day, the estate agent called. The young couple had sorted their mortgage. The flat was sold.

'Thank God for that. Now I can move up with a light heart.'

Twenty-fifth October came at last. Claire had spent most of her spare time doing a deep de-clutter to make room for Philip's belongings. She had taken the time off work, to be on hand when the removal van arrived – and also the following day, to help with the unpacking.

Just after one o'clock, the big removal van drew up, closely followed by Philip's Skoda. When the back doors of the van opened, her heart sank. Where on earth was all this stuff going to go? She doubted it would all fit into the garage. She was sure they'd find somewhere.

Somewhat optimistically, as it turned out.

When the removal men left, three hours and many cups of tea later, Claire and Philip sat at the kitchen table, almost too exhausted to talk. In spite of her efforts, the garage was chock-full. And so was the house.

'I'm sorry, my sweet,' Philip said. 'I hadn't realised I'd got so much stuff. We'll have to spend the next few weeks going through it all and doing some more trips to the dump. But I'm here!' His face lit up with an enormous smile.

'Yes, that's the most important thing,' she said. 'We'll soon get this lot sorted out. I think we need to get the kitchen, living room and our room done first. The rest can be done bit by bit. I need at least a few uncluttered rooms to live in!'

Philip laughed. 'We'll do it, I promise!'

'I'm going to Writers' Group this evening. Would you mind? Next month you can come along, too.'

'I'm too tired to mind anything. But come back soon. I want to savour our first night together.'

The next day was Philip's birthday.

'What's this?' he chuckled, picking up a large envelope.

'Your birthday present. Open it, open it!' She passed him the paper knife.

Philip slit the envelope open. Inside was an email, confirming two tickets to the *Harry Potter: A History of Magic* exhibition at the British Library on the coming Saturday. He sprang from his seat and hugged her.

'Claire, that's a wonderful present! Thank you, my sweet.'

'I booked it months ago, when I first heard about it,' she grinned, ridiculously happy. 'Now it's pretty much sold out until the end of the year. I've booked our train tickets too.'

After two long hard days of unpacking and discarding, arranging and re-arranging, the kitchen was back to its normal, orderly self, and so was the main bedroom. The rest would have to wait. But not for long. She hated living in a muddle.

The exhibition was enchanting. Each room was dedicated to a different subject on the Hogwarts curriculum, and held a mixture of artefacts, original pages of manuscript from J K Rowling, wonderful original illustrations by Jim Kay, and dozens of fabulous books from the British Library's collection, many of them illustrated. There were many interactive features too. They brewed up a potion in the Potions Room and had their fortunes told in Divination.

'Look, Claire,' Philip said in the Divination Room, 'Fortune-telling teacups!' When they looked more closely at them, they were amazed to see they dated from the 1930s. They hadn't realised that the superstition had persisted so late.

But what intrigued them most were the wide range of artefacts with tangential connections to the Harry Potter stories. They saw the real Nicholas Flamel's tombstone, two genuine witch's cauldrons, some ancient Chinese oracle bones, and many other items. Mesmerised, they moved slowly from room to room.

The manuscripts were also fascinating. It was so interesting for them, as struggling writers, to see pages from J K Rowling's actual manuscripts and marked-up typescripts, which showed how many changes she made in the process of writing the books. Her original illustrations were great fun too – including an aerial map of the grounds of Hogwarts, complete with giant squid.

Claire grabbed Philip's arm. 'Look at this! Her plan for *The Order of the Phoenix*.'

There were several manuscript pages, each set out in a grid, with the dates and chapter titles down the side, and columns for the plot and the main characters across the top.

'Wow! That is a totally brilliant way of planning a book. I'm going to go home and do the same for Dani. It's a great way of keeping track of what's happening and will make it easier to check for consistency too. But I think I'll do mine in Word, so that if I need to swap chapters round, it will be easier.'

She turned to him, beaming.

He hugged her, and said, 'You're right there, my sweet. It's an excellent idea. Good old J K Rowling!'

Having spent hours wandering through the rooms, they left via the exhibition shop, where Claire insisted on buying Philip the book of the exhibition, sweatshirts for them both, and a bookmark for herself. Then they wandered across the road to Pret a Manger for lunch before catching the train home.

'This reminds me of our first date. The *Radical Eye* exhibition. I remember travelling home in a daze. I'd expected to spend the day feeling so miserable and it ended up being so wonderful.' She squeezed his arm.

'Yes, that was a special day. And look where it's got us! I can't believe my luck. I'm so happy to have found you again, my sweet Claire.'

'Me too.'

Once home, they unpacked a few more boxes, and then, by mutual consent, came to a halt.

'I can't do any more tonight. D'you fancy a takeaway? I'm too tired to cook.'

'Sounds good to me.'

'Then we'll sit and blob. I have no further ambitions tonight.'

Philip laughed and kissed the top of her head. 'Blob we shall.'

The following Wednesday, Philip started his new job. He left at 7.30, not knowing the route, needing to arrive in good time. Claire waved him off, tidied round as far as she could, and set off for work. She was so glad it was only a few minutes' drive away.

Philip got home at half past six.

'How did it go?' she said.

'Oh, like all first days. I was given a tour of the building, introduced to so many people my head was spinning and finally set to reading various policy documents. I've got some induction training to do tomorrow and Friday, then I'll start to work properly next Monday.'

'Oh,' she said. 'Sounds a bit depressing. D'you think you're going to like it?'

'Oh yes, I expect so. I think I'm getting a bit old for new beginnings, at least of the work variety.'

'I've cooked us a lasagne for dinner. Hopefully you'll feel a bit better once you've eaten.'

As it was the beginning of November, they decided to sign up for National Novel Writing Month, NaNoWriMo. They wanted to use the imposed discipline of being expected to write a certain number of words a day to carry on with their current writing, rather than starting something new from scratch. So after dinner, they both repaired to the study, Claire at the desk, Philip in the armchair with his laptop balanced on his knee, and tried to produce their first 1,667 words.

For a while there were no sounds apart from the click of keys, then Philip sighed and closed his laptop.

'It's no good, Claire, I can't do it,' he said. 'I'm too tired. You carry on if you like, but I'm going to bed.'

Claire looked up. 'Oh, Philip! I'm so sorry. How much have you managed to write?'

'Only five hundred or so words, but it will have to do.'

'Well, if you really don't mind, I'd like to keep on going for a while. I'm in the flow.'

'That's fine. But I'm knackered. I'll probably be asleep when you come to bed. Good night, my sweet.'

Claire turned back to her computer. She plugged on for another half hour, but Philip's words kept getting between her and the keyboard. With Philip abandoning it – and her – for the evening, it was hard work. When she reached a natural break, having written about 1,200 words, she closed down her laptop and padded through to the bedroom. Philip was fast asleep.

The next day was All Souls' Day. Claire had booked the day off work. When she had attended it last year, it had given her some comfort in her grief over Jack. She walked down to the church and took her accustomed place.

It was a quiet and reflective service and she was moved by the prayers for the faithful departed, even though this year, Jack's name was not included in the telling.

What a difference a year made. Last year, she had been consumed by grief, functioning rather than living, and so alone. Who would have thought that only twelve months later, she would feel so much better, so less sad? Silently, she put up a prayer of thanks.

★

Bonfire Night was a village institution. Always held in the field behind the Lion, there was a huge bonfire, a Guy Fawkes, and a fireworks display.

Claire and Philip walked down, well wrapped up in coats and scarves, to have a drink before heading outside where they met Lucy, Sam, and his girls.

'Claire, Philip, this is Sam, and these are Sophie and Hannah.'

'It's lovely to meet you,' Claire said. 'I've heard so much about you.'

'Nothing bad, I hope?' Sam said, squeezing Lucy around her waist.

'Of course not.' She smiled at the girls, dressed in skinny ripped jeans, parkas, and woolly scarves. 'I'm glad you've dressed up warm. It's freezing, isn't it?'

Sophie smiled. 'Yes, but I do love Bonfire Night.'

'So do I,' Claire said.

'Me, too,' Lucy laughed.

It was clear night with little wind, which led to it being a magnificent, dazzling fireworks show – every colour imaginable – but, as always, it was over too soon. Everyone piled into the pub.

Although Claire was by now used to her Becks Blue, being in a pub was not the best way to avoid the smell of alcohol. Perhaps she shouldn't have come. When was she going to get over this? Surely she should be getting through it?

'Why don't you ask your sobriety group friends?' Philip said on the way home.

'That's a good idea, I haven't been on there for ages.'

Hello Everyone, Lent Lily here. I'm sorry I haven't been around for a while, but I'm still AF. Eight months now. Most of the time, it's just the way things are and I'm fine, but other times, like tonight, I catch a whiff of somebody's red wine, and am still filled with longing. Is this normal at this stage?

Hello LL, well done on eight months. That's brilliant! Yes, I'm afraid it is still normal to be caught out by the occasional craving. The demon drink doesn't give in easily. But every time you beat it, it gets easier. Log on here if you need to xx

Hello LL, I've been AF for nearly two years now and I still get the occasional longing. But I know that it will pass. It is fatal to give in to it. Keep on keeping on! X

So she wasn't abnormal. She could do this!

Claire's Dani novel was going well. Being a natural lark, she got up early every morning and wrote the required 1,667 words, or thereabouts. She had added Iona and Glastonbury to Oberammergau and the Camino and was about to start on Lindisfarne. It was wonderful how the discipline of having signed up to NaNoWriMo was keeping her nose to the grindstone. It was only the first draft, but this was the first time she had ever got as far as this. She might even finish it by Christmas.

Philip, however, had given up. 'I'll try again another year. I've just got too much on my mind at the moment, what with the conveyance on the flat and settling in to the new job. You carry on, Claire, don't mind me.'

'Are you sure you don't mind? I'm absolutely loving it. I hope you'll be able to come to Writers' Group at the end of the month?'

'Well,' he said, 'let's see how it goes.'

All the same, as it made her uneasy, she took it to Beryl the following Tuesday.

'I suppose I should have realised he'd be too tired to do NaNoWriMo this year,' she said. 'But I'm so disappointed. I was really looking forward to being able to write together. I'd hoped it was something we could share. But now he's backed out of it.'

'What on earth is Nano – what did you call it?'

Claire laughed. 'I'm sorry, Beryl. I should have explained. It's National Novel Writing Month, shortened to NaNoWriMo. The idea is that you sign up for thirty days in November and commit to writing 1,667 words every day, to produce 50,000 words by the end of the month. I'm managing fine so far – it's a challenge, but an exciting one.'

'Ah, I see. Well I'm not surprised that Philip has decided it is too much. He's in a new home, with a new job, and all the worries that go with both. Cut him some slack, Claire.'

'I hadn't seen it like that,' she sighed. 'You're right. It's more difficult than I had expected, this new sharing of life. I was naïve to think it would be all unicorns and roses.'

'Yes, you've both got a lot of adjusting to do. Be gentle with yourself, and him. I will be holding you both in my thoughts and prayers.'

Chapter Thirty Three

The following day, she picked Chas up from the station.

He greeted her as he walked through the exit, 'Hi, Claire. Is Dad still at work?'

'Hello, Chas. Yes, he won't be home until about half six. The car's over here. How's Jessica?'

'Good, thanks. We've got a pile of work done these past few days. But I'm knackered now. I've been travelling for more than six hours and had to change trains three times. I got a lot of reading done, though. I hope you or Dad will be able to take me back to York on Sunday.'

'I think Philip's planning to take you back.'

'What's for supper? I'm starving!'

'We won't be eating until your dad gets home.'

His face fell.

'But I've got plenty of snacks on hand.'

When they got to Brandleton, she showed him his room and left him to settle in.

A few minutes later, he poked his head round the kitchen door. 'About those snacks you mentioned?'

Claire had to laugh. 'What would you like? Soup? Cereal? Toast? Or I could make you an omelette?'

He thought for a moment. 'Toast, please. Have you got any peanut butter and jam?'

'Yes, I've got both. How many slices do you want?'

'Two for now, then I'll see how I feel. Thanks.'

'D'you want a drink? I've got tea, coffee, hot chocolate, lemonade, or Coke.'

'Coke, please.'

Five minutes later, he sat devouring his meal.

'Goodness!' she said. 'You must have been hungry. D'you want some more?'

'I wouldn't mind another slice, if that's OK. Then I'll go up and do some work.'

'That's fine. Come and help yourself to anything you want. This is your home now, Chas. I hope you'll be happy here.'

A couple of hours later, as she was putting the finishing touches to the evening meal, Philip's key turned in the front door. When he walked in, he hugged her.

'Did Chas get here all right?'

'Yes, he's upstairs. Dinner will be about another ten minutes. You've got time to get changed and say hello to your son.' She grinned. 'The poor lad was starving when he got here. He'd been travelling for six solid hours. It's a good job you're taking him back to York on Sunday.'

'At least it's not as far as it would have been from Bath. We're seventy miles closer here, which should shave an hour off the journey time, each way.'

'Well, if you're too tired, I could take him.'

'That's a wonderful offer, my sweet. Let's see how it goes.'

A few minutes later, the three of them were sitting round the kitchen table, chatting about what Chas had been up to the past few weeks and how the course was going this year. He was doing two modules this semester – one about the roots of modernity in England in the sixteenth to eighteenth centuries, and one about Britain in the twentieth century.

'I'm enjoying the twentieth century one more, 'cos I know more about it, but it's been fascinating learning how much England changed from the Tudors to the Georges. But I'm looking forward to next semester. We have to do a core module on issues in historical thought, which sounds dead boring, but an exploration module too, which goes on for two terms, and will link in to our Year Three dissertations. There are loads of subjects to choose from, and I can't decide which to do.'

Listening to him bubbling with enthusiasm, Claire was briefly envious. She had enjoyed her Librarianship course, but it had been an applied subject, and she sometimes wished she had studied something for the pure love of it.

'It sounds fascinating,' she said. 'I've always loved history but was no good at it at school – only scraped a C at GCE. But I love watching history documentaries and, from the sound of it, university level history is much more interesting.'

'Yeah, it's different all right. Some of the second and third-year modules look really exciting.'

After dinner, Chas went back to his room and they settled down to watch TV.

'You know,' Claire said, 'I'd love to go back to studying. Chas sounds so enthusiastic about what he's doing. It's made me realise that I missed out at uni.'

'Well, why don't you?' Philip said. 'There are loads of OU courses available. You can study from home then.'

'I'd love to do a creative writing course. But I'll have to wait until next year.'

She reached for her iPad, and googled 'Open University'. 'It looks as if you can only do it as part of a course, and I'm not interested in doing another whole degree. I wonder whether anywhere else does one? I think I've seen adverts in *Writing Magazine*.'

Philip smiled. 'I think we'd better get the house move out of the way first.'

'Oh,' she said. 'I'd forgotten about that. You're right, of course. But it's getting so late in the year now. And we won't know how much money we've got to play with until the sale of your flat's completed. I think we'd better wait until after Christmas to start serious house-hunting.'

'I'm not sure I've the energy for it right now. The daily commute is more tiring than I'd expected.'

'Oh, love. I'm sorry you're finding this so hard. Maybe we should move nearer –'

'I know how much this village means to you. I wouldn't ask you to give that up. I'll manage. It's early days yet.'

She reached up and kissed him.

'Come on, woman. Let's go to bed. We've both got work in the morning.'

'Will Chas be all right on his own?'

'Of course he will. Just tell him which food you *don't* want him to eat and he'll be happy to potter around. You'll be home by a quarter past five after all.'

The following Saturday Claire was up early to prepare for Peggy's visit.

Although she had spent most of the previous day tidying round and hoovering through, alternately helped and hindered by Chas, she wanted the house to look perfect. She sat down at the computer after breakfast and knocked out a few hundred words for NaNoWriMo, without thinking about it, just writing whatever came into her head. She'd have to go through it later. Her mind was not on it.

As the dining room was spick and span, they would eat there. She laid the table and shut the door. She didn't want Baggins prancing around, getting hairs over everything.

She was sticking to tried and tested dishes. Prawn cocktail to start, steak and all the trimmings for the main course, and her favourite pineapple cheesecake for the sweet. She suddenly remembered this had been the meal she and Lucy had eaten on the last evening before she gave up drinking. A good omen, perhaps.

When Philip came downstairs, the prawn cocktails were in the fridge and she was putting the crushed pineapple on to the cheesecake, before putting that, too, in to chill.

'Morning, my sweet. You're up early!'

'Yes, I've got to get everything ready. I'm not having her picking holes in anything I do.'

'You do sound fierce! I'm sure it's all going to be wonderful.'

'Don't patronise me! This matters!'

'Claire, sweetheart, I'm sorry. What did I say?'

'Oh, I'm sorry, love. I've just got myself really wound up about this meal. I don't want Peggy to look down her nose at me, so everything's got to be perfect.'

He swung her round to face him. 'Claire, my sweet Claire. I don't think you need worry. She'll be our guest., I'm sure she'll be on her best behaviour. Is there anything I can do to help?'

She smiled. 'Can you sort your and Chas's breakfasts and wash everything up afterwards? And then hoover through downstairs for me?'

'Of course I will. What time's she arriving?'

'She said noon, so I'm planning to have lunch at one, in case she's delayed. I won't start cooking the main course until she gets here. The rest is already sitting in the fridge. So I've just got to prepare the onions, mushrooms and steak before I head upstairs to get ready.'

'Well, it's only nine thirty now, so you've got oodles of time. D'you want a coffee?'

Claire brushed a strand of hair out of her eyes. 'Yes, that sounds good.' She flopped down at the kitchen table and sighed. 'D'you think I'm daft, getting so worked up about this?'

'No, I can understand it. But you don't need to worry. Like I said, I'm sure she's going to be on her best behaviour.'

'Let's hope so. I could murder a glass of wine!'

'Don't listen to temptation, Claire. You'll only regret it.'

She laughed. 'You sound like one of my sobriety group friends!'

'What are you giving Peggy to drink?'

'I was tempted to only offer AF drinks, but I bought a bottle of white wine on Friday. Boy, that was hard. It's the first time I've been down the booze aisle for months. I was so tempted to pick up a few bottles of red while I was there.'

'But you didn't! Claire, I'm so proud of you. That's huge.'

'It was a test and I only just passed.'

★

247

Peggy did not arrive until quarter to one.

'What a dreadful journey!' she said, still on the doorstep. 'The traffic on the M5 was terrible.'

'Come in, Peggy,' Claire said. 'May I take your coat? The living room's this way.'

'Where's my grandson?' Peggy demanded as she came in. 'Chas, where are you?'

'"Hello, Claire",' Claire muttered, stepping out of the way.

'Here, Grandma.' Chas appeared from the living room and was enveloped in a tight hug.

'Do sit down, Peggy. May I offer you a drink?'

'Thank you. I'll have a dry sherry, please.'

'I'm sorry, we don't have any. But if you'd like a tea or coffee? Lunch should be ready soon.'

'No sherry? Oh yes, I remember, you don't drink, do you?'

'No, I don't. But there will be wine with the meal.'

'I suppose I should be grateful for that.'

'Peggy!' Philip said. 'That's enough! We've invited you here for a pleasant lunch. Let's at least try to keep things civil.'

For a second or two, no one spoke.

Peggy glared at Philip, then looked down. 'I'll have coffee, please. White, two sugars, if I may.'

Claire fled into the kitchen. 'The old bat!' she told the kettle. 'How dare she speak to me like that in my own home?'

By quarter past one, they were sitting round the table in the dining room, eating their prawn cocktails. Claire excused herself, saying that she had to put the finishing touches to the main course.

Back in the kitchen, she plated up the steak and all the trimmings – oven chips, mushrooms, asparagus, and fried onions – then took the first two plates into the dining room and gave them to Peggy and Chas.

'Thank you, Claire,' Peggy said.

'Thanks, Claire,' Chas said. 'That looks lush!'

'Thank you, Chas. I'll just get mine and your dad's.'

Chas endured an interrogation from his formidable grandparent, about what he was doing at university, and how good his grades were.

Eventually, the last bite of cheesecake eaten, Claire stood up, ready to clear the table.

'I'll help,' Philip said. 'Chas, will you take Grandma through to the living room? Claire and I will be through once we're done.'

'OK, Dad,' Chas said. 'Come on, Grandma.'

'Thank you, Claire. That was delicious,' Peggy said, rising to follow Chas.

'You're welcome, Peggy,' she said, picking up some plates and nearly running to the kitchen.

'Did you hear that?' she said. 'She paid me a compliment!'

'You see?' Philip said, now in the kitchen with her. 'She's not so bad, sometimes. I think I caught her at the right moment. She'll be fine now, until she goes.'

Fifteen minutes later, the dishwasher was loaded, and the washing up done. They went back to the living room together, and Philip sat down.

'Would you like another coffee, Peggy?' Claire asked. 'And I've got some after-dinner mints too.'

'That would be very pleasant, thank you.'

The rest of the visit went well. Baggins made an appearance and Claire was so proud of him. He went straight up to Peggy and she unbent so far as to stroke him gently.

That'll show her what a nice cat is like! Good old Baggins.

For the next couple of hours, the conversation stayed on safe topics. Claire and Philip shared their experiences of walking the Camino and Peggy revealed that she was planning to go on a cruise with a friend in the spring. Chas sat playing with his phone and making an occasional contribution. Nevertheless, Claire was relieved when Peggy stood up, just after four o'clock.

'I really must go now,' she said. 'Hopefully the traffic will not be so bad on the way back. Thank you for inviting me, Claire. I look forward to my next visit.'

The three of them waved her off, then Claire turned to Philip and pantomimed wiping her brow in relief. He chuckled and gathered her in his arms.

'There, you see! You've survived ordeal by Peggy. She didn't bite and she only barked once.'

'Yes, it wasn't so bad, after all. Thank you both for your help. Now I'm off to get changed into my oldest tracky-bs and I have no ambitions for the rest of the day!'

Sunday, Philip and Chas lazed around while Claire went to the Remembrance Sunday service at St Mary's. Rev Martin reminded them that World War One had lasted for over four long, death-filled years and, that in almost every year since, human beings had been waging war somewhere on the planet. He said, 'It is a desperate irony that World War One was called "The War to End All Wars", and yet one hundred years on, humankind still seems unable to stop the fighting, the bloodshed, the cruelty, and wars continue to be fought the world over, for reasons of fear, and misunderstanding, the hunger for power, and the despising of the other.'

Claire joined in the responsive Commitment to Peace with fervour. It seemed so very sad to her that people could not live together in peace, sharing the plentiful resources of the planet, without resorting to violence at the drop of a hat.

Talking it over with Philip, later, she said, 'So many young lives wasted by war – it seems obscene. And we're still choosing violence over diplomacy. It makes me so sad.'

'But surely there are some times when war can be called just?' Philip said.

'I can only think of one instance when that was true,' she said. 'And that was World War Two – Hitler had to be stopped. But even then, I think it *stopped* being a just war when both sides started bombing civilians. None of the wars going on around the world today are just – they're about land and power and greed.'

'I'd no idea you felt so strongly about it,' Philip said. 'I'm not sure

I agree with you, though. I think that sometimes bullies have to be stood up to, and diplomacy doesn't work.'

'Hmm. I hate to say it, but I suppose you're right,' Claire said. 'But if nobody witnesses for peace, the world would be an even worse place. At least, that's what I think.'

'I think we'll have to agree to differ on this one, Claire.'

She shrugged. 'I suppose so.'

Chapter Thirty Four

Within a few weeks, Philip got used to his commute and was less tired in the evenings. The conveyance was slowly going through on the flat, which was one less worry for him.

Towards the end of November, Claire took him along to Writers' Group. She had found that month's assignment – writing a story set in a film studio – difficult, and wasn't looking forward to reading it. Sure enough, its reception was lukewarm. But at least she tried.

Philip enjoyed meeting the group and decided to join. The next assignment was to write a story about a ball game. On the way home, they discussed possibilities.

'I think,' Philip said, 'I'll write something about rugby. I used to love it when I was at school.'

Claire complained, 'I don't even like ball games. I can't catch for toffee. This is going to be really hard. I've got no ideas at all.'

'Leave it for a while. You've got most of December to finish it and you need to concentrate on NaNoWriMo for the next week at least.'

'That's true. It's amazing the difference it makes, the challenge of having to produce a certain number of words every day. I've fallen behind a bit but, I still reckon I'll have written more than forty thousand words by the end of the month. Of course, it's only the first draft, and I'll have to go through it all and polish it up, but it's something to have got the story out of my head and onto the page.'

'That's fantastic! Is the end in sight?'

'I'm not sure. I've taken Dani to most of the places I had in mind now but have no clue as to how to round it off.'

'I'm sure it will come to you. I'm looking forward to reading it very much.'

'Even when it's finished, I'll still have a shed-load of work to do on it. This is just the first draft. But I can't help feeling proud of myself – I've never tackled anything as long as this before.'

By the time Claire went to see Beryl in early December, Philip had been living at Brandleton for six weeks.

'Having Philip living with me is harder than I imagined,' she said. 'I thought it would all be wonderful – not having to travel down to Bath every other weekend, having him around all the time. But the reality is quite different.'

'Quite different?'

'There are times when I long to be in the house on my own again. I'm really enjoying my Tuesdays and Fridays, when he's at work, and I've got the house to myself. Is that dreadful of me?'

'But you must have known things would change.'

'Oh, I know. I realise it's not reasonable, but I'm finding it hard to adjust to some of his ways.'

'Such as?'

'Well, he's not as tidy as I am. Not by a long chalk. I'm forever having to clear up after him. And we *still* haven't finished the unpacking. I'm getting fed up of having everything in a muddle.

'And don't even get me started on Chas. He's been home for a reading week and he's eaten us out of house and home. I'm not used to having a student around the place. He leaves wet towels on the bathroom floor, used disposable razors on the sink, and his bedroom's a tip, or it was, till he went back on Sunday.

'And both of them seem to think it's acceptable to chuck their dirty washing out without turning it the right way out first. The socks are particularly infuriating. It takes for ever to sort the washing out these days.'

She took a deep breath. 'How can you love someone and still find them annoying?'

'Was Jack perfect?'

253

'Of course not! But I was used to him. We'd grown together over time – Oh.'

'Yes. These things take time. You had years of living with Jack and made the adjustments gradually. You've been with Philip for only a few months and already you're living together. It's not surprising some of the rough edges don't fit. And having a youngster around is a brand new experience for you too. I expect they find facets of your character equally infuriating.'

She blushed. 'Hmm. I hadn't thought of that. I suppose you're right. So you're saying just take it day by day, cut them both some slack?'

'Something like that, yes. Although it might be wise to share your concerns about Chas with Philip, rather than letting it fester. And be gentle with yourself, too. All relationships change when the first flush of romance is over, and the couple settle down to the serious business of making a life together. You can't expect anything different.'

The following Saturday was the village pantomime. They were going with Lucy and Sam, and Dawn. Claire and Philip walked down to the village hall early to get good seats. All five of them agreed it was a marvellous version of *Jack and the Beanstalk,* which thoroughly deserved the applause it got.

'Wasn't John brilliant as the giant?' Lucy bubbled as they came out. 'And Peter as the dame? His throat must be so sore, doing that falsetto voice for so long.'

'Yes, they were excellent,' Claire said. 'But my favourites were Simon and Maria as the sidekicks. They were so funny.'

'I really think it was one of their best,' Dawn chimed in. 'I wonder what they'll do for the spring play? I might even volunteer to join the drama group this time, now that I haven't got Mum to worry about.'

'That would be awesome, Dawn,' Lucy said. 'You'd be great, I know it!'

Philip and Sam glanced at each other and grinned.

When Claire and Philip were walking home, she said, 'I'm sorry,

Philip. I didn't mean to leave you out just now. It's just so much fun talking it over when you know all the actors.'

'I know you didn't. This time next year I'll know more of them. At least I hope I will.'

'This time next year? Blimey, it makes me dizzy to think of it! Beryl says we should take it one day at a time, so I'm trying to do that, enjoy you every day.'

She slapped her hand over her mouth.

'You've been talking to Beryl about us?'

'I didn't mean to tell you. But yes, I have.'

He stopped. 'Claire, this is important. You're not having regrets, are you?'

'No, of course not. It's just that, having lived on my own for eighteen months, I'm finding it hard to adjust, even with you.'

She looked at his stricken face. 'Oh, love, I'm sorry. I didn't mean that to come out like it did. I love you and I love being with you. There's a lot of adjustment to make. It's different being together every day from seeing each other at weekends. That's all, I swear it.'

'You're right. I've been struggling a bit too.'

'You have?' It was her turn to feel insecure. 'Why?'

'Well, if we're going to be honest with each other, it's hard for me to adjust to living in your house. Because it is *your* house, not mine. I think the sooner we move, the better.'

'Let's get home,' Claire said, 'have a cup of tea, and talk this through.'

They sat down at the kitchen table.

Claire cleared her throat. 'I'm sorry, Philip. I never meant to hurt you. It's hard, isn't it, this business of making a new life together?'

'You're not wrong, my sweet. Even with the greatest amount of love, adjustments have to be made. We're living in the daylight world now, not a romantic dreamscape.'

'That's just how I feel. Let's promise each other something. If anything one of us is doing bugs the other one, we need to be absolutely honest about it. And talk it through without blame and recrimination.'

'I agree. My main issue is what I said. I don't feel like I belong here, except as a guest.'

'I can understand that. It must be hard for you. It's so much easier for me. I haven't had to give up anything to be with you. You've given up your job, and your life in Bath. Let's start house-hunting straight after Christmas.'

He smiled. 'That sounds good. Now what about you? What's bugging you?'

'Well, it sounds so petty. But,' she paused, then continued, 'I've got pretty high standards of tidiness and it really gets to me when things don't get put back in their proper places. I know I'm being unfair. How should you know where the proper places are? But it does bug me. And I'd hoped we'd have finished the unpacking by now. And,' she added, 'I know it sounds trivial – but I wish you'd turn your clothes the right way out when you put them out for dirty. It takes me ages to sort the washing out these days. I'm sorry, but we said we'd be honest.'

'Well, turning my clothes the right way out I can do. But the first two are other reasons to move. If we make a new start, in a new house, that belongs to both of us, we'll have a chance to arrange it together and make it ours.'

'I agree. It needs to be our top priority, once Christmas is over. What's the completion date on the flat?'

'My solicitor's pushing for mid-January. So we can start looking now. Although I expect there will be more places on sale after Christmas.'

They looked at each other.

She smiled at him. 'Let's always share like this. I love you so much.'

'I love you too, sweet Claire. Let's go to bed and I'll prove it.'

Christmas was another unforeseen minefield. Each of them had certain family traditions they both expected to happen.

Claire spent the day after the pantomime writing her Christmas cards, which brought up the first problem. She generally scribbled a few lines inside the cards, succinctly telling her news. Philip, on the

256

other hand, produced an annual round-robin to include in some of them, complete with photographs of himself and Chas.

'I've always hated receiving these,' she said. 'So full of their precious offspring's achievements. They always remind me I don't have any children to share about, so I've never bothered.'

'But if I suddenly stop producing one, people are going to wonder why.'

'Tell you what, you write it and I'll read it and see what I think.'

'OK. What do you want me to put about you?'

'Me?'

'Well, you *are* part of the family now.'

'Say we got together in March and that you're now living up here and that we're planning to move in the spring. Then we both sign the cards. That should do it.'

'Fair enough.'

They agreed to spend Christmas Day in Brandleton, then to go to Peggy's for Boxing Day.

'We always go to Peggy for Boxing Day lunch. She'd be terribly hurt if we didn't.'

Claire pulled a face. 'Hmm. Not my idea of fun, but I guess you're right. At least it will give her a chance to see Chas over Christmas. OK, we'll go.'

They bought Chas a Kindle and a generous Amazon voucher. Philip had stopped giving Chas a stocking a couple of years before, as he didn't usually surface until nearly lunchtime on Christmas Day. 'So I just spend more on his actual present.'

But Claire dithered about what to get Philip. She had known Jack so well that the choice of Christmas present had been easy, but Philip was still somewhat of an enigma to her. Getting the wrong present would be worse than nothing.

After hours of thought, she bought him a copy of the writing software *Scrivener*, some Deep Water aftershave, and Stephen King's book *On Writing*, which Duncan had recommended at the last Writers' Group meeting.

The gift for Peggy was surprisingly easy.

'Oh, that's simple,' Philip said. 'We always buy her a bottle of Estée Lauder Beautiful. She loves it.'

So that was that. She added a bouquet of flowers.

The tree was extra bright and festive, with some extra ornaments from Philip's collection. The beautiful wooden nativity set from Oberammergau took pride of place on the mantelpiece.

'These are choice,' Philip said, as she put them out.

'I fell in love with them when we were in Oberammergau and had to have them. It was a devil of a job getting them back home. I was so scared they were going to get damaged. But by packing most of my toiletries in my case, I managed to carry them safely in my hand luggage.'

'They are a lovely memento.'

The next job was to pick up Chas from York. Philip was up to his eyes in work, so it fell to Claire to make the long trip. Fortunately, Chas wasn't required to vacate his room these holidays, so there was room in her car for everything. But it was a long and weary day, nonetheless.

That evening, she told Philip, 'I hadn't realised how far away York is. It must have been one heck of a trek from Bath. But he's home now and safe for a few weeks.'

The Friday before Christmas, Philip said he would have to go down to Bath the next day, something to do with the conveyance.

'D'you want me to come too?' Claire asked, hoping the answer would be no. As she had the final shop to do and last-minute tidying round, she didn't want to spend the whole day in the car.

'No, I wouldn't put you through that. I'll be as quick as I can.'

But he was gone for hours and came home shattered. 'The traffic was dreadful and the parking worse.'

'Why on earth did you have to go down, so close to Christmas?'

'Oh, there were documents to sign,' he mumbled.

Christmas Eve morning, she said: 'I always go to the midnight service at St Mary's on Christmas Eve. It's such a beautiful service. Do you want to come?'

His brow furrowed. 'I suppose it wouldn't do me any harm. It's a long time since I've been in a church, except for weddings, funerals, and sightseeing.'

'It would seem weird, now, to go and leave you at home.'

A blaze of candlelight welcomed them when they got to the church.

'It's a St Mary's tradition,' Claire said as they went in. 'The service starts at eleven thirty. At midnight, the baby is added to the crib, the final advent candle is lit and then we celebrate Jesus' birth.'

When Philip joined in the singing, Claire was surprised. She'd heard him in the shower, of course, but not like this.

They walked home arm in arm.

'Well,' she said, 'I didn't know you could sing!'

'Of course I can sing! I'm Welsh, aren't I? That was a good service, Claire. I really enjoyed it.'

Christmas Day morning, as Claire lay awake, waiting for Philip to stir, she remembered last Christmas.

She had been alone for the first time in more than twenty years, apart from the Christmas morning service at church, and hadn't even bothered to make a Christmas lunch. Instead, she had cooked herself beans on toast and had spent the day in front of the TV, sunk in misery, glugging down red wine.

Today was different. She was with Philip. No need to rush.

As there were only the three of them, she had bought the smallest turkey she could find and cooked it the day before, a tradition from her mother. It made Christmas Day cooking less fraught and, besides, she preferred her turkey cold. Philip had agreed to try it her way this year.

After breakfast, she led him through to the living room. 'I can't wait to give you your presents!'

'You're like a little girl!'

'I've always been this way about Christmas. I just love it! We needn't wait for Chas, do we?'

She gave Philip his presents one by one. He unwrapped the aftershave first, and promptly splashed it on all over.

She giggled. 'I'm glad you like it.'

Then he unwrapped the book. 'Ah, that's the one Duncan was talking about last month. Excellent. I'll look forward to reading that.'

Finally, he unwrapped the last parcel, the writing software. His face lit up. 'Oh, Claire! That's great. Just what I need to nudge me back into writing. Thank you, sweetheart. Now, it's your turn.'

He reached around the back of the tree and came back with three parcels in his hands. Like Claire, he doled them out one by one.

'I think you'd better open this one first,' he said, his eyes twinkling.

It was obviously a book and, when Claire opened it, she laughed. Another copy of Stephen King's *On Writing*.

'Two minds with but a single thought,' she said, and kissed him.

The next parcel was also book-shaped. A beautiful hardback journal. 'That's lovely. My old one is nearly full.'

Finally, he gave her a long, slim package. She ripped off the paper. A plain blue box. When she opened it, she gasped. A delicate silver necklace of linked daisies, which matched her bracelet exactly.

'Oh, Philip!' she said, on the edge of tears. 'It's perfect. However did you find it?'

He grinned. 'I sneaked a photo of your bracelet one day and asked a silversmith friend of mine in Bath to make it into a necklace. He finished it only last week. Hence my trip down on Saturday. I didn't have any documents to sign. I needed to pick that up. When you asked to come with me, I nearly had a heart attack.'

'It's so beautiful, and it matches perfectly.'

'Let me put it on you.'

With trembling fingers, he fastened it round her neck. They went into the hall to look in the mirror.

He kissed her softly on the back of her neck. 'Merry Christmas, sweet Claire.'

She turned and flung her arms around him. 'Thank you so much, my love.'

Chas appeared just before lunch and was well pleased with his

Kindle and Amazon voucher. When they had eaten, Philip and Chas cleared away, before joining Claire in the living room.

They spent the afternoon playing charades and other games, a Bateman tradition which she thoroughly enjoyed. In the evening, Chas went off to the Lion while Claire and Philip settled down to watch *It's a Wonderful Life* and nibble on leftovers.

'It's been a perfect day,' Claire said. 'Thank you, my darling. I'm not even worried about going down to see Peggy tomorrow.'

The next morning they set out for Peggy's early, much to Chas's discomfort. He rolled in quite late. Claire gave him a Recovery drink with his breakfast. His gratitude made her smile to herself. Glad this was in her past now, she knew so well how he must be feeling.

The visit to Peggy went well. Everyone was on their best behaviour and there were no incidents. Peggy was delighted with the perfume and thanked Claire for the flowers, unbending sufficiently to peck her on the cheek.

Claire was surprised to receive a present, a gift set of hand cream, moisturiser and soap. Perhaps Peggy was beginning to accept her.

As Chas was planning to meet up with friends in Bath, Claire and Philip left him with Peggy – which pleased her no end. He would then make his own way back to Brandleton in the new year – Claire and Philip had to work between Christmas and New Year.

Chapter Thirty Five

New Year's Eve, they Skyped Claire's parents at one o'clock, as their New Year started eleven hours earlier.

'Happy New Year, Mum! Happy New Year, Dad! I hope you've had a lovely Christmas?'

'Yes, thank you, Claire — it was quiet, but very enjoyable,' her father said. 'How was yours?'

'Really good, thank you. So different from last year. Mum, Dad, I'd like you to meet Philip. He's living with me in Brandleton now.'

'Philip? Who's Philip?' Her mother, imperious, as always.

'Hello, Mrs Henning, Mr. Henning. Claire and I have been friends for years, ever since university. We reconnected at a writing conference in February, and have been together since March.'

'Philip's made me so happy,' Claire said. 'I hope you can be happy for me, too.'

'Aren't you rushing things a bit, Claire?' her father said.

'No, I don't think so. After all, we've known each other for donkey's years.'

Her mother sniffed. 'Oh well, daughter. You know yourself best.'

'Thank you, Mum. I hope we'll be able to come out to New Zealand, some day soon. Then you can meet him in person.'

'That would be good, Claire,' her father said. 'Well, Happy New Year to you both.'

'Happy New Year,' Claire said. 'Bye now.'

'That could've gone better,' Philip said.

'Don't worry, they'll come round.'

After lunch, she shared another tradition of hers: the Year Compass.

'I've been filling one out for the past five years. The first half of the booklet is about the past year. Recording what's gone well, what's gone badly, what you've accomplished, what your challenges have been. The second half is about the year to come. Your hopes and dreams.'

'It sounds a bit airy-fairy to me,' he said. Then he sat down and started to fill it out. 'Hmm. I'd never have thought of doing something like this, but it certainly concentrates the mind.'

'I know. I love reading the previous year's one and seeing how many of my hopes and dreams have come true. I'm not one for New Year's resolutions, but I really enjoy this process. It's a spiritual practice for me.'

'Don't you do New Year's resolutions? I decide on three every year. They give me a boot up the backside for the days and months ahead.'

'That's a bit of an arbitrary process for me. When I make a resolution, it's when it's the right time for it, when I've done the research and made my decision. Like quitting drinking. It took me a good couple of weeks up to Ash Wednesday to really resolve to quit.'

'I guess everyone's different.'

'I'm a Questioner.'

'A questioner? What does that mean?'

'Have you read Gretchen Rubin's book *The Four Tendencies*? It's about habits, and it divides people up into four categories based on how they respond to expectations. Upholders, Questioners, Obligers, and Rebels. When I first started to read it, I thought I was an Upholder. Someone who responds well to both inner and outer expectations, but when I did the quiz, it said I was a Questioner. I'm good at keeping to inner expectations, but question those which are imposed on me from outside. It's fascinating. Why don't you do it? I've been trying to decide what you are and I think you're either an Upholder or a Questioner.'

He laughed. 'OK, I'll give it a try. But not today. What are your hopes and dreams for the new year?'

'To find a nice new home for us, to still be with you, and to finish my novel. How about you?'

'Pretty much the same.'

'This year has been marvellous, and I'm really looking forward to settling in together.'

They stayed in for New Year's Eve. The Lion would be packed, and Claire didn't fancy it. People would be getting steadily drunker and she didn't want to risk temptation. So they spent a peaceful evening in front of the TV. Philip introduced her to *The Expanse* – a sci-fi series he was following – and to her surprise, she was soon hooked.

'Lucy told me about this ages ago, but I never got round to watching it,' she said.

'Glad you like it!'

At midnight, they toasted each other in AF fizz.

'I really appreciate that you've quit drinking too,' Claire said.

'No problem,' he said. 'I never did drink very much. I don't miss it at all.'

The conveyance on Philip's flat was completed the first week in January. As soon as he had paid off Peggy, they put Claire's house on the market.

House-hunting then started in earnest and, after weeks of searching and many viewings, they came to a house on a small estate on the edge of Evesham.

It was in a cul-de-sac which – obviously – meant there was no through traffic. It had only one garage, but the kitchen was large with all mod cons, and they liked what saw in the rest of the property. The asking price was well within their budget.

The couple who owned it were downsizing, moving into a retirement village. Even better: there wasn't a big chain.

'We'll be leaving all the curtains,' the woman said, showing them around. 'The place we're moving into has smaller windows than here, so there's no point taking them.'

'Are you leaving anything else?' Claire said.

'The fridge freezer in the kitchen. It's huge. There won't be room for it where we're going. Oh, and the fitted bookshelves in the study. Do you want to buy the fridge freezer from us?'

'Yes, please.' She had always coveted one of those double-doored fridge freezers and her own single-door freezer was on its last legs. She loved the study on sight, with its walls of bookshelves. This seemed too good to be true. 'Have you had many viewings?'

'A few. In fact, a couple saw it this morning. They seemed quite keen, but you never know.'

She led them through the spacious living room into the conservatory.

'We had this built on a few years ago. It's south-facing, so it's a real sun trap and we often sit here on summer evenings. I'm going to miss it.'

'It's lovely, isn't it, Philip?'

'Yes, it is. Thank you. We'll be in touch very soon.'

When they got back into the car, Claire turned to Philip. 'This is the one. It's perfect! Let's make an offer straight away!'

'Are you sure? It's not in a village. I thought you wanted to be in a village.'

'Yes, that would be ideal. But we've been looking for weeks now, and this is the nicest we've seen. It's looking a bit tired. We'd have to redecorate all through, but otherwise I love it. The bookshelves in the study and the conservatory especially.'

'Let's go and make an offer. What do you think? Should we offer the asking price?'

'Of course. That couple who saw it this morning could snatch it from under us otherwise.'

A couple of days later, their offer was accepted.

'I can't believe it,' Claire said. 'I thought we'd have to look for months.'

'We struck lucky. Now all we've got to hope is we don't get gazumped.'

'Don't even think about it!,' Claire cried. 'Do people still do that?'

265

'Oh yes.'

'I'm sure the sellers aren't like that. They seemed such nice people.'

'Well,' Philip said, 'I only hope you're right. People can change overnight when it comes to money. All being well, we'll be in by May.'

It took only a couple of weeks to find a buyer for Claire's house – she decided to drop the asking price for a quick sale – which meant that, once she had paid all the solicitor's, surveyor's, and other fees, they wouldn't have much left to do all they wanted in the new house.

'But it should be plenty,' Claire said as they sat in their favourite Thai restaurant.

It was Philip's treat – to celebrate the successful ending of his probationary period, their imminent move and, last but not least, her birthday.

When he had left that morning, he had said, 'You'll get your present this evening.'

She ordered the chicken satay to start and the Kaeng Khiaw Wan, her favourite green curry, for her main course. Philip was more adventurous, going for fresh mussels to start and the Kaeng Pa, which had a three-chilli symbol next to it, for his main.

'I like my food spicy,' he grinned.

'Rather you than me! If it's too hot, I can't taste anything except the heat.'

After their starters and the waiter had cleared the table, Philip produced a small box from his jacket pocket.

'Your birthday present, my sweet.'

Then he went down on one knee. 'I love you so much, sweet Claire. Will you marry me?'

He opened the box to reveal a simple flower-shaped ring, with a glowing yellow citrine in the centre and six marquise-cut diamond petals around the outside. 'It was the closest thing I could find to a daisy.'

'Oh yes, Philip, yes.' Then she burst into tears.

'Hey, you're supposed to be happy, not miserable,' he teased. He took her hand, kissed it, then sat back down, to be greeted by applause from the waiter and the other diners. Claire smiled at everyone. Philip, shrugging his shoulders, blushed. 'I don't care who knows how much I love you.'

Claire pulled off her engagement ring from Jack, feeling quite a pang as she did so, and put it on the ring finger of her other hand. She took the daisy ring out of its box and slipped it on to her ring finger. It fitted perfectly. She marvelled at its beauty and simplicity. 'How did you know my ring size?'

'Oh, that was easy. I borrowed one of your other rings that I'd seen you wearing on the same finger of your right hand and hoped it would be the same size. Looks like I got it pretty much right.'

'Philip, it's more beautiful than I could have dreamed. I never imagined we'd get engaged so soon.'

'I'm not rushing you, am I?' he said. 'It just seemed like the right thing to do. We don't need to get married straight away. But I saw this in a jeweller's window in Warwick and fell in love with it. It matches your bracelet and necklace perfectly. So I pinched your ring that evening and went back the next day and bought it. It's been burning a hole in my pocket for more than two weeks now. I've been dying to give it to you.'

'It's perfect, and so are you.' Then her face changed. 'What's Chas going to say? Will he mind? I don't want him to think I'm trying to replace Angie.'

'I'm sure he won't. Let's give him a ring when we get home. Better yet, I'll text him now and ask him when it's convenient to Skype.'

Claire remembered little about the rest of the meal. She was in a daze. Every couple of minutes she would look down at the ring, then over at Philip, her heart full.

She floated back to the car on a cloud of contentment. Who needed alcohol? She was high on happiness.

At nine thirty, they Skyped Chas.

'What's up, Dad?'

267

'Nothing's up. We're fine. We just wanted you to know I asked Claire to marry me and she said yes.'

'Wow!' he said. 'I didn't see that one coming. When did all this happen?'

'In the Thai restaurant in Evesham, a couple of hours ago. We'd like your blessing, son.'

'I know I can never replace your mum, Chas,' Claire said, 'but I do love Philip so much. I hope you can be happy for us.'

'Um, yeah, I guess. Why are you asking *me*?'

'Because Claire will be part of the family now and it's bound to make a difference.'

He was silent for a moment. They watched him. 'Yeah, it's fine by me. I've seen how happy Claire makes you, Dad. Go for it.'

'Thank you, Chas,' she said. 'That means the world to me.'

'When are you getting hitched? Can I tell Jessica? Does Grandma know?'

'Whoa, slow down! To answer your questions. Not for a while, yes, of course you can, and no, not yet. We wanted to tell you first.'

'I don't envy you telling Grandma!' Chas grinned.

Then his mobile rang. 'That's Jess. Got to go now. Bye, you two.'

'Well, that went OK,' Claire said. 'I suppose I'd better let Mum and Dad know too. They're bound to want to come over for the wedding.'

'Are they up to travelling so far?'

'Hmm, I hadn't thought of that. Maybe we'd better honeymoon in New Zealand and drop in and see them then.'

'Then we'd better start saving now. The flights alone will cost a fortune. But it's an idea. I'd love to see some of the locations from the *Lord of the Rings* films.'

'When are we going to tell Peggy?'

'I'd rather leave it till the weekend, when we've got more time.'

'Then you'd better text Chas and warn him not to spill the beans first.'

'I'll do that now. Then we'd better hit the hay. You may not have work tomorrow, but I do.'

The next day was Friday, and Claire couldn't wait to get down to the Lion and show her ring to Lucy. She took her chance when Philip was at the bar, getting the drinks.

'Wow, Claire!' Lucy gasped. 'When did this happen? It's beautiful.'

'He asked me last night. Went down on one knee in the middle of the Thai restaurant in Evesham. I can't quite believe it, even now.'

'You're so lucky. Philip's a lovely guy. I wish I could find someone like him.'

'What about Sam?'

'Oh,' Lucy sighed. 'I've almost given up on him. I don't think he wants another serious commitment at the moment. He's too involved with his girls.'

'Ah, that's a shame. Give him time. I'm sure he's fond of you.'

'Oh, the sex is wonderful. But I want something more and I'm not sure he can provide it.'

'It's not like you to be so down, Lucy. You've only been together, what, nine months?'

'Well, you and Philip haven't been together much longer and look at you!'

'It's different for us. We've known each other for years and years. Everything's come together more quickly for us. Look, Lucy, if it's meant to be, it will be. Give him time.'

'I suppose you're right. Anyhow, enough about me. Tell me every little, teensy detail. I want to hear it all.'

'So, Peggy,' Philip said over the phone next morning, 'I hope you can be happy for us.' He smiled at Claire as she stirred her coffee.

'Well,' Peggy sniffed, 'I suppose I must offer my congratulations. But I have to say, I'm surprised, Philip. I still don't see how you can marry another woman after Angie.'

'I know,' he said. 'It's taken us both by surprise. But it isn't as if

269

I haven't known Claire for a few years, after all.' He gave Claire a quick smile. 'I like to think Angie would be happy for me. She was always very fond of Claire.'

'Well, I hope it all works out,' Peggy sniffed again. 'You know the saying, "Marry in haste, repent at leisure".'

Rolling his eyes at Claire, Philip sighed. 'We won't be getting married for a while, yet. We need to get the house move out of the way first.'

'What? You're moving house?'

'We both feel it would be better to make a fresh start together. The new place has four bedrooms, so you'll be welcome to visit any time.'

'Well,' Peggy said, 'I have to say it all seems too soon to me. But I suppose you'll do what you want, whatever I think. I wish you well. Goodbye.'

Raising his eyebrows, Philip stared at his phone, then switched it off. 'She's not happy. But she's accepted it . . . I think.'

'Thank goodness for that.'

'Yes, indeed.'

Claire emailed her parents to arrange a Skype session but as the time approached, she grew nervous.

'Hello, Mum. Hello, Dad. How are you?' As usual, she was shocked by how old and frail they were.

'We're all right, Claire,' her father said. 'Your mother's had a couple of funny turns but nothing to worry about.'

'Funny turns?' Claire's stomach did a somersault. 'What do you mean?'

'She's felt a bit sick but the doctor's checked her out, given her some new pills, and she's fine. Now what's this news of yours?'

Taking a deep breath, she said, 'Well, you know I told you I was in a relationship with Philip, one of Jack's old friends? That he'd moved up to Brandleton? We've been together for nine months now, and he's asked me to marry him and I've said yes.'

'You're getting married again? But Jack only died a few months ago. I'm surprised at you, daughter,' said her mother.

'It's been nearly two years, Mum. I've grieved deeply for him, but now I'm ready to move on. Don't begrudge me my happiness, please.'

'Two years? It can't possibly be that long.'

'Mum, he died nearly two years ago.'

'Who is this Philip? Do we know him?'

'You saw him when I Skyped you on New Year's Eve. I've known him for years. We were all friends at university and got back in touch a year ago at a writing conference and things happened from there.'

'Is he there with you? Let me see him!'

'Philip, come and say hello.'

'Hello, Mr and Mrs Henning. Nice to see you again. Mr Henning, I'd like to ask your permission to marry Claire. We love each other very much and both deserve a second chance at happiness.'

Over his spectacles, Claire's father surveyed Philip. 'If you can make my daughter happy, then of course I consent. How long have you known her?'

'As Claire said, we've known each other for years. We were all friends at university, Claire, Jack, Angie, and I.'

'Angie? Who's Angie?' said Claire's mother.

'Angie was my wife,' Philip said. 'She died six years ago. I have a son, Chas – Charles – who is now nineteen.'

'And what does he think of all this?' Claire's mother said.

'He was a bit surprised but he's happy for us. He likes Claire and says that if I have to be with someone after Angie, he's glad it's her.'

'When are you getting married?'

'Not for a while, yet,' Claire said. 'We're in the process of buying a new house. Philip's sold his flat down in Bath and has got a new job up here. We're not moving far, only to the outskirts of Evesham. But we both agreed that we needed to make a fresh start, together. We'd like to come out to New Zealand for our honeymoon. You'll meet him then. But you know how expensive the flights are, so we'll have to save up.'

'Hmph. I suppose that will have to do. Oh well, daughter, you know your own business best. I hope you are both happy.' Her mother nodded once, sharply.

'Thank you, Mum, Dad. I can't wait to see you again. Bye, now.'

Chapter Thirty Six

Ash Wednesday fell earlier this year. Claire went to the service again to give thanks for all the changes that had happened since the last Ash Wednesday. She then went to work for the afternoon. Last year, she had been jittery and nervous. Now, sobriety was an established way of life.

As it was also Valentine's Day, when she got home, she prepared a special meal. She remembered Philip's liking for her pork chops and pine nut pilaf. By the time he got home, it was all but ready. As he walked in, she ran to give him a hug and a kiss, nearly crushing the huge bouquet of flowers he was carrying.

'Steady on!' he laughed, freeing himself and handing them over. 'Happy Valentine's Day!'

'Oh, Philip! They're beautiful! Thank you so much.' Her face fell. 'But I didn't buy you anything, except a card. Jack and I didn't do presents on Valentine's Day.'

'That's OK. I saw these and thought of you. Give me a kiss, woman!'

Claire did as she was told, happy to be in his arms. 'Dinner's nearly ready. I'll just put these in water. You've got time to get changed.'

When Philip came down, the flowers were in a vase on the kitchen table. When he saw what was cooking, he said, 'See, you have given me a present.'

With her first proper Soberversary coming up fast, she wondered how to celebrate it. Her first thought was a bottle of champagne. She had to fight temptation to the floor once again.

The next week was Beryl's birthday. Claire sent her a card. *'Dear Beryl,'* she wrote. *'Have a fabulous birthday. Thank you for all you do for me. Love, Claire.'* She couldn't wait to see her the following week, to tell her all about the engagement.

For her own personal Soberversary celebration, Claire booked an appointment with a tattoo artist recommended by Dawn, to have her first tattoo, a daisy, on her shoulder. She wanted a permanent reminder of this momentous year.

'This is such a good idea of yours, Claire,' Lucy said as they waited. 'I've never dared to have a tattoo. Dawn's got loads now and I love the way they look. Maybe one day.'

'I'm feeling pretty nervous,' Claire said. 'I hope it's not going to hurt too much. Dawn said shoulders hurt more than arms, but I want it on my shoulder.'

'You can still change your mind,' Lucy said.

'No, I don't want to do that. But, God! I'll be glad when it's over.'

Lucy took Claire's hand and gave it a reassuring squeeze. 'You can do this!' she said.

'Claire Abbott?' the young woman asked. Both her arms were fully covered in tattoos and so was her chest, what they could see of it.

'Yes, I'm Claire,' she said.

'I'm Charlotte. I'm ready for you now. What size do you want the daisy to be?' She showed Claire a couple of stencils of daisies in different sizes.

'Which do you recommend?' she said.

'It's up to you,' Charlotte said.

'What do you think, Lucy?' Claire said.

'I'd go for the bigger one, myself,' Lucy said. 'You're making a statement with this, after all.'

'I guess you're right,' Claire said. 'OK, Charlotte, I'll go for the bigger one, please.'

Ninety minutes later, the job was done. It had hurt more than she had expected, a lot more at times, but she was thrilled with the result.

'Keep the film on it for a few hours,' Charlotte said. 'Then bathe it two or three times a day in warm water. Dry it by patting, not rubbing, then use a moisturising skin cream to protect it from drying out. Whatever you do, don't scratch it. It's probably better to have a shower rather than a bath to avoid soaking it while it's healing. After a couple of weeks any scabbing should be gone. But you'll see a silvery skin for another week, after which it will be healed.'

'Thank you, Charlotte. I'm made up with it,' Claire said.

'Yes, it's beautiful,' Lucy said.

'You're welcome.'

The day before her first Soberversary, she got out the new journal Philip had given her for Christmas. It seemed right to be christening it with a reflection on the changes of the last year.

My first Soberversary is tomorrow. How do I feel? I'm not really sure, which is a shame. Because it is a Fantastic Achievement. This time last year, I was struggling with the idea of giving up wine. It frightened me so much. I'm not sure, looking back, what was horrifying me most – the hold it had on me or the prospect of never drinking again. About even, I think.

Then I began to realise how much control it had over me. It was a strong daily habit that took some courage and guts to break and to keep on breaking. I was numbing the pain of Jack's passing and (without realising it) numbing my whole life in consequence. Now I've been AF for a whole year tomorrow, in the face of many opportunities and provocations to start again. Not to mention downright encouragement from well-meaning but misguided idiots, like some of the folk down the Lion, who say things like 'Just one wouldn't hurt' or 'If you just have a drink today, you can go back to being sober tomorrow.'

No, I can't. It's exactly like giving up smoking. You either do or you don't. For me, unlike other people, there is no pleasant halfway house of the occasional glass at a weekend. I know myself well enough to know that if I once started again, it would soon be back up to between half and one bottle of red wine a night, just like the old days.

275

So I'm going to stick to my resolution, remain AF, and maintain my self-respect. I've got through the crucial first year – first anniversary of Jack's death, first holiday, first Christmas, first New Year. And I've Done It. And that is something to be proud of. And to celebrate.

But I couldn't have done it without Philip and without my sobriety group friends. I owe them so much.

I guess the reason why I don't feel much like putting the flags out is two-fold:

1. The automatic way it occurs to me to celebrate in this drinking culture of ours is still by having a drink. Not Good. In the past year, these are the times I have found hardest – when there has been something to celebrate – getting together with Philip, our holiday along the Camino, him proposing, stuff like that. The automatic reaction is, 'Let's drink to that.' And I feel very left out and kill-joyish. Which I'm not. I've also found I get pretty bored at social functions, when all around me are getting slowly pissed, and loud and happy with it, and I'm just sitting there. Not so bad if I have access to my beloved Becks Blue, but dire otherwise.

2. Contrary to my expectations, I haven't lost any weight. Unlike friends who have travelled the same journey as me and lost shedloads of weight, mine has remained the same. Because I've been eating more, to compensate, I guess. Good job I go to the gym!

But I have never regretted my decision to go AF and am exceedingly proud to have nearly made it through the first year. With a lot of help from my friends. There is still the odd difficult day, but they are getting fewer and further between, and I have been able to overcome the temptation and stay AF.

And that is my life. I'm sober, and likely to stay that way. I'm proud of my achievement and can't see myself changing, not now. I've got Philip, we're moving to a new home together, and life is good.

She closed her journal and logged on to Facebook to share her news.

She noticed a plaintive post from someone she hadn't seen before, a new member of the group.

276

Hello, I'm new to this journey – it's five days since I've had a drink. And I'm finding it impossible to sleep. Is this normal? Thanks, BT

Claire smiled, then reached out to reassure her:

BT: well done on five days – that's great. And yes, I'm afraid it is. Because your body is used to being sedated to sleep by booze, and misses it. If you're anything like I was, you'll start to sleep much better after two or three weeks. Hang on in there! Post as often as you need to, and stay sAFe! LL xx

Acknowledgements

I would like to thank all the Soberistas who supported me in the early years of my own sobriety journey: Mike Richards for his encouragement and excellent advice; fellow members of Northampton Writing Circle for teaching me how to receive feedback gracefully; and Greg Rees for his efficient editing. And last, but not least, Maz, David and Becky Woolley, for being the best family in the world.

Addictive thrillers. **Gripping** suspense.
Irresistible love stories. **Escapist** treats.

For **guaranteed brilliant reads**
Discover **Headline Accent**

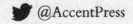 @AccentPress

ACCENT